Pra  **s**

'We are predicting extremely big things for this
new adventure seri

Jake Djones

the limelight' – *Telegraph*

A time travelling detective tale. There are
desperate chases, hair-raising escapes . . . and more
comical or eccentric secondary characters than you
could shake a wand at' – *Guardian*

'A cocktail of time travel, secret societies, double agents
and edge-of-your-seat excitement . . . You won't be able to
put it down. Pure magic!' – *Glamour*

'The next big thing' – *Observer*

'Today's answer to *Harry Potter* crossed with
The Hunger Games' – *Tatler*

'History can be fun too! Damian Dibben's books
have got kids' imaginations going – and cultivated
their interest in the past to boot' – *Sun*

www.**totallyrandombooks**.co.uk

Also available in
The History Keepers **sequence:**

The History Keepers: The Storm Begins
The History Keepers: Circus Maximus

THE
HISTORY
KEEPERS

NIGHTSHIP TO CHINA

DAMIAN DIBBEN

CORGI BOOKS

THE HISTORY KEEPERS: NIGHTSHIP TO CHINA
A CORGI BOOK 978 0 552 56430 4

Published in Great Britain by Corgi Books,
an imprint of Random House Children's Publishers UK
A Random House Group Company

This edition published 2014

1 3 5 7 9 10 8 6 4 2

The Random House Group Limited supports the Forest Stewardship Council®
(FSC®), the leading international forest-certification organisation. Our
books carrying the FSC label are printed on FSC®-certified paper. FSC is
the only forest-certification scheme supported by the leading environmental
organisations, including Greenpeace. Our paper procurement policy can be
found at www.randomhouse.co.uk/environment.

Corgi Books are published by Random House Children's Publishers UK,
61–63 Uxbridge Road, London W5 5SA

www.randomhousechildrens.co.uk
www.totallyrandombooks.co.uk
www.randomhouse.co.uk

Addresses for companies within The Random House Group Limited can be
found at: www.randomhouse.co.uk/offices.htm

THE RANDOM HOUSE GROUP Limited Reg. No. 954009

A CIP catalogue record for this book is available from the British Library.

Printed and bound in the UK by CPI Group (UK) Ltd, Croydon, CR0 4YY

For my brother Justin

. . . and all the brothers and sisters of the
Lowrys & Ansteys – warm, witty and wise.

1 THE SENSATIONAL SECRET SERVICE

The day that death came to the Mont St Michel had begun as the most festive the castle had ever seen. It was a hot June afternoon and a wedding was due to take place between two agents of the History Keepers' Secret Service.

The sky was cloudless, the sea like glass, the Mount festooned with scented flowers. On a lawn at the edge of the Atlantic, neat rows of chairs had been set out for the ceremony, and the guests – almost a hundred of them from different corners of history – were now busy assembling, here in 1820, chatting in many languages.

Miriam Djones urgently threaded her way through the crowd. She wore a giant puffball gown and a towering headpiece of exotic fruits and palm leaves. 'Have you seen Jake? Jake, anyone?' She

1

received nothing but shakes of heads and shrugs. 'He's supposed to be an usher,' she sighed irritably.

'Someone's making a hullaballoo in the fencing chamber,' a deep-voiced man volunteered. 'Perhaps it's him?' He was dressed as a crusader knight and sipping a champagne cocktail.

Miriam smiled curtly, turned on her heel and swept towards an outbuilding where agents practised combat and sword technique. As she approached, she heard music booming out at full volume – Wagner's *Ride of the Valkyries*. It was certainly Jake in there: he had been listening to this feverish piece of opera over and over for weeks. She flushed with irritation and, holding onto her hat, flew inside.

The music was ear-shattering; it came from an old phonograph and was amplified through speakers (of course, these inventions had been imported from a later time than 1820, but the commander, a keen musician herself, allowed *restricted* use of them). On the far side of the room, a fifteen-year-old boy, dressed only in breeches and a loose shirt, was practising sword-fighting with a mechanical warrior.

His opponent had a solid metal body and eight

robotic arms, each lunging, thrusting and slicing at lightning speed. The boy was riposting at the same frantic pace, making it appear as if he had eight arms himself! The whole operation was being witnessed by a dog, a chunky mastiff, whose eyes followed every movement his master made.

'Jake!' Miriam shouted over the racket of the Valkyries. She flew over to the phonograph and swung the needle off the record with a piercing screech. Silence at last. '*Jake!*' The dog's ears went back.

The boy finally turned round. 'Mum, I didn't see you there.'

Miriam did a double-take. Jake was growing at such a rate, he seemed more adult every time she looked. He had turned fifteen three months ago and had shot up several inches even since then.

'Is everything all right?' he asked as the machine carried on slicing and lunging behind him.

'No, everything is *not* all right,' his mother began. 'Your aunt is getting married in five minutes' time, you're an usher – and you're not even dressed— Jake, watch out!' she shrieked as a blade went spearing towards his back. He dodged it breezily. 'I hate that machine, it gives me the

3

heebie-jeebies.' She pushed a lever to switch it off. One by one, its various arms fell still. 'Wedding, now.' She clicked her fingers and bustled out.

Jake's clothes were laid out on a wooden horse. Rose Djones, a lifelong lover of all things Indian, had chosen a Mughal empire theme for the nuptials, and the ushers had been given traditional Indian uniforms to wear: knee-length jackets and silk turbans. Jake hurriedly put his on.

His aunt was marrying Jupitus Cole. It had come as a total surprise to everyone when they made the announcement: for decades they had apparently hated each other – he being fussy and austere, she hot-headed and fun-loving. But on their last mission together – a trip to ancient Rome in which Jake had been involved – things suddenly changed. And now here they were.

'Come on, Felson,' Jake called to his dog, who bounded straight to his side.

As he approached the lawn, he took in the sea of people, all dressed in clothes of far-off times and places. The sight of many History Keepers together always gave him a thrill, but he had never seen a collection as large and diverse as this. There were guests from colonial America, from Inca Peru, from

China, and indeed from Mughal India (the extended family of Dr Chatterju, head of inventions). Jake saw a stout woman in Elizabethan dress smoking a cheroot as she talked to a slim musketeer. Next to them, two young French aristocrats in powdered wigs showed off their pocket watches to a pair of blushing bridesmaids from Persia.

Jake had been called up to the History Keepers' Secret Service almost a year and a half ago. Back then, he had learned, quite out of the blue, that his parents had been covertly working for the service for decades – and that they had recently gone missing in sixteenth-century Venice! He had joined the mission to find them, and ultimately to stop Prince Zeldt in his attempts to destroy the Renaissance.

They had been successful on both counts, but soon more danger was afoot: Zeldt's sister, Agata, the so-called 'most evil woman in history', had launched her own diabolical stratagem. Jake and his friends had been dispatched to AD 27 – the height of the Roman empire – to locate and stop her. In the end, largely through the sheer grit and courage of Jake and his young fellow agents, her plan had been foiled.

Most extraordinary of all, Jake had discovered

that his beloved brother Philip, assumed dead in an accident at the age of fifteen, had also been a History Keeper . . . and that there was a chance – just a tiny one – that he was still alive, somewhere in the past.

Jake now knew many people on the island of Mont St Michel, but his *real* allies were those his own age, and it was towards three of these – two boys and a girl, all supposedly showing guests to their seats, but actually busy chatting – that he made his way.

One of the boys was tall and broad with a winning smile. He'd accessorized his Mughal outfit by tucking a great curving scimitar into his belt and fixing a huge ruby to the front of his turban. The other was shorter, wiser perhaps, and had a brightly coloured parrot – Mr Drake – sitting on his shoulder.

The girl, who was dressed identically to the boys, had long tresses of honey-blonde hair and indigo eyes that were warm and mysterious in equal measure.

These three were Jake's best friends – really the best friends he had ever had: Nathan Wylder, Charlie Chieverley and Topaz St Honoré.

'What I'm trying to ascertain,' Nathan was saying in his distinct Charleston drawl, 'is whether these spectacles make me look more intelligent . . . or just blind . . .' To ensure that Charlie and Topaz gave him the right answer, he made his eyes smoulder behind the lenses.

'I'd verge more towards blind,' Charlie replied.

'Cross-eyed, at the very least,' Topaz added.

'You're both being absurd,' Nathan huffed. 'Jake, what do you think of my new look? Better *with* or *without?*' He demonstrated by taking the glasses off and then putting them on again, this time lowering them halfway down his nose like a university professor.

'Do you need glasses?' Jake asked.

'Of course I don't *need* them. My visual acuity is second to none. On a clear night I can see across the English Channel, not to mention the rings around Saturn. I don't need them, no. But do they add a certain *je ne sais quoi?*'

As Jake was mulling it over, Charlie chipped in mischievously, 'He wants to know because he's trying to impress some mystery girl from the mainland.'

'That's right,' Topaz added. 'Having spent his life

breaking hearts, someone *finally* seems to be returning the favour.'

Nathan went as red as the ruby on his turban and
protested, 'Those are outrageous and unfounded
allegations – I have no idea what's got into everyone
today. The nuptials are obviously making you all
giddy.' He was so flustered he got the hilt of his
scimitar caught in his jacket. As he tried to right it,
the ruby popped off his turban, which unfurled
about his shoulders. He grunted, snatched it all up
again and disappeared into the throng.

'I definitely think spectacles make you look more
intelligent . . .' Jake couldn't resist saying to his
friend's disappearing back.

'And we're so looking forward to meeting her,'
Topaz called after him.

The three young agents fell about laughing.
'There is nothing more satisfying in the whole wide
world,' Topaz said, 'than pulling Nathan's leg when
he's serious about something.' She and Nathan
had been raised together on the island by
his parents, Truman and Betty Wylder, so she
knew him as well as a sister could know a
brother.

Just as they were about to take up their ushering

duties, a voice called out, 'Would one of you youngsters do me a favour?'

It was Galliana Goethe, Commander of the Secret Service. She always cut an elegant figure, tall and slender, with long silver hair swept sharply back from her face. She was accompanied by Madame Tieng, head of the Chinese bureau. Tieng and a handful of other agents had been staying on the island for over a year now, having sought refuge after their own bureau had been ransacked.

'My daughter has vanished again,' Madame Tieng sighed. She looked like a bird of paradise in her silk robes, wafting a fan against her pale face.

'The ceremony is about to begin' – Galliana smiled – 'so would one of you find her immediately?'

'Jake or Charlie can go,' Topaz jumped in quickly. 'If I ask "Miss Yuting" to do anything, she'll make a point of doing the opposite.'

'I can't,' Charlie said. 'The cake's arriving and I need to check it's all in order.' The crowd was parting, cooing with delight, as two men brought out a vast iced confection. It was a replica of the Mont St Michel itself, topped with figurines of the bride and groom.

'Jake, then? Would you . . . ?' Galliana asked.

It was his turn to blush. 'Of – of course,' he stammered.

As Jake, with Felson at his side, stepped into the heart of the fortress, in search of Madame Tieng's daughter, his stomach flipped. Even though Miss Yuting had been here for ages, Jake still didn't know what to make of her; he felt nervous around her.

On an island full of eccentrics, she was one of the oddest mixtures of all: opinionated, reckless, shockingly beautiful. She was almost exactly his age (they had celebrated their fifteenth birthdays in the same week), but she seemed to possess decades of worldliness in her tiny frame. With ideas above her station, she had asked people to call her by her *formal* name – Miss Yuting – but had recently given Jake permission to use her nickname: Yoyo. He was the first to be granted the privilege.

Yoyo was as accomplished as she was striking. It went without saying that she was a brilliant fighter, but she was also a master mathematician and an exceptional code-breaker; she could speak as many languages as Charlie, draw like Michelangelo and play a dozen musical instruments, including the harp and the Scottish bagpipes. She was good at everything; everything except making friends.

She had insulted Topaz within two minutes of her arrival. Topaz had gone to greet her, upon which Yoyo had handed her her cloak and asked her to run her a bath, assuming that she was her maid. She hadn't got on any better with the others – belittling Nathan's dress sense and Charlie's skill in the kitchen. No, it was only to Jake that she showed any warmth, and he had no idea why.

After scouring the whole building, he eventually found her on the roof. At the top of the tower he saw her silhouette outside the casement window.

'Miss Yuting?' he called.

The small figure rippled in the heat, then a voice called out: 'Didn't I tell you to call me Yoyo?'

'Wait here, there's a good boy,' Jake said to Felson, climbing out of the window. Remembering that he was wearing a turban, he pulled it off and stuffed it in his pocket; then mussed up his hair, squared his shoulders and stepped across towards her. It was precarious, the tiles steeply raked and loose in places. Distant sounds carried up from below. Everyone was taking their seats now.

'I think the wedding's about to start,' Jake offered as he drew near. She had her back to him and was busy fixing a harness around her chest. It was connected, via ropes, to a large pyramidal bamboo frame, which held a sail-like canopy. It was a perplexing sight. 'What are you doing?'

'I'm going to test this parachute,' she replied without looking round. 'I have made it to Leonardo da Vinci's precise specifications.' Like her mother, Yoyo spoke English with an almost perfect cut-glass accent. 'It was successfully tested in 1485, so I am not unduly worried. I'm going to jump off the gantry there.' She pointed to a thick metal beam that stuck out from the top of the building.

'Really? Is that a good idea?' Jake found himself asking. He adjusted his voice down a tone. 'I mean, it looks . . . dangerous.' This was an under-statement: she was going to throw herself off a two-hundred-foot-high building trusting to nothing but a bit of wood and tarpaulin.

Yoyo looked round at him and smiled. 'If it wasn't dangerous, it wouldn't be worth doing.' Her face was a shock of beauty: perfect alabaster skin, eyes like emeralds and a mouth of carmine red. She was clothed like a mythic princess in a dress of coral silk, belted at the waist, with a sword and dagger slung from her hips. 'Wish me luck,' she said, picking up the sail and stepping onto the narrow beam.

Jake's stomach flipped again as he looked down at the sheer drop. He had a sickening premonition of the celebration suddenly turning to tragedy; of the device failing and Yoyo thumping to her death in front of everyone. 'Miss Yuting, I really don't think this is a good idea,' he insisted.

She held the sail up towards the sky. 'If you don't start calling me Yoyo, I'm going to get angry,' she said, suddenly accelerating and leaping into the void. 'Victory!' she shouted as air filled the parachute.

There were cries from below, and Jake could see a swathe of guests standing up, pointing towards them. He heaved a sigh of relief when he realized that Yoyo's contraption was, after all, effective. Eddies of warm air carried her away from the castle and back again, and within a few seconds she had landed right next to the wedding party. She unfastened herself from her harness, brushed down her dress and took her seat as if her mode of arrival had been not the slightest bit unusual.

Jake saw his mother shake her head in astonishment, then look up at him, holding out her hands in disbelief. He hurried back downstairs, Felson scampering at his side. They took a shortcut through the stateroom, along the corridor of the communications wing and down towards the armoury.

As they hurried through the door, Jake noticed the animal sitting on her haunches in the centre of the room; it was as if she was waiting for him. It was Josephine, Oceane Noire's 'pet' lioness.

Jake wasn't fond of the beast; no one on the island was, except her owner. As a cub, Josephine had been sly and devious, but now she was worse – unpredictable and spiteful, as if she viewed everyone as an enemy. Charlie, a great animal lover, had made a huge effort, cooking her special meals and taking her for walks. In return, she'd bitten his hand. Since then, Commander Goethe had insisted that the lioness be kept locked in Oceane's quarters or on a leash when exercising. Jake had not seen her for weeks, and now she looked more ferocious than ever.

'Where's your mistress?' he asked her. 'Is she at home?' Oceane had shut herself up in her suite for weeks, avoiding anything to do with the wedding. She had still not forgiven Jupitus for betraying her by taking up with her arch-rival, Rose. Jake advanced cautiously, wondering if he might be able to herd Josephine back to her quarters, but he stopped when she gave a low growl, sitting up and fixing him with her amber eyes.

He gulped, quickly glancing at the wall of weapons, working out how best to defend himself if she suddenly went for him. But Josephine just twitched her ears, turned and padded across the room. She gave him one last sly look, then pushed the door open with her nose and slipped out.

Jake took a deep, calming breath before hurrying after her, and emerged at the top of the grand staircase. The lioness was nowhere to be seen.

'Where did she go?' he asked Felson. The dog appeared as perplexed and unnerved as his master. The life-sized portraits of all the past History Keepers stared at them silently as they went down the stairs. Jake felt sick with worry – Josephine shouldn't be roaming around when there were so many guests on the island! He had to alert someone. He rushed back to the lawn, but by the time he got there the congregation was standing and the orchestra already playing a Mughal *Wedding March*.

'Where on earth have you been? What were you doing on the roof?' Miriam demanded, flushed with anger, as Jake sat next to her in the front row.

'I was told to find Yoyo . . . Miss Yuting.' He shrugged defensively. 'I didn't know she was going to throw herself off the building, did I?' He was aware that his tone was rude – that it so often was these days when he spoke to his mother. 'But listen, I'm worried about Josephine, she's—'

'Just put your clothes on properly,' Miriam snapped, pulling his scrunched-up turban out of his pocket, unwilling to hear more. She peered round at Yoyo. 'That girl's not right in the head.'

Jake did as he was told, hoping the lioness had taken herself back to her own quarters – though he found himself glancing round the edges of the lawn nervously.

Suddenly a spontaneous round of applause went up at the appearance of Rose Djones, carried triumphantly on a sedan by four men, including Jake's dad, Alan, dressed in the Mughal style. Rose – looking like an Indian queen in a headdress and layers of bright crimson silk – reclined on velvet cushions, surrounded by garlands of flowers. The spectacle was only slightly spoiled by the presence of her trusty carpet bag bundled up next to her.

'Do you think I'm mad,' Rose called down to

Miriam as she passed by, 'marrying a man who folds his socks before he gets into bed?'

Miriam couldn't stop giggling. She'd already forgotten all about her little spat with Jake and squeezed his hand in delight.

The litter bearers carefully set down their load and Alan escorted his sister to the altar, where Jupitus Cole was waiting with a stiff smile that gave the impression he might still make a run for it. The ceremony began: the marriage of Rosalind Aurora Djones to Jupitus Tarquin St-John Seneca Cole.

It wasn't until the moment came for the rings to be exchanged that Jake noticed Felson suddenly sit up and prick his ears, then stare at the banqueting table and growl softly. It was covered with a white cloth that went down to the ground, and Jake saw the material rustle as something moved underneath. Then, halfway along, Josephine emerged. With everyone's eyes on the ceremony, only Jake had seen her. For a moment the lioness stopped, staring at him as she had done in the armoury.

All at once a little girl – one of Dr Chatterju's nieces – caught sight of the beast and screamed. The sound was so shrill that everyone turned at once and a great shout went up.

Josephine was momentarily confused. Then she bounded forward towards the bride and groom. There was a gasp of horror as she sprang towards Rose. The two gold rings, one halfway onto Rose's finger, went flying into the air. Josephine snapped, her teeth taking hold of the many layers of silk, shaking Rose around like a rag doll.

2 SUMMER SLAUGHTER

Rose threw herself backwards into Jupitus's arms, shuddering in horror as the lioness came away with a mouthful of silk, which she spat out. As a mass of people bore down on her, Josephine swung round, skidded on the grass and smacked into the banqueting table, sending the Mont St Michel cake tumbling to the ground.

'Are you all right? Are you hurt?' Jupitus asked Rose, his voice trembling. She looked down: her gown was shredded and her arms scratched and bleeding, but there was no serious damage. 'That beast will draw no more blood! A gun!' he cried. 'Does anyone have a gun?' He tore off into the building, leaving Rose in the hands of Alan and Miriam.

Nathan had already drawn his scimitar and Yoyo

had also armed herself with her sword and dagger. Having no weapon, Topaz took hold of a candlestick. They all vied for the best position to strike as Josephine – certainly a pet no longer, but a wild, angry beast – patted the cake with her giant paws, crushing the effigies of the bride and groom. Nathan lunged first, but she dodged him, springing up and landing on the table, making it buckle under her weight. She skidded along, sending everything flying – an eruption of smashed crockery, cutlery and food. When she alighted upon a vast joint of meat, she took it in her jaws. Meanwhile Nathan bounded forward again, sword raised, ready for the kill.

But Josephine was too wily. She dropped the joint before leaping back to the ground and heading along the lower terrace.

'Where is that woman?' Jupitus roared with rage, rushing back from the fencing chamber with two pistols in his hand. 'Oceane Noire!' he called out. Jake had never seen him so red in the face.

'May I?' said Nathan, taking one of his guns and heading off in pursuit of the lioness. Jupitus, Topaz and Yoyo followed.

'Wait for me,' Charlie called out, bringing up the

rear, Mr Drake bouncing on his shoulder. 'She can be stopped without bloodshed, you know . . .' He couldn't bear to see animals suffer.

'I'm coming too,' Jake shouted, arming himself with a sword.

'There's enough of them already, darling,' Miriam said, trying to block his path. 'Why not leave it to one of the professionals?'

'I *am* one of the professionals, aren't I?' he replied tersely, pushing past her.

He caught up with the others as they followed the track around the Mount. They skirted a turreted watchtower and continued round to the ocean-facing side of the island. Here, the path narrowed, winding between the ramparts on one side and the craggy rocks of the foreshore on the other. They were forced to walk in single file, aware that the beast might leap out at them at any moment. They were on the right path for sure: Josephine had left faint footprints of icing sugar.

The track led to a low door at the base of a sheer wall of battlements – the back entrance to the interior harbour where most of the Keepers' fleet was moored. The door was hanging off its hinges where Josephine had crashed through it. Nathan darted through, pistol at the ready. He checked there was no immediate danger and nodded for the others to follow.

Despite the urgency of the situation, Jake felt a thrill, as he always did, stepping into this dramatic place. It was a vast domed limestone cave, secreted in the very heart of the Mount. A quay curved round one side, lined with a succession of ships of all sizes, their masts bare, rigging furled.

Nathan edged along the quay and up a flight of stairs to another doorway, which was closed. 'This is the only exit,' he called back quietly, 'so she must be in here somewhere.'

The six of them scanned the empty decks of the ships. There was no obvious sign of life. 'We search each in turn,' Nathan commanded.

'I suggest we use this to stop her,' Charlie said, scooping up a large fishing net. 'She has every right to a fair trial.'

'No one appreciates your sensitive side more than I, Charlie,' Nathan drawled, 'but the creature did just try to tuck into the bride – not to mention that unfortunate gateau. Use your net by all means; I'll put my trust in this.' He brandished his pistol and started his search at the far end of the quay, vaulting up onto the deck of a Norse longboat. Jupitus, Topaz and Yoyo were about to follow suit when a thump came from the hold of the *Campana* – a square-sailed merchant galley – docked next to her.

Everyone froze.

Jupitus cocked his pistol. Yoyo gave him a knowing look and creaked up the steps, her sword clutched firmly in her hand, while Nathan tiptoed across from one deck to the next. An anxious Mr Drake dug his claws into his master's shoulder. In unison, Nathan and Yoyo threw open the cover of the hold, ready for the kill. But their faces fell.

'Rats. Having their own wedding party, it seems,' Nathan deadpanned. 'Rowdy little things, aren't they?'

Jake couldn't help but smile. Then his face froze as he became aware of a sound just behind him, from the shadows of another ship, the *Hippocampus*. He turned to see the lioness crouching at the top of the cabin steps. Her lips curled back to reveal her incisors; otherwise she was as still as stone.

Jake tried a friendly nod of recognition. He might as well have spat at her, for suddenly Josephine launched herself into the air and he felt a rush of air as she leaped off the ship towards him.

Like lightning, Charlie cast his net over her, slowing her slightly, but she still hit Jake with tremendous impact. His sword went flying as she brought him down, forcing the air out of his lungs.

She scrabbled with her gigantic paws, trying to free herself from the net. Jake felt her hot breath on his face as she opened her jaws, and he lashed out, hitting her on the nose. He heard a crack of bone, and as she turned, stunned, Jake tried to kick his way free.

Josephine was just about to lunge for him again when Jake heard a shot ring out, and then another, the second grazing her back. This served only to enrage her further. She sank back onto her haunches and let out a tremendous roar, when Mr Drake dive-bombed her, slashing out with his claws. In the chaos, he got caught in the net, and there was a cacophony of squawking and roaring; Charlie screamed and all the others shouted in alarm.

Suddenly Jake felt the weight lift off him. He rolled over and saw the lioness charging up the steps, trailing the net behind her, with the poor parrot a blur of colour, still tangled up in it.

'Mr Drake!' Charlie wailed as she hurtled through the door, smashing it to pieces. He snatched the gun from Nathan and followed swiftly behind.

From the hall, Charlie looked up at the grand staircase where the portraits of old History Keepers stood guard. He couldn't see anything at first, but he heard squawks echoing around the vaulted space. He hurried on up the stairs; ahead of him, Mr Drake finally broke free of the net and tried to fly towards him – but his broken wing jerked uselessly and he fell to the floor. Josephine turned and snapped at the bird, but he used his last ounce of energy to flap free, before collapsing and plopping down the steps one by one.

Charlie's face was filled with fury. He pointed his gun at the lioness – but his finger froze on the trigger. Could he kill an animal in cold blood?

His hesitation was fatal. Josephine roared and leaped forward, swiping the gun out of his hand. Charlie's eyes widened in shock as he toppled backwards; he lost his balance completely and went flying, his shoulder smacking into an oil portrait. Sejanus Poppoloe, the founder of the History Keepers' Secret Service, was ripped in two, and Josephine, no longer hindered by the net, bore down on Charlie, sinking her teeth into his ankle.

Jake heard the bone snap as she flipped him right over, about to start on the rest of him . . .

Jake lunged forward, picked up the gun and took aim. But an ear-splitting shot rang out from behind him; a cloud of acrid smoke rose into the air. Josephine froze in surprise. Then blood started to seep out of a black hole in her chest – just trickling at first; then pouring, as thick as oil, down the steps. She looked around in confusion, then her legs gave way and her body thumped to the floor. As Jake gazed into her eye, it grew cloudy, flickered one last time, and then she was still.

Josephine was dead. On this day of celebration, death had come to the Mont St Michel.

Jake turned to see Oceane Noire coming down the steps. In her hand she held a shotgun – for it was she who had killed Josephine, her own pet. Her face was expressionless as she knelt down and picked up a limp paw. She closed her eyes and then let out a cry of pain, low at first, but building to a crescendo.

Jake went over to Charlie. His face was pale, but he managed to ask: 'Mr Drake? Is he . . .?'

Jake looked round at the lifeless coloured bundle. Topaz was tending to the fallen parrot. He was moving, but it didn't look good.

Then he turned to see the wedding party standing in silence at the bottom of the staircase, Rose at the front in her torn wedding gown.

Oceane picked herself up and, like a zombie, made her way down the steps. Jake had never seen her look so dishevelled, an old shawl thrown over her bony shoulders. At the foot of the stairs she reached out her hand to Rose and stroked her cheek, smearing it with vivid blood.

Her lips trembled as she asked bitterly, 'Happy now?'

3 MONSTER FROM THE DEEP

On the other side of the world, in a far-off part of history, a ship was sailing through the night in the South China Sea. It was a trading junk – in 1612, one of the largest vessels in the world: two hundred feet long, with five masts supporting a cluster of giant fin-shaped sails. The vessel had set off from Canton two nights previously, bound for the ports of Persia and Arabia.

In a candlelit cabin at the stern of the ship, three distinguished-looking merchants, the owners, sipped tea and pored over maps, charting their route around the world.

Beneath them, in the many compartments of the hold, was an extremely precious cargo: chests of jade, jet and lapis lazuli; porcelain and ebony; rolls of fine silk and crates of tea, ginger, cinnamon and peppercorns. Guards patrolled the narrow corridors between the compartments.

Meanwhile, on deck, bare-footed sailors checked the rigging, their brows beading with sweat against the humid night; others sat cross-legged, playing dice. Watchmen in breastplates and pointed helmets kept a lookout across the dark sea for anything dangerous – pirates in particular.

All was quiet . . . when suddenly there was a huge jolt.

In the merchants' cabin, candles were overturned and a cup of tea spilled on a chart of the Indian Ocean. Above them, the sailors froze, some halfway up the rigging, and looked round at their shipmates. The watchmen held their lanterns out over the water to see if they had hit anything. But the vessel was now continuing normally, with the wind in its sails.

In the hold, one of the guards went along a corridor to investigate a strange sound – a heavy insistent tap coming from the hull. He bent down, his ear to the floor. All at once there was a surge of noise. The wood shattered and a metal tentacle, sharp-tipped, and as thick as a human leg, punched through the timbers, just missing him. A torrent of water gushed in. Then, as quickly as it had appeared, the tentacle retreated, sliding back through the hole.

The three merchants stumbled out of their cabin and looked down into the hold, stunned. They heard a deep rasp from beneath the hull, and suddenly a second steel arm smashed through, cracking open the wall of a compartment; its precious cargo tumbled out. Terrified, the merchants hurried the other way, up the stairs onto the main deck.

The ship was listing: its stern was sinking, while its prow stuck up out of the water. Many of the sailors and watchmen were clustered together on one side, swords drawn, shouting. The merchants stumbled over, and saw another of the sea creature's limbs rising up. There was a cry as it reached into the sky before curling round towards the deck. The crew tried to fight it off – and it was only when their swords made contact that they realized it was made of metal! The tentacle took hold of the ship's rail and pulled.

The merchants turned and ran across to the other side, where the rest of the sailors were lowering a small skiff. The ship's owners scrambled aboard and it thumped down onto the water. Immediately another tentacle shot out, smashing the boat to pieces, tossing them all into the water, before reaching up for the other side of the ship.

The entire vessel, now coming apart at the seams, was drawn down under the water. Two of the masts snapped in two, one tumbling onto the remaining sailors. The ocean churned as the junk quickly disappeared below the surface.

It was lunch time on the Mont St Michel. Jake sat by Charlie's bed in the castle sick bay. He'd been watching over his friend for three days, often accompanied by Nathan and Topaz, as they waited for him to wake up properly.

Josephine had shattered Charlie's ankle, along with three bones in his foot. The attack had left him in a state of deep shock. Dr Chatterju had operated on him immediately, and now Lydia Wunderbar was in charge of his recovery. She was the larger-than-life head librarian – as vivacious as she was fearsome – who doubled up as a brilliant nurse (apparently she'd once been a friend of Florence Nightingale).

'Miss Wunderbar, something's happening,' Jake whispered, seeing Charlie's eyes flicker open properly for the first time.

She approached the bed, and Charlie looked up at them both, blinking in confusion. Then a terrible thought struck him. 'Mr Drake? Where's Mr Drake?'

'He's a very fortunate parrot,' Lydia said, smiling. She indicated a basket by the bed, containing a poorly looking bird stretched out on plump velvet cushions, wing bandaged in much the same manner as Charlie's leg. She and Jake watched, tears in their eyes, as Charlie picked up his beloved pet and held him next to his heart.

'How are you feeling?' Jake asked.

Charlie looked down at his leg uncertainly. 'I don't know. How *am* I feeling, Miss Wunderbar?'

'In time, you'll make a full recovery,' she said, 'but there'll certainly be no assignments for a while.'

Charlie nodded grimly; then he remembered something else. 'It's all a blur, but I suppose Josephine . . . did she make it after all?' Despite everything, he couldn't help feeling dreadful about what had happened. Jake's face told him the answer. 'And Oceane?'

'She's been locked in her room for three days – she's opened her door just once, to receive a delivery of red wine and cigars.'

'She must be inconsolable,' Charlie said quietly. 'What about the wedding? Did Rose and Jupitus tie the knot in the end?'

Jake and Lydia Wunderbar shared a look. The librarian busied herself cleaning up the sick bay as Jake explained: 'Actually, they're not on speaking terms. They had a huge row – Jupitus said something about the garish colour of Rose's wedding dress being like a red rag to a bull, and she flew off the handle. It ended up with her tossing her engagement ring into the sea.'

'Into the sea? Hell's bells and Bathsheba . . .!' Charlie sat up, trying to get comfortable. 'So, anything else I've missed?'

'Tomorrow my parents are going back to London, for a month,' Jake told him.

'I'd forgotten. Modern London?'

'Yes, where I'm from – where you and I met for the first time,' Jake remembered with a smile. 'Their two oldest friends, Martin and Rosie, are turning fifty. Also, they feel they should sort out the bathroom shop – don't ask me why: no one's ever going to find them in the nineteenth century. They wanted me to go with them, of course, and then *we* had an argument too. As usual, they threatened to take me back for good. I don't know who they're fooling – they love it here just as much as I do. Anyway, in the end I managed to get out of it. Emotional blackmail. Today is, you know . . .' He didn't finish the sentence.

Charlie frowned, trying to remember what day it could be; then it came to him. 'The twenty-first of June?'

Jake nodded. 'My brother's birthday. He would have been nineteen.'

Charlie squeezed his hand. 'He *is* nineteen; let's think of it that way.'

Jake changed the subject. 'I promised to go and tell the others when you woke up. I'll be back in a minute. Don't go anywhere,' he joked as he left the room.

With the news that Charlie had woken up, the sick bay quickly filled with people. Nathan arrived first with his father, Truman, both talking loudly and knocking things over. Topaz followed behind with Alan and Miriam. Jake's mum had made chocolate brownies and she offered them round, oblivious to the expression of horror on people's faces. (Miriam's brownies were infamously as hard as granite and usually tasted of petrol.) Jupitus followed, and then Signor Gondolfino – the head of costumiery. Then Dr Chatterju dropped in, along with his ninety-year-old mother, who had stayed on after the non-wedding. Rose brought up the rear and, excited at finding such a jovial party, started to entertain them all – and annoy Jupitus – with stories from her 'crazy days' as a young agent in Constantinople. One rather risqué tale made Gondolfino feign deafness.

It was when old Mrs Chatterju snapped a tooth on one of Miriam's biscuits, creating a terrible scene, that Lydia Wunderbar insisted that enough was enough. She allowed Jake to stay, but booted every-one else out.

After all the excitement, Jake sat back down and promptly fell asleep across the end of Charlie's bed.

'Jake?' Lydia whispered.

He sat up with a jolt, disorientated. 'What time is it?'

'It's almost ten o'clock. Lights out.'

Jake saw that it was almost dark outside. He stretched and turned to see Charlie sitting up, ensconced in a book, Mr Drake nestled next to him.

'This is absolutely fascinating,' Charlie said, holding up the tome. 'Miss Yuting lent me this book about China, and something incredible has just occurred to me. I don't know why I never thought of it before . . .' He raised his eyebrows and dropped his bombshell: 'The Han dynasty and the Roman empire existed at the same time.'

Jake gave Miss Wunderbar a sideways glance; he didn't have a clue what his friend was talking about.

'I mean, think about it,' the invalid continued, 'it's the first century BC and you have two of the biggest civilizations the world has ever known. In the west: Rome, Julius Caesar, vast empires, huge armies, all sorts of inventions. And four thousand miles away, you have the Han empire of China, just as grand, massive and all-conquering. And yet' – he held up his finger to emphasize his point – 'they knew next to *nothing* about each other. Well, all right, there was some silk and silver going back and forth, but basically, no cultural exchange what-soever.'

'Charlie, are you sure you're not hallucinating?' Jake asked.

He shook his head and looked them both in the eye. 'What I'm trying to say is this: east and west, they were once utterly divided. We take that for granted. And we shouldn't.' His gaze was unsettling.

'Enough now,' Lydia Wunderbar tutted, taking the book away. 'I know I'm a librarian, but I wonder sometimes, Charlie, if you should take an interest in more mindless things – like Nathan Wylder does. Anyway, bedtime, both of you.'

'Why don't we talk about it tomorrow?' Jake said, pulling Charlie's blankets up and giving Mr Drake a stroke. His friend nodded and they said their goodbyes.

At the door, Jake whispered to Lydia, 'He's going to be all right, isn't he?'

'Thanks to you, he's going to be fine.' Lydia would never let it be known that she had a favourite, but she was particularly fond of Jake. She gave him a peck on the forehead as he left.

Jake strolled back to his room. Usually he loved the castle at night, when its corridors were deserted. He could appreciate the history of the building; imagine the young agents of yesteryear setting off on missions, their stomachs in a knot of excitement. But tonight he felt different. He had tried to avoid thinking about his brother, but now that he was alone, a black cloud crept over him. Midsummer's

Day – 21 June, the longest day of the year – used to be one of his favourites; a day of laughter and madcap family expeditions. Now he dreaded it.

He is *nineteen*, Charlie had said. It didn't ring true any more. A year had passed since Jake had last heard anything about Philip. The traitorous Caspar Isaksen, before he died on the rooftop of Agata's palace in Rome, had confessed: *Yes, I've seen him. I've even tortured him. But I expect he's dead now.* The last phrase Caspar uttered was the worst of all: *He thought you'd forgotten all about him.*

The notion of Philip locked up in a dark dungeon in a distant corner of history tormented Jake. How could his brother ever think he'd been forgotten? *Never. Not until my dying day will I ever forget him.*

Galliana had been so intrigued by the discovery of even a tenuous link to Philip, she'd managed to persuade Fredrik Isaksen, Caspar's father, to let her come and look through his dead son's possessions in the Isaksen family mansion, situated in northern Sweden of the 1790s. For reasons of security, one of the most solemn rules of the History Keepers was that the Isaksen laboratory – where atomium, the substance they needed to take when travelling through time, was laboriously manufactured – was out of bounds to anyone but the Isaksens; even to the commander herself. However, the disappearance of Philip Djones had been so momentous, so keenly felt by everyone, that the Isaksens had waived the rules – though Galliana had had to submit to being blindfolded for the journey.

She had found nothing. She and Fredrik had spent an entire week going through every drawer and cupboard in the castle, scanning every piece of paper. There had been no mention of Philip anywhere. That had been many months ago now.

As Jake closed his bedroom door, Felson came to greet him, tail wagging. He gave Jake a quick lick of the hand before retreating to his basket.

Jake opened the window and breathed in the balmy night air. Across the bay he could see twinkling lights on the mainland and hear the distant sounds of a party – a band playing, accompanied by cheers of delight. Despite the hour, the sky was still streaked with crimson and pink.

He got into his pyjamas, but found that he was no longer tired. He didn't want to start thinking about Philip again, so he jumped onto his four-poster bed and – remembering Charlie's ideas about the Han dynasty – picked up the book that Yoyo had given him. (She was very patriotic and had circulated books about China to everyone; though she had annoyed Topaz by giving her one called *Chinese Manners and Morals*.)

Jake's volume was all about the adventures of Marco Polo, a young Venetian who had voyaged to China in 1272 and ended up staying for twenty-four years; the first European ever to reach that mysterious country. He'd met the grand emperor Kublai Khan, staying in his summer palace and even spending time as his ambassador.

Jake was two pages into a chapter about brilliant Chinese inventions when he heard a thump on the roof above him. His room was at the top of a turreted tower – the highest bedroom in the castle apart from Nathan's. He froze, checking that his sword was leaning against his bed (it was now a habit to sleep with a weapon at hand). Felson lifted his head. When another thump came, the dog growled softly as Jake carefully reached for the hilt of his blade. Someone, or something, was creeping along to a point just above his window. Jake tiptoed across the room, sword at the ready, and threw open the casement.

'Who goes there?' he demanded in the deepest tone he could muster.

He gasped as a figure in a balaclava abseiled down from above. '*Who goes there?*' said a voice. 'A little old fashioned, isn't it?' And with that, Yoyo ripped off her disguise. 'May I come in?'

Jake stood back and she jumped down into the room, cheeks rosy with excitement. She looked different, dressed in the French style of the 1820s, in a floaty, high-waisted gown and her hair up in a loose bun. Felson gave a welcoming *wuff* and went to say hello.

'Nice to see you too, Felson, old chap,' said Yoyo, putting on an English accent, ruffling his head, which made him bark again.

'All right, back to bed,' Jake told him, and he curled up in his basket again.

Jake felt a little self-conscious in his pyjamas. 'Wh-wh-what are you doing here?' he asked Yoyo. 'Not that it's not nice to see you . . .'

Yoyo went around examining his room, looking at the portraits of explorers and inventors on the walls. 'Ah, you're reading the book I recommended!' she exclaimed, seeing it lying open on the bed.

'Yes. It's amazing. I can't believe how clever the

41

Chinese are. I never knew they invented the compass.'

'The first great maritime nation in history,' she said proudly. 'But that was only the start of it. How about steel? Paper? Mirrors? Fingerprints? Sunglasses? And how about a little thing called gunpowder?'

'Yes, gunpowder certainly changed a thing or two.' This was an understatement: in the last seven hundred years, Jake had learned, it had been the basic ingredient of every war that had taken place on earth.

There was an awkward silence. 'I've never seen you dressed like that,' Jake commented. 'Are you going somewhere?'

'*We* are,' she corrected him. 'We're going to the party over there.' She pointed in the direction of the mainland, a big smile on her face.

'Really? Er . . .' Jake mumbled. 'Isn't it late?' Immediately he gave himself a mental note to start sounding more daring.

'It's Midsummer Eve, the most magical night of the year . . . and they're dancing the *waltz*. Have you ever heard of the waltz? It's from Vienna, but in France it's considered indecent.' She sounded scandalized. To Jake, the waltz was the most old-fashioned thing in the world, but he reminded himself that he came from a different place in history from Yoyo: he was from twenty-first-century London, while she was from imperial China.

'So? Shall we go?' Yoyo persisted. 'I have a boat moored at the pier. We could be there within the hour.'

Jake glanced out of the window at the midsummer sky, now a deep ultramarine. It still wasn't quite dark. Yoyo's plan was certainly tempting: it would chase his sorrows away. And he had only been to the village twice, on errands with his parents, and never at night. During the day it seemed quite ordinary, but he had the feeling that it would somehow be magical this evening. Even so, he was undecided. 'I'm not really sure, Miss Yuting . . . Yoyo. For a start, my mum and dad would definitely not appreciate—'

'Jake, I'm disappointed. I heard that you were a daredevil. Chariot racing in the Circus Maximus, someone told me! And as far as your parents are concerned . . . don't tell them. That's the easiest course. I don't tell my mother anything. Parents say that they want you to be honest with them, but when you are, they get upset.' Yoyo shrugged, then added: 'I have a feeling your mother doesn't really like me.'

'What? No, of course she likes you,' Jake replied hurriedly, his cheeks flushing at the lie.

'I don't mind, Jake,' she said softly, before putting on her English accent again. 'As you say in jolly old England, I'm not everyone's cup of tea. Anyway, let's find you something to wear.' She had just gone to his chest of drawers and started riffling through it, when there was a knock at the door.

Jake froze and Felson pricked up his ears.

'Are you awake, darling?' his mother called.

Panic engulfed Jake; he looked round at Yoyo. 'Not really,' he called back.

'We'd love to have a word . . .' Miriam cooed.

We? Jake thought. His dad was there . . . even worse. He turned to Yoyo. She was hiding under his bedcovers. 'Not there,' he hissed.

But it was too late.

'What was that, darling?' Miriam answered, coming into the room with Jake's father. Felson bounded over as Jake sat down on the bed, leaning back to mask the lump under the blankets. His dog started barking excitedly, jumped up, and rammed his nose into the bulge where Yoyo was.

'Back to bed,' Jake commanded, rather more harshly than usual, making Felson's ears droop as he sidled back to his basket.

'We won't be long, darling,' said Miriam, pulling up a chair and sitting down. 'We just wanted to check you were all right.'

'Today is not a happy day for any of us,' Alan added, putting his hand on his son's shoulder.

'I'm fine,' Jake replied hastily. 'I'm sad, obviously. But, you know . . . I'm used to it.'

His parents exchanged a look, mistaking the source of his anxiety.

'You know we're leaving tomorrow?' Miriam continued.

'Of course – you've been talking about it nonstop for weeks.' Again Jake realized he sounded sullen. *Where did it come from?* He tried to soften things by adding, 'I'll miss you.'

'Well, before we go, there was something else we wanted to talk about . . .'

'It's a matter of some gravity,' added Alan in the voice he only used on very serious occasions. He had an ancient-looking book under his arm, which he put down on the chair. Jake noticed a picture of the Egyptian pyramids on the cover.

'Do you remember that on your way back from Rome,' Alan began, 'Rose told you a secret . . . that you had travelled to history before, as an infant?'

'Of course I remember,' Jake replied. How could he forget? He had spent a year trying in vain to find out more.

'You see, the thing is,' Miriam carried on carefully, 'we've kept another secret from you, and we think it's time now that you were told.'

'Told? Told *what*?' Jake replied. He felt Yoyo shift under the covers, obviously cocking an ear to hear whatever secret was coming.

His parents looked at each other.

'Well, that wasn't the first time you went back in history.' Alan sat down on the bed and a muffled cry went up: fifteen stone had landed on Yoyo's foot.

Miriam peeled back the covers to reveal . . .

4 THE LAST WALTZ

'Evening, Mr and Mrs Djones,' Yoyo mumbled with a timid smile. She got up and straightened her clothes. 'Jake and I were just . . . It's Midsummer Eve!' she added for no particular reason.

Miriam bristled with anger. 'I think you had better go back to your room, Miss Yuting. Immediately.'

'Mum, don't be so embarrassing.'

'Embarrassing? You're fourteen, Jake.'

'Fifteen. I'm fifteen. I have been for three months.'

'Well, you're just a boy,' she snapped. 'You're far too young for . . . for . . .' Unable to produce the word, she waved her hand at Yoyo.

This only threw Jake into a fury. 'We were *talking*!'

he fumed, raising his voice. 'Is that against the law?'

'I wouldn't speak to your mum like that,' Alan chipped in. 'Not a good idea.'

'Well, I'm sorry if I'm *so* embarrassing,' Miriam continued, 'but I have a duty of care to Miss Yuting's mother.'

'And that's your only concern?' Jake muttered. 'Your own reputation?' He had no idea why he felt so angry.

'It's all right, Jake. She's quite right,' said Yoyo, trying to calm things down. 'It's very late.' She picked up her things, turned to Alan and Miriam and bowed. 'I'm so sorry to have upset you.' She turned towards the door, but Jake jumped up and intercepted her.

'Well, I don't want her to leave,' he declared defiantly. 'We were talking. Please sit down again, Miss Yuting,' he added self-consciously, pointing to a chair.

Now Miriam lost patience. 'I have no idea what's got into you lately. No idea at all. But I think it's best if you two see less of each other. Now, Miss Yuting, would you please return to your rooms. This instant.'

Yoyo nodded, squeezed Jake's arm, headed for the

door. She stopped and looked back one last time. 'Mr and Mrs Djones, can I just say, for your own piece of mind, that your son was entirely innocent. I came to pay him a visit, that's all. I panicked when I heard you and hid under the bedclothes. I was to blame – but the crime was no more than this. I wish you both a good night.' And with that, she vanished.

Jake went after her.

'Jake, you stay here,' his mother commanded.

'Is it all right if I say goodnight?' he asked tersely. Without waiting for the answer, he left the room and collared Yoyo just outside. 'I'll see you on the pier in fifteen minutes,' he whispered.

'Maybe not tonight,' she replied quietly.

'It has to be tonight. It's midsummer,' he insisted.

Yoyo looked up at him; there was fire in his eyes, and suddenly she was excited again. 'We have a deal.' She rushed off down the passage as Jake returned to his bedroom.

Miriam was already looking sheepish, the flush of anger gone. 'I'm sorry. But you have to learn that you can't always do what you want.' Jake shrugged and got back into bed. 'We'll see you before we leave. All right?' She kissed him on the forehead.

'What about this big secret?' Jake asked.

'Let's talk about it in the morning,' Alan said, slipping the book with the picture of the pyramids back under his arm. 'You sleep well, son.'

Jake hid under his duvet until he heard them leave. Suddenly he wanted to run after them, to apologize for being rude, to tell them that he loved them really. But something prevented him. He waited until their footsteps had disappeared down the stairs; then he got up and went over to his chest of drawers to find something to wear for the dance.

Fifteen minutes later, Jake was creeping across the lawn and down the steps to the pier.

He'd gone for what Nathan called 'the rakish look': buccaneer boots, shirt half hanging out of his breeches, a belt with his favourite sword, a scarf with a skull-and-crossbones pattern and a ruby earring. The earring in particular – on loan from Nathan – made him feel very grown up. In modern-day London, he wouldn't have had the courage to wear a big jewel on his ear, but in these romantic times it was the ultimate symbol of daring; although in truth the clip hurt his earlobe.

There was a rowing boat moored on the far side

of the quay; obviously the one that Yoyo had pre-pared earlier. Jake jumped down into it and waited, heart thumping. A warm breeze carried across the water and a giant moon inched up over the Mount.

The bells from the clock tower chimed eleven. Jake looked impatiently towards the main doors, checked that his earring was still in place and teased his scarf into a carefully casual knot. No one appeared. After ten minutes more, Jake's spirits started to deflate.

As he lingered, he noticed something he had never seen before: the stone piers to which ships were moored were each engraved with the History Keepers' symbol of two planets whizzing around an hourglass. He gazed at them, and remembered his earlier conversation with his parents. He was suddenly desperate to know what it was that they'd been about to tell him. *Well, that wasn't the first time you went back in history,* his father had said. When had he been before? What was the significance of that old book? He would have to wait until the morning to find out.

Finally Yoyo pattered excitedly down onto the pier. 'Sorry – my mother was patrolling.' She was breathless with excitement. She jumped into the boat and planted a kiss on Jake's forehead. 'Let's go,' she said as they took an oar each and set off towards the mainland.

Behind them, the castle slept. All the windows were dark – except for one, high up in a turret. Here a candle flickered and someone looked down with a telescope, watching the craft make its way across the bay.

Smiling at each other, Jake and Yoyo glided towards the mainland, while the giant silhouette of the Mont St Michel diminished behind them. Gradually the music grew louder, clear as crystal across the placid sea.

As they neared the little port, Jake saw that it was hectic with activity; even the pier was heaving with revellers who had come down to take a break from the dance and enjoy the night air.

They moored and stepped ashore, Yoyo leading the way. A cluster of merrymakers watched her as she sliced through them with the assurance of an empress. (Even dressed in the style of the day, Yoyo couldn't help standing out.) One woman, rouge plastered over her worn face, put her nose in the air in imitation of the new arrival. Yoyo paid no attention, but Jake smiled timidly at the woman and gave a little bow.

'*Trop jeune, hélas, chéri,*' the woman said, pinching his cheek and making the whole company fall about laughing. *A little too young for me, my dear.*

Jake reddened and hurried on, fiddling nervously with his earring. Yoyo was waiting on the edge of the square, where the dance was in full swing: at least twenty couples whizzed around, shrieking with delight, as the fiddlers played at the far end.

'That's the waltz?' Jake asked, wondering where he had ever got the idea that it was boring.

'Wonderful, isn't it?' said Yoyo, stepping back as a particularly swift couple spun past.

Jake remembered the last village dance he had been to: his first mission with the History Keepers had taken him to the banks of the Rhine in Germany. That dance had been entrancing; this was far more riotous, with a midsummer madness in the air. Around the edge of the square, innkeepers served cider, brandy and absinthe from makeshift bars, while cooks spit-roasted whole pigs over hot braziers. Swelling the numbers of locals, there were dozens of raucous young soldiers from the local garrison in navy and white uniforms, merry on wine and singing army ditties.

'Come on, then,' said Yoyo, taking Jake's hand and pulling him onto the dance floor.

He had no time to protest. He knew he wasn't much of a dancer, but he threw himself into it, holding onto Yoyo as they swirled round. 'Sorry, sorry,' he kept saying as he thumped into other couples. But they were all too carried away to even notice him. Yoyo seemed to pick up the waltz immediately, and she helped guide him. After a bit of practice – and half an eye on people's feet – Jake started to find his rhythm. As he spun, he noticed the distant outline of the Mont St Michel across the water and felt a pang of guilt.

Meanwhile, another small vessel had docked next to Jake and Yoyo's boat. It carried a single passenger: a man in a high-collared trench coat, and a stovepipe hat worn so low that it all but hid his mane of auburn hair and cast his face into shadow. He stepped ashore and darted to the edge of the square, watching Jake and Yoyo closely.

'Thirsty work,' Yoyo panted as the dance came to an end. 'Something to drink?' Without waiting for a reply, she headed for one of the bars.

As Jake followed, the band struck up a new tune.

It was evidently a favourite, and a great shout went out as everyone rushed onto the dance floor. A young girl bumped into Jake and his earring pinged off, a shot of red flashing across the ground. He went to pick it up, but it was kicked away by another dancer. He had to get down on his hands and knees, making a nuisance of himself, before finally retrieving it.

He found Yoyo being served by a man with an immense belly, long lank hair and a deeply un-welcoming look in his eye. He sloshed some of the contents of an open vat of murky liquid into two wooden beakers and shoved them across the table. Yoyo paid with a single silver coin, claimed her drinks and held one out for Jake.

'What's that?' he asked apprehensively.

'It's cider,' she announced with a sparkle in her eye.

Jake knew that cider was alcoholic. He had only tried alcohol a couple of times. On the second occasion, at a dinner party thrown by his parents, he'd secretly drunk two glasses of red wine and had been sick on the family sofa, ruining the evening for everyone. 'I don't think my mum and dad would really—' he began.

'You mustn't worry about them so much,' Yoyo insisted testily.

Jake found his gaze flicking again towards the island in the distance. He didn't want to disappoint Yoyo, but on this point he was clear: his parents were leaving early in the morning and he needed to say goodbye to them properly (not to mention discovering this secret of theirs). 'Thank you, not for me,' he said decisively.

'A man of conviction.' Yoyo smiled. 'I like it.' Then her eyes flashed as she recognized someone on the other side of the square. 'That's Nathan, isn't it?'

'What?' said Jake.

'Nathan Wylder. There . . . with the top hat.'

Jake tried to peer through the crowd to where Yoyo was pointing. He spotted someone in a coat and hat, but couldn't see his face. Then the man, perhaps sensing that he had been rumbled, turned sharply and collided with someone. As his hat went flying, Jake saw that it was indeed his friend.

'Nathan!' he called overexcitedly. The American was retreating up a side street, away from the square. 'Nathan!' – again to no avail. 'He obviously hasn't seen us,' he said to Yoyo. 'Wait here a minute . . .'

Jake flew after him. 'Nathan, it's me,' he panted, on finally catching up with him.

His cover blown, Nathan turned and gave a dazzling smile. 'Jake, you old rogue, how nice to see you,' he said innocently. 'What brings you to these shores?'

'It's a long story,' replied Jake, a little sheepishly. 'Yoyo and I thought it might be fun to come to the dance. Obviously we're breaking every rule in the book—'

'Yoyo?' Nathan interrupted.

'Miss Yuting – she's just over there.'

'Yes, I've seen her,' Nathan said impatiently. 'She lets you call her Yoyo?'

Jake was a little confused by his friend's strange, abrupt manner. 'It's her nickname, I think,' he replied carefully, wary of falling into a trap. 'So what are you up to?' he asked – then suddenly remembered what Charlie had said on the night of the wedding: that Nathan had fallen for someone from the mainland. This was clearly why he was behaving so oddly.

'I know you don't really get on with Y— Miss Yuting, but would you like to come and say hello?' Jake asked.

'I suppose it wouldn't kill me . . .' Nathan

57

shrugged. 'As long as she doesn't say anything rude about my outfit. I may be a perfect specimen of manhood, but I do have feelings too, you know.'

As Jake led him back into the square, he reached into his pocket, took out his spectacles and hurriedly put them on. 'I've grown used to them,' he explained. 'Find them rather reassuring on my nose.' He unbuttoned his coat, revealing a smart tunic beneath. 'Good evening, Miss Yuting,' he said, coming face to face with Yoyo and bowing formally. 'What a lovely coincidence bumping into you both. They're very colourful, these local dances, aren't they?' He sounded more like an old professor every minute. 'I heard the music across the water and couldn't resist it.'

'That was our thought entirely,' Yoyo agreed, fondly pinching Jake's cheek. Nathan flinched at the gesture.

Just then, three young soldiers swaggered towards them. They were a little older than Nathan, and if not taller, certainly broader. The leader – a lieutenant – went up to Yoyo and, without even glancing at her companions, ordered with a Gallic shrug: '*Dansez avec moi.*' It was not a question. Though no more than eighteen, the youth was dripping with medals, and the muscles rippled underneath his half-unbuttoned tunic. His features were those of a boxer – square chin, bold nose – finished off with a sneer, and his ear was pierced with a gold stud. *Now* that's *the rakish look*, Jake couldn't help thinking.

Yoyo looked him up and down, before whispering to the others, 'He's so pompous, I *have* to do it.' She presented her hand.

'Excuse me.' Nathan stopped the soldier with a delicate tap on his shoulder. 'Just the one dance. *Pas plus qu'une danse, d'accord?* She's with us, you see.'

He and Jake watched Yoyo take the floor. Despite his appearance, the lieutenant was a surprisingly good dancer.

'So, Jake,' Nathan began nervously, 'I'm going to come right out and ask it . . . Are you two an item?'

'What?'

'You and "Yoyo" – as she has deigned to let you call her – are you . . . *together?*'

'*Together?* No – no of course not,' Jake stammered, the very word throwing him. 'We're just friends.'

'I can't begin to tell you how relieved I am.' For the first time that night, Nathan gave a genuine smile.

59

Jake's voice was cold. 'You're being a little hard on her. Actually she's – she's lovely when you get to know her.'

There was no reply. They both watched the dance for a minute before Nathan spoke again. 'I'm not bragging, am I, when I say that I have a certain reputation with the young ladies? A particular *je ne sais quoi*? How could I not? Ravishing looks, a winning sense of style, bucketfuls of charm – not to mention my kindness to children and animals. You'd agree?'

'Absolutely. Bucketfuls of everything,' Jake concurred, his eye on Yoyo as she whizzed past.

'So, getting the attention of the fairer sex has never been a problem. Ergo I have never felt the need to commit to any one person. Love has always struck me as an absurd waste of energy, the bringer of a great deal of angst. And it's a well-known fact: angst adds lines. Who wants to get old before their time?'

'Who indeed?'

'Besides, why tie yourself down when you have the whole of history to choose from?'

'Exactly,' sighed Jake, wishing that Nathan would get to the point.

'Then *she* arrives. Miss Yuting. The perfect specimen. Good at everything.'

Jake turned to his friend, the truth of the situation suddenly dawning on him.

'She pretends not to be dazzled . . .' Nathan continued. 'That's fine. I work a little harder, dress a little sharper, smoulder a little bolder. Nothing. *Rien. Nada.*'

'There *is* no girl in the village, is there . . .?' Jake asked.

'She won't even laugh at my jokes. And she questions my intelligence – forcing me to wear spectacles.'

'You don't dislike her at all, do you? Quite the opposite.'

'I mean, look at me! How could you turn this down?'

'Did you follow us here? Is that why you came?'

'And *then* she starts challenging me to duels – with sabres, pistols, crossbows. Beats me hands down every time. No one *ever* beats me – except Topaz on very rare occasions. And do you know how that makes me feel? It has only made me like her more, Goddammit – excuse my French. It's insufferable.' Nathan took off his glasses and looked

Jake in the eye. 'Do you have any idea how painful it is?'

Jake decided it was time to make his own confession, if only to shut Nathan up. 'Yes,' he replied defiantly. 'I know *exactly* how painful it is. Because I feel the same about her. And in answer to your question, we're not *together* – as you put it – but I wish we were!'

There was a moment of stunned silence. 'Really?' Nathan replied. 'Well, that might be a problem, old boy.' (Nathan was using phrases like *old boy* a lot these days; a half-English, half-Charleston affectation.)

Just then, the dance ended. Jake and Nathan watched keenly as Yoyo thanked her partner and turned to leave the dance floor. But the soldier grabbed her hand and pulled her back. She shook herself free and spoke sharply to him.

'That's it!' Nathan declared. 'I've seen enough.' He barged his way into the square, followed swiftly by Jake, and they positioned themselves between Yoyo and the lieutenant.

'That's all for tonight,' the American drawled. 'Run along now.'

As the three History Keepers retreated, the

lieutenant gave Nathan a kick in the pants, so that he lost his balance and fell to his knees. Rage flashed across his face.

'Kicking a man from behind?' Nathan hissed as the others helped him up. 'You really are as dumb as a bucket of rocks, and not much prettier.' He was about to draw his sword when Jake interceded, firmly placing his hand on the hilt.

'Better not,' he warned; 'not in the village.' It was one of the golden rules of Point Zero: the inhabitants of the island should avoid drawing attention to themselves. It was, after all, a *secret* organization.

But the soldier, whose sidekicks had now closed ranks with their leader, had not finished: '*Vos cheveux sont ridicules*,' he said, unsheathing his own weapon and flicking Nathan's curls. '*Vous ressemblez à une fille.*'

'I look like a girl?' replied Nathan, his hand going to his sword again.

'That's right,' the soldier sneered, before nodding at Yoyo. 'And she dances like a man.'

In unison, Jake and Nathan drew their swords.

The soldiers followed suit. Nathan attacked first, lunging at his foe, as Jake set upon the two sidekicks, slicing expertly, relishing the opportunity to show off his new-found skills in front of Yoyo. In the last year he had become almost as gifted a swordsman as Nathan.

Gasps went up amongst the villagers, many retreating in alarm, as the two young agents, with just a handful of strokes, disarmed their three opponents without even breaking sweat.

'If you spent a little less time prancing around on the dance floor,' Nathan gloated as he scooped up the Frenchmen's swords, 'you could make something of yourselves.'

'Behind you!' Jake shouted, as an entire platoon of soldiers surged across the square towards them.

'Is that really necessary?' his friend sighed. 'It's got nothing to do with them. Hold this a moment,' he said, chucking his sword to Jake before turning to one of the spit-braziers and grabbing hold of the giant spit. 'My apologies,' he offered to the cook as he launched an entire roast pig into the air. It thumped to the ground, rolling towards the on-coming guards and knocking them down like skittles. As they landed one on top of the other, a stray helmet flew out. It struck Jake full in the chest, whereupon he tottered backwards and fell into a vat of cider; it collapsed, the contents spilling out across the dance floor.

Furious, the hulking innkeeper grabbed him by his scarf, pulled him up out of the wreckage and drew his fist back to sock him. Jake dodged the blow, and as the innkeeper lunged forward again, helped him on his way with a firm kick on the backside. There was a chorus of discordant fiddles as he crashed into the band.

Now the entire village had got caught up in the fight, locals and soldiers with one common enemy: the two young upstarts who had arrived by boat (Yoyo had sensibly retreated into an alleyway at the start of the brawl). Madness raged until two pistol shots rang out. Everyone came to a standstill as a stout man with a tricorn hat and enormous red sideburns stepped into the square, a look of thunder on his face.

The two boys edged closer to each other. 'Just our luck.' Nathan rolled his eyes. 'That's Poing de Fer, the local sheriff.'

Poing de Fer subjected them to a tirade of abuse – in the most colourful French that Jake had ever heard – before giving orders for their immediate arrest.

Yoyo watched with a sinking heart as they were handcuffed and led away.

They were locked in a tiny stone cell with a single barred window looking out onto the dark sea. They were a sorry sight: Jake's clothes were torn, he stank of cider and he had the beginnings of a black eye. The jail was next to the army garrison, one of a cluster of old stone houses on a headland half a mile from the village. The boys had begged the sheriff to show mercy for their *moment de folie*, but their pleas had fallen on deaf ears. When Nathan persisted, Poing de Fer told them that the pressgang would be round in the morning to assess them for military service.

As Jake stared through the bars at the dark shape of the Mont St Michel, he was filled with disgust at himself. In a few hours' time he was supposed to be saying farewell to his parents. Even worse, he and Nathan had broken one of the most solemn rules of the organization by drawing attention to themselves.

'We have to find a way out of here!' he exclaimed, shaking the bars. But they were set solidly in the stone wall.

5 FAMILY IN RUINS

An hour later, a voice whispered from outside: 'It's me.' Jake and Nathan looked up to see a familiar face looking through the window and immediately leaped to their feet.

'Sorry to keep you waiting,' Yoyo said quietly. 'I've been waiting for the guard to doze off – not to mention the whole platoon next door. But I have a plan to get you out of here . . .' She produced two sticks of dynamite. 'Borrowed from the army stores,' she explained.

The sight of the explosives gave Jake a jolt. He hadn't come across dynamite since Agata Zeldt had detonated her bombs in ancient Rome, creating pandemonium and carnage during one of the largest public events in history.

'It's an interesting notion,' Nathan told Yoyo, 'but these walls are three feet thick. We'll just end up drawing more attention to ourselves, and no doubt losing some limbs into the bargain – and I'm rather partial to mine. No, I'm afraid we have only one option. Miss Yuting, you need to get help from Point Zero. The commander has an understanding with Poing de Fer. She's the only person who can get us out of here.'

Jake's heart sank. Involving Galliana Goethe was the last thing he wanted. Losing a limb was almost preferable to the disgrace he would suffer once their misconduct became common knowledge. But he knew that Nathan was right. They had to do everything they could to limit the damage.

Yoyo reluctantly agreed, and moments later Jake and Nathan saw her rowing back across the bay.

Nathan turned to his companion. 'Jake, old boy,' he said, 'can we agree on something?'

'What?'

Nathan was clearly in a serious mood: his voice was low and deep. 'Not to fall out over Miss Yuting?'

Jake looked back at him, half smiling – and nodded. Nathan held out his hand and they shook on it.

'Friendship is more important than anything,'

Jake declared solemnly. Then he started to laugh; though it hurt his head. 'I can't believe you followed us here.'

'Well, no one needs to know about it, all right? I'd be a laughing stock if it ever got out.'

'God forbid that anyone should laugh at you.'

They both chuckled, but then sat in silence, listening to the sounds of the dance in the distance.

The night passed slowly, the noise dying down by degrees. At dawn, Jake heard the sound of splashing oars. He pulled himself up. His head throbbed and the bruise around his eye was sore. He saw a small craft with navy blue sails approaching the mainland. It was Galliana's yacht, the *Kingfisher*, and he could see her standing at the prow. There was a gentleman with her, in a top hat – Jupitus Cole.

Jake frowned. 'Why's he here?' he said to himself, his spirits plummeting still further. He watched as the boat docked at the pier. When the pair disembarked, Jake noticed that Jupitus was carrying a heavy crate. They headed towards the town and disappeared from view.

'Nathan,' Jake called quietly to his friend, who had fallen asleep in the corner. The American opened his eyes and sat up. 'They're coming.'

Jake tucked in his shirt, combed back his hair and tried to clean his face with his skull-and-crossbones scarf. It didn't make much difference: he still looked dreadful.

'*I* do the talking,' said Nathan, smartening himself up. 'This is *my* mess.'

Jake shook his head. '*I* was the one who came here in the first place.'

Voices came from beyond the door. Jupitus had started talking – in slightly broken French – but Galliana soon took over. She was completely fluent and spoke with authority. Whatever she was saying must have been reasonable, as Poing de Fer seemed to put up no fight at all; his tone became almost jovial.

Five minutes later there was a clinking of keys and the door swung open. Jake froze as Jupitus entered, eyes cold and mirthless.

'Your parents leave within the hour,' he spat contemptuously to Jake. 'I believe they would like to speak to you before they go.'

'Mr Cole' – Nathan beamed – 'may I start by saying, this is clearly not as bad as it looks.'

'You may do nothing of the sort,' snapped Jupitus. 'Your jangling voice is unwelcome at the best of times, but before breakfast it is unendurable.'

'Jangling?' Nathan shrugged to himself. 'That has quite a pleasant ring.'

'Mr Cole, I'm so sorry,' Jake began. He had a whole speech worked out. 'I am completely to blame—'

Jupitus silenced him with a hiss. 'I have even less interest in *your* point of view. I'd conserve your energies for those you have hurt the most.' He turned and left. Jake and Nathan eyeballed each other and followed him out.

Galliana was waiting, equally stony-faced. Jake had never seen her dressed so soberly – almost like a schoolteacher – and with such attention to period detail (where clothes were concerned, she tended to be as eccentric as her friend Rose). Jake offered her a smile, but she ignored him.

'*Merci*, Monsieur Poing de Fer,' she said, turning to the sheriff. '*C'était un plaisir, comme toujours* . . .' She patted the crate that Jupitus had brought from the boat. It contained nine ancient-looking bottles of golden-brown liquid. Jake guessed that she had used them to bribe him.

Jupitus led the way back to the pier, where Galliana's boat, with its distinctive dark blue sails, was waiting. Nathan attached the skiff he'd brought over to its stern, and they set off for the island. Not a word was spoken for the entire journey.

As they approached the quay, Jake saw that a group of people had gathered there. Usually the departure of agents on missions to distant lands and times was a cheery affair. This time, the *Escape* was being prepared for his parents' journey in almost total silence.

Mr and Mrs Djones stood at the front. It was a shock seeing them dressed in modern clothes again – Alan in his corduroy trousers and Miriam in an old woolly jumper and a denim skirt over leggings. Next to them was a piece of luggage that always seemed to presage bad news: a red suitcase, bulging in readiness for the journey.

Galliana's boat docked, and she and Jupitus stepped ashore, followed by the boys. Jake felt everyone's eyes on him; Yoyo was also watching from a distance, her tight-lipped mother standing guard next to her. Topaz, waiting with Nathan's equally concerned parents on the quayside, offered Jake a glimmer of a smile, but she looked sad, and Jake realized that he had let her down, along with everyone else at Point Zero.

He approached his parents, his head bowed, barely able to look them in the eye. 'I'm glad I managed to see you before you left,' he offered in a quiet voice.

Miriam shook her head and asked, 'What is it that we did wrong?'

'Nothing.' Jake shrugged.

'Are you proud of your behaviour?'

'No.'

'Do you have any idea what the commander had to do to get you out of jail?'

'Mrs Djones, may I just say—' Nathan began.

'You may not! I'm not impressed with you, either. You should be setting an example,' Miriam snapped without taking her eyes off Jake. 'I asked if you had any idea what the commander had to do to get you out of jail?' Jake shook his head. 'She had to bribe the police with cognac left to her by her dead husband! It was two hundred years old. It was priceless.'

'No, I didn't . . . I mean, I didn't ask her to . . . I mean, I'm sorry.'

'So what did we do wrong?' Miriam asked again.

'You didn't do anything wrong!' Jake shouted, suddenly losing his temper.

'That's how you speak to me? Do you hear how he speaks to his mother?' Miriam asked her husband. Alan shook his head; Jake had never seen him look so disappointed. Suddenly Miriam broke off. She leaned forward and sniffed Jake's shirt. 'You've been drinking . . .'

'No.'

'You stink of alcohol, Jake! Don't lie to me.'

'I'm not lying.'

'Actually, Mrs Djones—' Yoyo interrupted from the back; but her mother silenced her with a glare.

For a moment Miriam closed her eyes and shook her head. 'This is your two-week warning, Jake,' she said in a baleful tone that Jake had only heard once in his life; it sent shivers down his spine. 'Do you hear me? We shall return from London, collect you and go straight back again. You will be going back to school, so you can start saying your goodbyes.'

Jake could feel his face heating with anger. 'Really?' he hissed. 'Every time the same threat—'

'This time we mean it! *We mean it!*' Miriam swore. 'You've become impossible.'

'Well, maybe you *did* do something wrong. For a start, you lied to me my whole life.'

'What?' Miriam gasped.

'Now, Jake, let's not get carried away . . .' Alan began.

Rose tried to intervene. 'Come on, now – everyone's a bit tired and emotional.' She took Jake's hand, but he shook her off.

'Well, you *did*. You lied about everything,' Jake continued, gathering momentum. 'You lied about working here – the bathroom shop – everything in London . . . all lies!'

'We did that to protect you,' Miriam said. 'You *know* why we did that.'

'And you lied about Philip. My own brother!' Jake stared at her, eyes flashing with fury. 'I hate you.' The phrase hung in the air for a moment; then he turned, pushed his way through the crowd and ran up into the castle.

Miriam sobbed as Alan pulled her into his arms.

A few minutes later, leaving the murmuring crowd on the pier, Alan and Rose went looking for Jake.

He had gone to Dora's stable and slammed the door behind him. He often took refuge with the elephant when he felt low: just being close to her calmed him down. Of course, she was only an animal, but she seemed wise all the same. He fed her some carrots, stroked her ears and searched her ancient eyes for the answers to his problems.

When he heard his father and aunt calling his name, he hid in a little compartment where the straw was kept, covering himself completely.

After a while the shouts stopped. Jake lay there a little longer. He was exhausted, his eyelids feeling heavier and heavier.

Suddenly a vision came to him – he wasn't sure if it was a dream or a hallucination – of his mother crying out. The *Escape* had been holed in a storm and was being dragged down under the foaming waves. His eyes shot open and he sat up with a jolt. 'I have to stop them . . .' he muttered, running out of the stable and down the path to the other side of the island. But the pier was deserted, save for a single person, and the *Escape* was disappearing towards the grey line of the horizon.

'*Nooooo!*' Jake yelled.

Signor Gondolfino was watching the retreating ship. Jake flew past him, to the very edge of the pier and called out again at the top of his voice: 'I'm sorry. I'm so sorry . . .' The sea seemed to mock him: there was no chance anyone on that ship could hear him.

Signor Gondolfino approached, tapping his way carefully along the quay with his ivory cane. '*Mi dispiace tanto*, Jake,' he said softly, laying a hand on his shoulder. 'My deep regrets. Your mother gave me this for you.' He handed over a note:

> *You're my special boy, I love you.*
> *Mum*

Jake watched the ship disappear over the horizon; then his face crumpled and he started to cry. Signor Gondolfino put an arm around him. '*Piangi, caro mio.* You cry – it's good for you. It's so hard to be grown up. *Magari fossimo bambini per sempre.* If only we could be children for ever.'

A drop of rain fell from the sky, splattering onto Gondolfino's silk jacket. Then another; and another. Soon they were soaked to the skin.

6 THE DOOM BELL

Jake was wide awake, tossing and turning, the events of the day haunting him. It was gone two when he heard a single deep toll from somewhere far below. There were many bells that rang on the island for many different reasons, but this one had a distinctive tone that was unfamiliar to Jake. It sounded ominous.

A few moments later, he heard doors slamming and footsteps clattering along corridors; then urgent voices coming from the quay. He went over to the window and looked down. Galliana, hurriedly fastening her cloak, was issuing orders to two boatmen. As they started preparing a ship – the *Tulip*, a craft that Jake had sailed in on an ill-fated expedition to Stockholm – Jupitus Cole emerged, buttoning his jacket and putting on his top hat, followed swiftly by Dr Chatterju with a bulging leather case.

Jake *had* to know what was going on. He threw on some clothes, put on his boots, and hurriedly made his way down to the ground floor.

'What's happened?' he asked the doctor on arriving at the pier.

'The doom bell just rang!'

'The *doom bell*?'

'SOS. Someone's got into difficulty trying to enter the north-western horizon point!' Horizon points, Jake knew, were the places where agents could leap through time.

He felt sick, fearing the worst. 'Is it my parents?' he asked, remembering his terrible vision.

'No,' Chatterju said. 'The mayday signal came from the past, the 1790s. Your parents were heading the other way.'

'But perhaps they got lost in time?' Jake persisted. It wouldn't have been the first time they had taken a wrong turn.

'All we have is an SOS,' the doctor replied, opening his case to check the contents: it was full of medical instruments, bottles of medicine and syringes.

Galliana and Jupitus rushed aboard the *Tulip* and started up the engine. Chatterju bustled up the gangplank after them.

Jake was desperate to follow. 'Can I assist in any way?' he called hopefully. Galliana and Jupitus stared at him, their opposition clear.

'The more hands the better . . .' Dr Chatterju offered. 'Who knows what trouble they might be in . . . Whoever *they* are.'

Reluctantly Galliana agreed. 'Quickly, then.'

Jake hurried up the gangplank, the boatmen untied the rope, and a second later the vessel lurched away from the sea wall. Behind him, he heard the main doors crash open; then more hurrying footsteps, and Nathan appeared, followed by Yoyo.

'What's happened?' the American shouted from the quayside.

'SOS from someone entering the north-western horizon point,' Jake called back.

His two friends watched, powerless, as the ship sped off. It flew into the night, guided by the gold rings of the Constantor towards the horizon point.

From time to time, Jake glanced at Galliana standing at the helm, the wind in her long grey hair.

He realized that he only knew her in the context of the island, as an administrator – not as an adventurer. Now, for the first time, he got a sense of what she must have been like as a young agent in the field, determined and calm. Suddenly he longed to know about the missions she had undertaken. 'Commander,' he ventured, 'may I ask, how can we be sure that the SOS did not come from an enemy faction?'

'Mayday signals are encrypted like all Meslith messages,' she replied, her eyes glancing at the Constantor, 'but of course, there is never a hundred per cent certainty.'

Jupitus illustrated the point by removing pistols from a chest beside the helm. He handed one each to Galliana and Chatterju – but none to Jake.

'Everyone to be armed, Mr Cole,' the commander declared coolly.

Jupitus passed another weapon over, saying, 'As a precaution only, you understand?' Jake nodded.

As the three golden discs on the Constantor began to align, they became even more vigilant, scanning the ocean for any sign of a vessel in trouble. Sturdy waves rolled across the Atlantic.

Jake, watching from the starboard rail, noticed it

first: a soft whistling in the air. He looked around, scanning the dark water. The mysterious sound grew shriller and louder. 'There's something here,' he called, and Jupitus and Chatterju rushed over. As they watched, bubbles foamed on the surface; then the water began to curve in on itself, creating a hollow in the sea: the imprint of the hull of a ship that hadn't yet materialized through time. Jake felt a pulse of fear.

As Jupitus and Chatterju cocked their guns, there was a sudden intense rush of air, then an explosion of spectral light, immediately followed by shouts and the creaking of timbers as the vessel suddenly took shape, filling the void.

She was a small sailing yacht, half the size of their own ship. It was certainly not the *Escape*; not his parents. But who could it be?

'Right hand down!' Jupitus yelled to the commander, fearing they might forge straight into it. She obeyed, narrowly missing the yacht.

Jake could see that the other ship was in danger: her prow was sinking and water foamed up through the smashed timbers of the deck. A man in a high-collared coat, seemingly the only person on board, stood with his legs braced as he shouted for help over the tumult. He was Galliana's age – in his fifties, Jake guessed – and had the bearing of an adventurer. His thick hair was still blond despite his age, and seemed oddly familiar to Jake. He was obviously not the enemy, as Jupitus and Chatterju immediately threw down their weapons.

Without hesitation Jupitus jumped up onto the rail and flung himself over the foaming water onto the troubled ship, sliding down the raked deck towards the man. 'Are you all right? Are you hurt?' Jake heard him ask. The man nodded to his arm, indicating that it was broken. 'Are you alone?' A firm nod.

Jupitus clasped him around the waist and led him up the deck, calling out to Chatterju to throw him a rope. Jake noticed that the man was clutching a leather satchel under his good arm.

'Who is that?' Jake asked the commander.

For a moment she did not reply; just stared at him, perplexed. 'It's Isaksen,' she replied in a worried tone. 'Caspar Isaksen Senior – or Fredrik, as we know him.'

Jake's eyes went wide. The name Isaksen sent a shiver down his spine. This was the head of the famous producers of atomium; the father of the double-dealing Caspar Junior – that's why Jake had recognized his blond hair.

'What's he doing here?' Galliana murmured. 'In twenty years, he has not once left Sweden.'

Jupitus was using the rope to pull Isaksen towards the *Tulip*, when there was a splintering of wood. The yacht cracked in two and suddenly sank, almost dragging them down into the vortex with her. Jupitus held onto the rope as his top hat went swirling away, but Isaksen lost his footing. Jupitus reached out to save him, grabbing his broken arm and making the man howl in agony. Jupitus, sinews stretching to their limit, managed to hold onto the man's coat, while Jake and Chatterju, hooking their feet onto the rigging, hauled the two of them up onto the deck. As the injured Swede was lifted over the rail, he dropped his leather satchel into the sea.

'No!' Isaksen bellowed. 'Save it! You must save it.' He looked like he was about to throw himself back into the water.

Jake acted on impulse, leaping onto the rail and diving into the roiling sea. First there was a shock of cold, then blindness. It was like being inside an avalanche, with debris smashing into him from all sides. But he knew where the sack was. He grabbed its strap and kicked back with all his might. Twice he was pulled down again, but finally he surfaced.

The others, shouting from the *Tulip*, threw a lifebelt. Jake caught hold of it and they yanked him up onto the deck.

He stood there shivering, and Galliana wrapped a blanket around him. 'That was brave of you, young man,' she whispered, her eyes glinting with pride. 'It was worthy of the Djones name.'

Jake grinned: it had been worth it just to hear that. He handed her the leather satchel, and she turned to Isaksen, who was sitting on a trunk, while Dr Chatterju felt carefully along his arm to see where it was broken.

'Good morning, Fredrik,' she said. 'I must admit, you were the last person I was expecting.' Isaksen looked up at her and gave a little grunt. 'You know Dr Chatterju, of course; and Jupitus.'

'It's – it's been a while,' Isaksen stammered hoarsely.

'And the boy who saved your satchel,' she said, pointing, 'is Jake Djones.'

At the sound of the name, Isaksen's head came up, and he studied the boy keenly, before offering a smile. 'Good to meet you, Jake.'

'Good to meet you too, sir,' Jake answered back, intrigued by Isaksen's reaction.

'So what happened, Fredrik?' Galliana asked.

'I was mad, completely mad to make the journey on my own. It's been decades since I've set sail and I'm rusty at the helm,' he said. 'I was in such a hurry to leave 1792, I didn't chart my journey properly. I struck some rocks. It wasn't until I was two leagues from the horizon point that the ship started listing and I realized that the hull had been ruptured. That's when I sent out the mayday. Thank God you came.'

'Why the terrible hurry?' Galliana asked.

'Because I found something late last night – something important – and I wanted to hand it over immediately. In person.'

Jake looked at the man. There was something in his tone that made his heart beat faster. Jupitus had turned the *Tulip* round to head back towards the coast, but he too was now listening closely.

'What did you find?' Galliana asked gravely.

'Open it,' Isaksen said, nodding towards his satchel.

She unbuckled it and withdrew a bound portfolio. It was old and cracked, and stuffed with odd pieces of paper. As Galliana turned to the first page – holding onto it tightly so it wouldn't take off in the wind – Jake noticed Isaksen scrutinize him once again. The commander glanced over a few more sheets, then, without comment, put them back in the bag.

'Thank you for bringing this,' was all she said.

His examination complete, Dr Chatterju spoke. 'Well, you've fractured your humerus, no doubt about it. We'll have to deal with that later. In the meantime I'm going to pop your radius back in its socket. The sooner, the better. You might feel this.' Without a moment's hesitation, Chatterju took hold of the patient's forearm and, pivoting it at the elbow, snapped it back into place, making Isaksen roar once again and thump his good hand against the trunk. 'All done.' Chatterju grinned, trying to make as little of it as possible. Isaksen panted, teeth clenched, until the pain receded.

Soon, the distinct conical shape of the Mont St Michel came into sight. Nathan, Yoyo, Rose and a few others, mostly still in their dressing gowns, were waiting on the pier. They got to their feet as the *Tulip* drew near, squinting up at the deck to see who was aboard. Rose recognized the newcomer first.

'Good grief,' she said. 'Fredrik Isaksen. What on earth is he doing here?'

They watched as the group disembarked.

'Thank you all for waiting,' Galliana announced brusquely as she came ashore. 'It's late, and our new arrival needs attention. So quickly to bed now, everyone, please. In the morning I will make an announcement. All History Keepers are to convene in the stateroom at eight o'clock sharp.' With that, she swept into the castle, the leather satchel still in her hand.

Jake was exhausted, and soon dropped off to sleep.

He woke just after dawn and dressed quickly, desperate to know why Isaksen had been in such a hurry to get to the Mont St Michel. With time to spare before the meeting, he took Felson for a brisk walk, popping into the stables to give Dora her breakfast of cabbage and apples.

On his way back, he found himself drawn to the History Keepers' memorial stone, where agents who had perished in the course of duty were remembered. Set upon a plinth in the shadow of a willow tree, it was a statue of an hourglass, carved out of silvery black marble. Dozens of names were engraved on it, some of them quite recently. Jake sat there for a long time, lost in thought. All those lives . . . Thinking of his recent behaviour, he wondered if he was worthy of them. Rescuing the satchel had made him feel better about himself, but would he ever become as great as these History Keepers?

When he reached the stateroom at a quarter to eight, it was already buzzing with activity. Nearly every seat around the long conference table had been taken, and groups of History Keepers were standing chatting. 'Make way — convalescent coming through,' a voice called from behind. Jake turned and smiled at the sight of Nathan pushing Charlie into the room in an ancient bath chair. A holdall attached to the side of the chair contained Mr Drake, perched on a velvet cushion, evidently enjoying all the attention.

'It's good to see you up and about,' said Jake. 'Can I get you anything?' he asked, nodding towards the breakfast counter.

Charlie was sniffing the air. 'I can smell something intriguing. What is that . . .?' Then it came to him: 'Macaroons! Yes, please. A much-maligned but nonetheless magnificent pastry.'

Jake went to get him some, and returned with

a plate piled high. Charlie took one immediately.

'So' – he spoke with his mouth full – 'do we know any more? Fancy Fredrik Isaksen turning up. It's like being visited by royalty. Galliana Goethe might be the commander, but Isaksen holds the *real* power.'

Just then, Topaz appeared at Jake's side. She leaned forward and gave Charlie a kiss on each cheek. 'How's the invalid this morning? *Tu te sens beaucoup mieux aujourd-hui?* And you too . . .' She gave Mr Drake a tickle under his chin, then turned her warm smile on Jake and Nathan. 'And I trust you two have recovered from your night on the town?'

Jake nodded sheepishly, while Nathan added glumly, 'The less said about it the better.'

Suddenly the chit-chat subsided and Jake looked round to see Jupitus in the doorway – with Fredrik Isaksen at his side. The Swede's arm was in a sling and he was gazing around the room in admiration. Charlie was right: it was as if royalty had arrived. The women were particularly fascinated. Fredrik was handsome, in a rugged way – especially next to the pale and imperious Jupitus. Last night, Jake hadn't really noticed the distinct twinkle in his eye.

'How wonderful to see you again, Herr Isaksen,' Lydia Wunderbar trilled, forcing her way through to the front. 'May I say how super you look, after all these years. How long has it been? Two decades?' She smiled coquettishly, her hand going to her immaculately coiffed hair.

Isaksen smiled roguishly as he struggled to recall who she was.

'Don't tell me you've forgotten!' Lydia gasped in horror. 'Lydia Wunderbar. Of the Munich Wunderbars. Remember we played eight hands of quite frantic Canasta together while waiting for that ghastly ferry in Genoa? I'm afraid I rather trounced you,' she added, shrieking with laughter.

'Of course I remember,' Fredrik purred. It was obvious to Jake, if not to Lydia, that this was a lie. 'We must do it again sometime.'

'Anytime! Anytime at all!' She clapped her hands together in delight. 'But I am being so rude. You are injured, and here I am chatting away. Do sit down.' She indicated a chair next to Rose's.

On seeing her, Fredrik's face lit up. 'Miss Rosalind Djones,' he said. 'Now there's a face to bring back memories. Do you remember Persia?'

Rose blushed and fiddled with the clasp of her

carpetbag. 'One doesn't easily forget a fleet of five hundred ships coming for you up the Red Sea.'

'The Persians wore chain mail and you wore bronze.'

Jupitus seemed irritated by their exchange. 'I think Herr Isaksen would be more comfortable on the armchair there,' he declared, leading the new arrival away from Rose and installing him in a Louis XIV *fauteuil* by the window.

Jake whispered to Topaz, 'Is he married?'

'For forty years. Fru Isaksen is exceptionally long-suffering.'

The hubbub died down once again as Galliana swept in, her greyhound, Olive, trotting behind her. She was still clutching Isaksen's portfolio under her arm. 'Good morning, everyone,' she said. 'Thank you for being so prompt.' She stopped next to Jake. 'Would you join me at the front?' she asked him. 'I may need your advice on something.'

Jake did as he was told, feeling proud, without knowing what she could possibly need his advice on.

Galliana took a seat. Jupitus joined her on one side, while Jake sat, rather self-consciously, on the other. He noticed Rose smiling at him and nodding, just like she had on his first time in the stateroom.

'You've probably all had a chance to say hello to our distinguished visitor,' Galliana began. 'I speak on behalf of everyone, I'm sure, when I say he is most welcome on the island.' There were murmurs of assent. 'Now, straight to business—'

The door at the back suddenly burst open and Yoyo came in. 'I'm sorry – I didn't realize everyone had started.' She grimaced, not looking sorry in the slightest.

Topaz gave Charlie a sideways glance and Nathan jumped up, calling, 'There's a free seat here, Miss Yuting.' Yoyo glanced over, but took a stool by the fireplace instead. 'Don't mention it,' Nathan muttered to himself, sitting down again.

The commander carried on. 'The reason I have gathered everyone together this morning is this . . .' She held up Isaksen's portfolio. 'It was discovered only yesterday, in Fredrik's time, hidden in his mansion in northern Sweden. It contains documents and papers belonging to his late son, Caspar.'

At the mention of this name, a ripple of disquiet went around the table. Rose looked over at Jake with a concerned smile. For his part, Isaksen hung his head in shame at his son's treachery.

'As you all know, when we discovered that Caspar had been working as a double agent for Agata Zeldt – and after his unfortunate demise – extensive searches were carried out in his rooms and all over the Isaksen estate. So anxious were we to glean any more intelligence of Caspar's dealings, the Isaksen family allowed me to help. We discovered nothing.'

Jake looked at the bundle of papers in her hand, desperate to know what they contained.

'Then, yesterday, as refurbishments were being carried out, the hidden safe was discovered behind wooden panels in Caspar's *pâtisserie*. Most of the handwriting on these papers is indeed Caspar's.'

'*Pâtisserie?*' Truman Wylder asked (Nathan's father was just as loud as his son). 'What on earth is a *pâtisserie?*'

'I believe it was a room Caspar had set aside for the creation of pastries and such like,' Galliana replied. Charlie's jaw dropped at this.

Despite the gravity of the subject, Jake couldn't help smiling at the thought of Caspar's *pâtisserie*. Of course he would hide his secrets there – Jake had never met anyone quite so obsessed with cakes.

'The papers have revealed a shocking truth.' Galliana gazed sternly around the room. 'I am sorry to say it, with his father present, but it seems that Caspar Isaksen had ambitions beyond anything we had imagined; that he offered his services in more than one direction . . . In short, that he had forged links not only with Agata Zeldt, but also with another of our greatest enemies – Xi Xiang.'

The History Keepers – already on the edge of their seats – gasped in unison and started talking. Jupitus had to stand and tap a teaspoon against his coffee cup to remind everyone that the commander was still speaking.

'As we all know,' she carried on, 'since an incident a year ago at the Chinese bureau, we have been trying to establish Xi Xiang's whereabouts. He has always been one of our most dangerous adversaries, not least because there is rarely method in his madness. He seeks chaos, pure and simple. He is also a master of disguise and loves nothing more than to disappear into thin air. Moreover – and I need hardly go into details here – he is *categorically* the most cold-blooded murderer that we have ever come across.'

On this point there was a cool murmur of agreement. Jake knew why: amongst the many horrors he had committed, Xi Xiang had been personally responsible for the murder of Galliana's husband and only child. He had drowned the five-year-old boy by tying weights to his legs and dropping him into the Sea of Japan, laughing as he did so. Jake studied the commander to see if her face showed any emotion, but she remained impassive.

'All this is bad enough,' Galliana resumed, 'but we have feared for some time that he was planning a new atrocity. The content of these papers seems to confirm this. Luckily they also offer clues as to his whereabouts – his geographical location as well as his temporal one.' Ignoring the exclamations that met this piece of information, Galliana poured herself some water, took a sip and carried on. 'Xi Xiang was actually Indonesian, born on the volcanic island of Krakatoa, but he adopted China as his home in his early twenties—'

'Tabuan,' Yoyo interrupted.

'Excuse me?' the commander replied tersely.

'The island of Tabuan was where he was born, just off the coast of Sumatra. His family moved to Krakatoa when he was two. I am an expert on Xi Xiang.' The older History Keepers muttered, shocked – interrupting the commander was a no-no, especially for new arrivals. Yoyo sensed everyone's disapproval and gave a cool shrug. 'My apologies for pointing it out.'

'She's right, of course,' Nathan piped up. 'Tabuan it was.'

'That will do,' Galliana interjected. 'Miss Yuting, I have no doubt that you are an *expert* on this subject – as you are on so many things – but we have a lot to get through. As I was saying . . . as Xi Xiang based himself in China, that is where we focused our search – particularly the South China Sea, where he has many associates.' She opened up the folder and took out the first batch of papers. 'These documents must alter our thinking drastically. It appears that Xi Xiang has a hideaway in the west; it seems he has spent a good deal of time here over the last few years. There is a chance that he may still be there now. The location is unexpected.'

She held up one particular page for everyone to see. It was a city map, old and frayed around the edges. Jake had to crane his neck to see it. It was hand-drawn and inscribed with faded curling letters, but there was something familiar about the shape of the river that twisted its way across.

'London,' Galliana said. 'Jacobean London, early

seventeenth century. If he is not physically there himself, he certainly has quarters in the city.'

Jake understood why she had asked him to come and sit with her: he had grown up in London.

Galliana continued. 'It makes sense. In addition to his obsession with chaos and murder, Xi Xiang has another mania: plays, actors, showmanship, magic – of course, he sees himself as a great performer. There is no more important place for drama in all history than Shakespeare's London – and, of course, it is the last place that anyone would think to look.' She traced her finger along the centre of the map. 'The city of London, the Thames, the White Tower, London Bridge, old St Paul's . . . And here' – her finger rested on one point – 'north of the river, just beyond Blackfriars, the symbol of an octopus – the moniker of Xi Xiang.'

'Which is where we think he may be hiding,' Jupitus clarified.

'We don't know for sure,' Galliana said, 'but it is the only lead we have. This afternoon I will be sending a team to investigate.'

There was another eruption of noise, of people putting their hands up, all asking questions at once.

'Silence, please,' she called over the hubbub.

'Silence. I have one more important matter to discuss . . .' She waited while everyone settled down. 'The last tranche of documents in this folder have thrown up one more discovery – perhaps the most alarming of all.' She took a deep breath and put her hand on Jake's shoulder, glancing at him before continuing. 'These documents pertain to another young man, who it seems was also working with Xi Xiang and Caspar . . .'

And then she dropped the bombshell:

'Philip Djones.'

7 THE SIGN OF THE OCTOPUS

Rose put her hands to her mouth, Charlie choked on his macaroon and Signor Gondolfino dropped his ivory cane on the floor. Jake stopped breathing altogether. The agents were in uproar. Only Yoyo was mystified by the reaction.

'Settle down!' Galliana called. 'Settle down, everyone.'

'Is this true?' Truman Wylder boomed. 'What evidence do you have?'

'There are various indicators,' the commander told him, fishing out one particular page. 'This Meslith was received by Caspar at some point.' She adjusted her spectacles and read: '*XX and I arrived London . . .* XX is evidently Xi Xiang. *XX goes east in one week. Send more atomium for journey. Philip D.*'

Again everyone started talking at once. Someone

said, 'That doesn't prove anything.' Another added, 'Anyone could have written that.'

Jupitus interjected, 'We know that Caspar talked of Philip in ancient Rome, that they likely met; but Caspar claimed that Philip was tortured.' As he spoke, with a typical lack of delicacy, Galliana kept a firm hand on Jake's shoulder, which was now rigid. 'Perhaps his association with Xi Xiang was a façade: he was working as a spy and he was found out, hence the torture. But that leads to an even greater mystery: why on earth would he not maintain contact with us prior to this? No, indeed, it is my gut feeling that he went over to the other side. He was always hungry for power.'

'Excuse me!' Rose called from the other end of the table. 'Philip working for the enemy? Hungry for power? Have you lost your mind?'

'I knew it would be an unpopular view' – Jupitus shrugged – 'but once you have heard all the facts—'

'Jupitus Cole, you have sunk to new depths,' Rose exclaimed. 'How dare you! How dare you say such a thing!' Jupitus just shrugged and took another sip of coffee. 'Thank God our wedding never took place – thank *God*!' she thundered.

'You're a brute. Not to mention a parsimonious, petty-minded—'

'Resort to shouting, Rosalind, to hurling insults, like you always do. So incredibly grown up.'

'Don't call me Rosalind. I hate that name. I've always hated it! You have no right to call me by that name.'

'Stop!' Jake yelled suddenly, thumping the table. '*What* facts, Mr Cole? Is my brother alive?'

The room was silent. Rose fell back in her chair, embarrassed by her outburst. Even Jupitus looked guilty.

'I'm sorry, Commander,' Jake went on quietly.

'That's all right,' she replied. 'You are quite within your rights. This is harder for you than anyone.' She turned and looked at Jupitus, adding sharply, 'Some people around this table should remember that. I have seen more decorum in a circus!' She waited a moment for her anger to subside. 'Jake has quite rightly asked for facts. On this score, it seems that there may be one in particular. This sheet was the last in Caspar's file.'

Galliana now took a piece of paper from the very back of the portfolio – this one much newer and stiffer than the rest – and set it down on the table in front of Jake. 'Is this in any way familiar to you?'

His eyes went wide as he looked at it. There were two hand-drawn diagrams of guns – one small, one large, both shown from various angles – along with studies of how each mechanism worked. They were covered in detailed notes in tiny writing.

Every eye in the room was on Jake as he reached out and touched the paper. Philip used to love sketching intriguing things: machines, ships, artillery . . . When he was just ten, he had come across a book of Leonardo da Vinci's inventions. At first he had copied Leonardo – even writing his notes back to front – but soon he developed his own distinctive style. These two weapons, one a slim revolver, the other a sturdy bazooka (or *flame thrower*, as the writing under the lower diagram called it), were depicted in intricate detail, both taking the fantastical shape of a golden dragon, the head and mouth serving as the barrel.

'Is the writing familiar?' Galliana asked again. Jake nodded. 'I recognized it too,' she said softly, before turning to the other History Keepers. 'We believe that these sketches – *blueprints*, as we assume they are – were drawn by Philip Djones. There is an embossed seal at the top of the page: the symbol of an octopus.'

Topaz, Nathan, Charlie and Rose all sat, frozen, their eyes trained on Jake.

Galliana carried on: 'Dr Chatterju has spent the night examining the diagram, testing its age.'

'It's not an exact science,' the doctor chimed in, half standing, 'but ink, once exposed to air, changes its properties over time. It depletes. I use a chemical compound to see roughly how *dry* it has become.'

There was silence for a moment, then Rose asked: 'And how dry was it, Dr Chatterju?'

He looked at Galliana, who nodded back at him. 'I would guess that this drawing dates from just over a year ago.'

There was a collective intake of breath. As this news sank in, Jake's bottom lip started to tremble. He was on the brink of tears, but he did not cry. Galliana squeezed his shoulder even tighter.

'Just over a year ago?' he asked.

'That is our guess.'

Silence again.

'But it was just over a year ago that Caspar claimed Philip was probably dead.'

'This is a shock, I know,' Galliana resumed,

deadly serious, 'but we need to get to the bottom of it. For the time being, let us not assume the worst. Let us, for now, be thankful that we have a lead at all.' She took a deep breath. 'So . . . to the operation at hand: I will be sending a team of the following agents to London, 1612: Topaz St Honoré, Nathan Wylder' – she paused for a second before uttering the third name – 'and Jake Djones. Topaz will be in charge of the operation. Charlie, sadly, is unable to travel.'

Jake heard his name, and despite his shock, he felt a pulse of pride, of consolation. *He had been picked*, without even putting up a fight.

'Hear, hear,' Rose called solemnly from the other end of the table. 'About time too.'

The choice of agents did not surprise anyone. A History Keeper's *valour* – his or her ability to move in time and travel great distances – was far stronger in the younger agents, and even more pronounced in 'diamonds': those who could see sharp diamond shapes when they scrunched their eyes shut. Nathan, Topaz, Jake – and, indeed, Charlie – were all diamonds. Jake's parents and aunt were too. There were exceptions to the rules: Jupitus was not a diamond, but his valour, even at his age, was still very strong.

'I will leave these drawings in your hands,' Galliana said quietly to Jake. 'Take them with you.' She slid Philip's sketches across the table and he took hold of them as if they were priceless relics.

Yoyo put up her hand and waited for the commander's nod. 'I would also very much like to put myself forward for the mission,' she said politely.

Her mother put her finger to Yoyo's lips to silence her.

'That's kind of you, Miss Yuting, but not this time.'

Yoyo's smile did not falter. 'As I have said, I have studied Xi Xiang extensively,' she persisted, 'and it goes without saying that I have great expertise in all matters related to the east.'

'I have no doubt of that. You are a valuable member of our team. But we will not be going east on this occasion.'

'But it concerns the east. Xi Xiang is Chinese – I mean, he *operates* in China.'

'Well, I'm sorry, Miss Yuting, but the answer is still no.'

'But I would strenuously—'

'And I would strenuously advise you to be quiet

now,' Galliana snapped. 'You have not been a good influence here recently.'

Now Yoyo's smile finally slipped.

Madame Tieng stood up, blushing. 'My daughter is sorry—' she began.

'Don't answer for me, Mother. I am not sorry in the slightest. It is ridiculous for me not to be included. I am more capable than the three of them put together. I fight better and I think better.' With that, she stood up, stared at them all dismissively, then stormed out of the room and slammed the door behind her.

There was a stunned silence as the dust settled. '*Che dramma*,' Gondolfino muttered under his breath to Dr Chatterju.

Galliana did her best to appear unruffled. 'Would the team please make their way to the costumiery, before collecting your weapons in the armoury. You will set sail on the *Thunder* at ten a.m. There is no time to lose. That will be all.'

Immediately Topaz and Rose leaped up and ran over to Jake; Charlie followed, pushed along by Nathan, who had one eye on the door in case Yoyo came back.

'Everything will be all right, Jake,' Topaz consoled

him as they all gathered around. 'We're going to get to the bottom of it.'

'I'm fine,' said Jake, shrugging it off. It was a lie: he was far from fine; he was in shock, more confused than ever. Was Philip dead or alive? Was he working for the enemy? It was too much to think about. 'Let's go,' he said decisively, Philip's drawings clutched tightly in his hand.

In the costumiery, a rail of Elizabethan outfits was trundled over to the fitting area.

'The early 1600s,' Nathan explained to Jake, 'is all about the exaggerated collar – the *ruff*, to give it its correct name.' He was trying to keep his friend's mind off Philip. He ran his hand along the bands of tightly pleated silk. 'Biggest is best, and I intend to push things to the extreme.' He chose one that was nearly twice the circumference of his head, wrapping it around his neck and checking himself in the mirror. 'Hello, handsome,' he laughed, winking at his reflection.

'Just wait your turn,' Gondolfino snapped, snatching the ruff back. 'Miss St Honoré first.' His face creased with a smile as she stepped forward. He adored Topaz and was not ashamed to show it.

'Now, I see you in velvet and brocade,' he trilled, running his ancient hand along a rail of clothes that he had already picked out for her.

After Topaz, Gondolfino got going on the other two, and when his work was done he clapped his hands. 'Let's have a look at you all together – *tutti insieme*,' he said, adjusting his eyepiece. The three of them lined up. '*Incantevole!*' he exclaimed. They made a strikingly attractive group, in their dark clothes and white ruffs.

When they reached the armoury, Dr Chatterju was waiting at a work station with Amrit, his cheeky young nephew who doubled as his assistant. 'Over here,' the doctor called. 'I have something to show you.'

'Treats! That's what I like.' Nathan grinned when he saw that the doctor had a number of gadgets laid out before him.

'To commence, may I introduce our new crossbow arrow gun,' said Chatterju, picking up the first item. It was halfway between a crossbow and a revolver: a squat bow and stock, customized with a cylindrical ammunition chamber and fitted with a trigger and hammer, like a normal gun. 'The revolving chamber carries ten bolts and can be replaced

in half a second.' He demonstrated by swiftly un-
clipping it from the stock and fitting another one in
its place. 'For extra effect, the tips of the arrows may
be dipped in poison.'

'May I, sir?' Nathan asked, itching to get his
hands on it. Chatterju passed it over and the
American shot off half a round at the marks on the
far wall of the chamber – quick flashes of steel –
thwack, thwack, thwack – into the target. 'How's
that for sport? Almost five bull's-eyes!'

Topaz took the weapon from him and tried it for
herself. Five arrows struck absolutely dead centre in
one solid cluster, making Nathan mutter under his
breath, 'Obviously more of a girl's weapon.'

Jake wanted to try his luck, but Chatterju
signalled that it was time to move on. 'There are a
variety of other firearms in here,' he said, indicating
a trunk. 'Non-explosive, of course, and appropriate
for the early seventeenth century.' He moved on to
show them the contents of the shelf. 'Now, you will
also need ink and quill, a standard feature in
Elizabethan London; but write with this and you'll
get more than you bargained for. Amrit, will you
demonstrate.' The grinning boy put on a protective
visor and chain-mail gloves, then picked up the quill

and dipped it into a pot of ink. 'Once it has come in contact with the ink,' the doctor explained, 'it starts to react.' He was right: they could all hear the nib make a fizzing sound.

Amrit crossed to the other side of the room and placed the quill on a metal stand, then backed away. The feather suddenly threw out a brilliant white light before exploding in a cloud of smoke. Amrit was sent flying, clattering into a pile of shields and helmets. He wasn't bothered in the slightest; he simply picked himself up and giggled as he brushed down his laboratory coat.

'A poison pen.' Nathan nodded his approval. 'I like it.'

The last device on the shelf was introduced as 'quite an ingenious *outboard motor*'. The box looked like a scruffy tea-chest, but Chatterju carefully pulled out a machine of many interconnected parts, some polished wood, others gleaming metal. He twisted the sections until it took shape: a rudder, engine and propeller, all connected in one clever mechanism. 'It can be fitted onto the back of any small craft.' The doctor folded it up again and replaced it in its case. 'It's the prototype and I am particularly proud of it, so do take care.'

With only a short time remaining before they set sail, Jake, Nathan and Topaz returned to their rooms to pick up anything they might need for the journey. Jake went straight over to the chest by his bed, and took out a photograph. It was of the Djones family, taken the Christmas before Philip disappeared. Jake studied his brother's smiling face. What was going on under the smile? Could there really be treachery? 'Of course there couldn't,' he muttered. He placed the picture, along with Philip's diagrams, inside a portfolio and packed it in his bag.

As he emerged from his room, Nathan came bustling down the corridor with his own bag slung across his back. 'I know you have other things on your mind, old boy,' the American said in his version of a whisper, 'but what did you make of all that business with Miss Yuting?' He didn't wait for Jake to reply. 'I mean, what she said about being more capable than us was a little uncalled for, but still . . . an odd business, wouldn't you say? I just went to talk to her,' he confessed. 'I wanted to say goodbye. She pretended she wasn't in her room, but she was there all right, swishing a sword.'

'Well, there's not much we can do about it.' Jake shrugged. 'She'll have got over it by the time we get back.' As he said this, an unsettling notion suddenly struck him: *What if he didn't come back?* Missions were dangerous, and the truth was, not everyone in the history of the secret service survived them. The memorial stone under the willow tree was proof of that. All of a sudden Jake, like Nathan, didn't want to leave without speaking to Yoyo. 'Let's go and see her, then,' he said. 'Quickly, though – we have to leave in five minutes.'

They rushed up to find her room empty, the door wide open. There was no time to search further, so they headed down to the quay, frustrated.

A small farewell party was gathered next to the *Thunder*, a little merchant frigate with blue sails and a complicated lattice of rigging.

'Charlie, you old rogue, I'm going to miss you. It won't be the same without you,' Nathan said, squeezing his friend's arm. Jake and Topaz said goodbye too, hugging him tightly.

'All the best,' he replied. 'And will you promise to do me a favour? Get to the Globe and see some original Shakespeare. I want solemn promises, do you hear?'

'It will be *top* of our list,' Nathan announced grandly, while shaking his head at Jake. (Jake had no idea why Nathan wasn't keen on the theatre or the opera, being such a dramatic person himself.)

Galliana handed Topaz a small casket containing the atomium and the Horizon Cup, and they spoke briefly. 'If you locate Xi Xiang, or any of his people, be wary. There are so many layers of deceit to that man. And such depth of cruelty.'

'We will be careful, Commander,' Topaz promised her.

'You're going to stay with Aunt Rose for a few days,' Jake said to Felson, giving him a fond stroke. 'She'll spoil you rotten.'

'Quite right,' Rose agreed – adding for Jupitus's benefit, 'Who needs humans to snuggle up with at night?' She gave her nephew a hug. 'Look after yourself, darling boy. If Philip's alive somewhere, you'll find him, won't you?'

'I'll do my best. Goodbye, Rose,' he said, but suddenly Jake had that morbid thought again – that he might not come back at all. He gave her an extra special hug and picked up his bag. He was just about to climb aboard with the others when Yoyo appeared. Her puffy red eyes were fixed on Jake.

'Were you looking for me?'

Jake was self-conscious, knowing that everyone

was watching. 'W-w-we were just saying goodbye . . .'

Yoyo took him by the hand. 'I really hope you find your brother.' As she stared into his eyes, he felt a peculiar thrill. No one had ever looked at him quite so directly before. 'Get back safely, won't you?' she said.

'Yes, I will,' he replied in a daze.

Then she leaned forward and kissed him on the cheek. Her mouth was warm, and it made the hairs stand up on the back of his neck.

Nathan let out a snort of disbelief and a few others raised their eyebrows.

'Look after Jake, won't you?' Yoyo said to Nathan, before pushing her way through the group and disappearing into the castle.

'And I'll just look after myself, shall I?' Nathan called after her. 'Someone has to,' he muttered under his breath. 'I make all that effort, and that's what I get in return. Charming.'

He was so put out that he didn't bother with his usual 'impromptu' speech about the perilous mission ahead. There was a last flurry of goodbyes as they boarded the ship, and then they cast off.

Jake watched the island retreat into the distance,

the people getting smaller and smaller. There was more of a jumble in his mind than ever: the revelations about Philip, the look in Yoyo's eyes . . . and the dreadful feeling that they were heading to their doom.

8 RETURN TO THE THAMES

Once they were at sea, Topaz carefully calibrated the Horizon Cup, added the atomium, poured out three doses and passed them round. Any History Keeper wanting to travel through time had to possess a natural ability; but then the journey time and distance had to be carefully calculated and the golden-coloured atomium mixed before being shared out. Any error, and an agent could end up spinning in time, their atoms even bursting apart. Every journey carried a risk, and the agents had to be focused when they reached the horizon point.

'Is anyone's stomach rumbling apart from mine?' Nathan asked as he swigged his atomium back with a grimace. He glanced down into the empty galley. 'If Charlie was here, he'd already be rustling something up by now – one of those clever soufflés of his.'

'I'll go and make something,' Jake suggested.

Nathan shook his head. 'No offence, old boy, but cookery skills don't really run in the family. No, there's nothing for it . . .' he said. 'I shall create one of my special Charleston brunches. With so many skills, it's easy to forget my talent with a wooden spoon. Topaz, would you take over?' He relinquished the wheel and clattered down into the galley.

The grey morning had brightened, and now the sun shone down, making the sea sparkle. Topaz looked over at Jake. He sat leaning against the rail, basking in the warmth.

'Miss Yuting and you looked quite . . .' Topaz began.

Jake squinted at her. In the hazy light, she was an apparition, a head floating on a silk ruff.

'We looked quite . . .?' he asked.

Topaz shrugged. 'Attached to each other?'

Jake laughed. 'You don't like her at all, do you?'

'What?' Topaz floundered. '*Je la connais à peine.* I hardly know her really. She's not someone you would forget in a hurry.'

'You're not jealous, are you?'

'Jealous? Of course not!' Topaz protested – a little too vehemently, Jake thought. 'You and I are friends, aren't we? What should I be jealous of?'

Jake suddenly felt mischievous and threatened to tickle her. Topaz claimed not to be ticklish in the slightest, but couldn't stop giggling. He chased her around the deck until the ship lurched and they had to dash back to the wheel.

Gradually noises started coming up from the galley. First they heard Nathan talking to himself, then a frenzy of clanging saucepans, smashing plates and very colourful swearing. At one point he exclaimed out loud, 'No, you can't do that! I won't let you.' Jake looked below and saw that he was shouting at strips of charcoal that had once been bacon. In the end, the American let out a howl of rage, came back up the steps and plonked down a loaf of bread and some tomatoes. 'Here!'

'What happened to your famous Charleston brunch?' Jake teased.

'It's off,' Nathan fumed. 'I've never met such obstinate ingredients in my life. It's like they had a personal vendetta against me.'

Soon they were approaching the horizon point. It was a little further north than the one where Jake had intercepted Fredrik Isaksen, and was considered one of the safest portals to deeper history. In Jake's experience, no two horizon point episodes were ever the same, and this one was different again.

Although all History Keepers had an out-of-body experience when travelling to history, they usually experienced it separately, unaware of the others around them. This time, however, when the rings of the Constantor aligned, Jake launched off with his friends beside him; they held hands as they soared into the stratosphere. As usual, Jake saw an explosion of diamond shapes (when taking off from a horizon point, History Keepers always saw shapes – squares, oblongs or diamonds, depending on the strength of their valour). Sometimes, transitions through time could be full of horrible visions or flashbacks; but this time it was exhilarating, and by the time Jake returned to his body on the deck of the *Thunder*, he felt full of energy.

The afternoon passed as they made their way across the English Channel and forged on towards the vast mouth of the Thames, an otherworldly delta stretched between distant marshlands. *I'm coming back to London after all*, Jake thought as they sailed into the estuary and began the last leg of their journey. It was curious to think that his parents were here too – though in a completely different era.

The river started to fill with ships heading to and from the capital – galleons and trading craft from many corners of the world, creaking under their heavy loads.

'I think we're getting close,' Jake called from the prow, too excited to turn round. A warm breeze ruffled his hair as he watched the river twist left and right, and a hum started to fill the air, barely audible to begin with, but deepening – a far-off chorus of city life.

Finally they glided round a headland, and as the sun started to set, London, Shakespearean London, opened up before them.

Since joining the History Keepers, Jake had arrived at a number of ancient ports – Venice, Stockholm and Herculaneum – but he had never seen anything like this, with so many ships crammed into such a narrow stretch of water. They lined the banks on either side, in some places two or three deep, creating a thicket of masts and rigging. As well as the larger merchant galleons, there were hundreds of smaller craft – rowing boats, yachts and single-sail vessels – all weaving in and out of each other as they crisscrossed the river.

Beyond the banks, the city radiated out in an endless, zigzagging jumble of tenements, halls and palaces as far as the eye could see. The houses – mostly timber – were all of a similar height, but occasionally a church spire soared above the city. Spindly chimneys rose up, a thousand slender fingers pointing into the dark sky.

This London was unrecognizable to Jake at first: there were no tall buildings, none of the modern sounds of traffic. A curious drone emerged from the unseen streets, as if the whole metropolis was whispering.

Gradually he started to piece the geography together. 'The Tower of London,' he gulped on seeing a fortress sweep by on his right. In 1612, this was a simple construction: two circuits of thick walls, both set with several fortified turrets, surrounded the keep of the White Tower, which was much taller and grander than Jake remember-ed. He shuddered as they went by Traitors' Gate. Only now did he realize that they had passed the point where Tower Bridge crossed the river. It was nowhere to be seen.

'If you're looking for what I think you are,' Topaz said, 'it won't be built for another two hundred and seventy years. You won't recognize St Paul's either.' She pointed at a cathedral on the north bank. Gone was Sir Christopher Wren's famous domed construction, replaced – or rather foreshadowed – by a stately Norman church with a huge round stained-glass window. 'The Great Fire of 1666 will wipe out three quarters of the city.'

'My sister loves London,' Nathan commented, opening a vanity case and producing tweezers and a little mirror. 'Personally, I can't bear the weather. The whole place is like a cold waiting to happen – all those damp streets and chestnuts roasting on fires.' He started carefully plucking his eyebrows.

'You are, of course, speaking to a Londoner,' Topaz pointed out. 'This is where Jake grew up, remember?'

For once, Nathan looked embarrassed. 'Unforgivable of me. I meant to say that, culturally, it is wonderfully vibrant. And personally, I love chestnuts.'

'I'd just ignore him if I was you,' Topaz suggested.

Jake took her advice. 'So how many bridges are there?' he asked, trying to square this vision of the city with the one he remembered from the present.

'Just the one,' she replied. 'London Bridge, straight ahead. Possibly the most famous bridge in history.'

At first, with all the jumble of ships, Jake couldn't make it out: the buildings that lined the bank seemed to continue right round in front of him, as if the river came to a dead end. Then he realized that the bridge *was a building itself* – or rather a whole collection of them, crossing the water on top of nineteen sturdy arches. 'First erected by Henry the Second in the twelfth century,' Topaz continued. 'There are roughly two hundred houses and shops on it. There's even a church and a small palace called Nonsuch House.'

Satisfied with his eyebrows, Nathan put away the mirror and tweezers, took out a silver file and started working on his nails.

'So can ships get beyond the bridge?' asked Jake.

'Actually there's a drawbridge in the middle,' Topaz told him, 'but you need permission. Obviously smaller craft can get through the arches, but the currents are perilous.'

'And did you also know,' Nathan chipped in, 'that there is a multi-seated public toilet overhanging the parapets and the locals can merrily discharge their' – he fumbled for the phrase – 'their *reconstituted chestnuts* into the river below.'

'Nathan!' Topaz sighed. 'Why don't you do something useful? Here . . .' She passed him Isaksen's map. 'Work out our best route to the location.'

Nathan perused it sulkily, continuing his manicure.

'What are those things there?' Jake pointed to a collection of objects sticking up from an arch on the southern end of the bridge. They looked like giant pins.

'Those are severed heads,' Topaz replied matter-of-factly. 'The heads of traitors, dipped in tar and impaled on spikes. Some of them have been there for decades – like the Earl of Essex, once a favourite of Elizabeth the First.'

Jake stared at the gruesome sight and Topaz went on, 'These are cruel times, like so much of history, but they are incredible too. London in 1612 is possibly the first truly *global* city. Look at it . . .' She indicated the busy wharves. 'There are traders here from Africa, South America, India and China. Goods are arriving that, even a decade ago, people could only have dreamed of: tea, spices, dye, perfume, jewels – potatoes.'

'Not to mention those funny curly shoes,' Nathan chipped in.

'And things are not just arriving; they're leaving – the British are exporting technological marvels: clocks, maps, guns. Twenty-odd years back, the country was crippled by debt, and at war with Spain. Now look at it. An Englishman – Francis Drake – has sailed around the world, and the East India Company – the world's original trading corporation – has been doing business for a decade. This is the gateway. It's no coincidence that Shakespeare called his theatre the *Globe*.' Topaz's eyes glistened with passion as she spoke. '*Non, c'est un age magnifique*. An age of exploration, of enquiry, of curiosity, of acceptance.'

'And where *is* the Globe?' Jake asked, remembering Charlie's request.

Topaz pointed under the bridge towards the south bank, and Jake squinted through the forest of ships. He could just make out a white, octagonal building set within a copse of trees.

Topaz docked carefully at a timber pier on the north side of the river. As Jake jumped ashore and secured the mooring, an incredible thought struck him. He was in the very place where he had first boarded a ship with the History Keepers. Then, the embankment had been half deserted and overlooked by nondescript office buildings; now it was teeming with life – sailors, crewmen, merchants, all shouting at once as crates, barrels and trunks were winched back and forth from ship to shore.

A self-important-looking young rake with a velvet cape slung across one shoulder approached a man in a small sailboat; he tossed him a coin and ordered that he and his friends were taken across. 'Westward ho!' the ferryman called as he cast off.

'Taxis for the rich,' Topaz said under her breath. 'It's the quickest way to travel around here.'

They put on their capes, Nathan immediately copying the jaunty style of the young man, and jumped onto the bank. 'This way,' he shouted, and they set off.

On the river behind them, a small boat with navy blue sails was entering the port of London. At the helm, a young man in black doublet and cloak steered with one hand while scanning the shoreline with his telescope. He watched Jake and the others turn off the quayside and disappear up a flight of steps.

The three History Keepers came to a wide thoroughfare that led from the northern end of the bridge into the heart of the city.

'With just one crossing over the Thames,' Topaz explained, 'this is the main route into London from the south. At busy times it can take hours to cross the bridge.'

Now Jake understood why the rich took taxis. London Bridge was a bottleneck of carts and carriages, their wheels rattling on cobbles, along with foot travellers and herds of cattle and pigs, all trying to funnel through. The queues snaked back for miles.

Jake gazed around, taking in all the sights and sounds. He could hear foreign voices – a group of Frenchmen were deep in discussion about the prices of the inns, and a pair in turbans and long robes spoke in an unfamiliar dialect as they unpacked bolts of cloth from a wagon.

'Here is all the world . . .' Topaz swept her hand along the highway. 'Africans, Italians, Dutch, Persians and Moroccans; visiting, living, sightseeing.'

Rich and poor jostled side by side. They saw an aristocrat's coach drawn by four white mares, its roof laden with trunks and caskets. A man in a feathered cap peered out at the mayhem through curtained windows, while his wife held a nosegay to her face. There were farmers with loads of vegetables, herbs and fresh flowers, and traders carrying pewter, tin, candles and books. There were young men on horseback and beggars ambling along barefoot. On each side, innkeepers and ostlers plied their trade, and locals played at cards and dice or smoked tobacco from clay pipes.

At last they turned into a wide road that ran parallel to the river. It was less frenetic here, peopled mostly by well-dressed Londoners. Like the rake on the pier, many of the men strutted like peacocks, chins up to display their oversized ruffs, their swords hanging down behind them, some so long they dragged in the mud.

'Length of sword,' Topaz explained, 'is one of those ridiculous status symbols in Elizabethan London.' Nathan slyly checked his own, pushing his belt down so that the tip of his scabbard caught on the ground.

Here they passed shop after shop: jewellers, glass-makers, glove-makers, embroiderers, silversmiths, apothecaries and furriers. Jake noticed one window stacked with scientific instruments and another with a giant golden tureen filled to the brim with peppercorns.

'In case you were wondering,' Nathan said, 'the pepper costs ten times more than the gold. These are crazy times.'

The next shop was a cartographer's; a large map in the window showed the misshapen continents of Europe, with Asia and America either side. A sign next to it read: ENTER TO DISCOVER THE NEWE WORLDE. Around it, there were pictures of mythical beasts – unicorns and winged tigers.

Ahead, a throng of people jostled and shouted as they queued up outside a bow-fronted store. Two elderly ladies in fur-trimmed coats almost came to blows over who was the first in line. Jake craned his neck to see the object of their fascination.

'Porcelain,' Topaz told him. 'There is no greater obsession in the west than porcelain from China. In fact, *everything* from China: silk, nutmeg and, of course, the drink of the century – of the whole modern age – tea.'

Jake got a glimpse of the blue and white ware, of the frantic shoppers and the besieged assistants. It looked like Christmas in Oxford Street, and he realized that people's habits changed very little through time.

'And that, if I am not mistaken' – Topaz pointed to a building looming ahead of them – 'is the head-quarters of the East India Company. It was founded just over ten years ago, but it's already one of the richest companies in the world.' There were four storeys of mullioned windows rising up like a medieval skyscraper; but more eye-catching still was the giant coat of arms stamped in the centre, and the mural above it – a galleon. The *pièce de résistance* was a larger-than-life statue of a voyager astride two dolphins.

The three youngsters were struck by the ostentation of the thing. 'What's amazing,' Topaz said, 'is that buildings like this are going up all over the world, from Amsterdam to Cairo to Canton. This is the age of trade.'

Nathan checked his bearings, then led them into a labyrinth of narrow streets. 'This is where things get a little more pungent,' he said, holding his nose. The roads – now little more than dirt tracks – were slimy with refuse, though a network of planks made walking a little easier. Overhead, the crooked houses hung right over, leaving just a thin band of sky. A window opened above them, and a hand emerged to empty a chamber pot, its gloopy contents narrowly missing Nathan as they splattered down.

'Don't you just *love* those reconstituted chestnuts?' he muttered, stepping gingerly past.

At last they came out onto the waterfront again. Jake scanned the river. Dusk was falling and the watermen, their boats lit by lanterns, glided across in every direction. Jake couldn't get used to this city – so different from the London he knew. It seemed incredible that nearly all this would be washed away by history. He could see the Globe more clearly now, its white walls luminous against the crimson sky. 'On Bankside, on the *south* of the river,' Topaz explained, 'the laws are different, less strict – so that's where most Londoners go to amuse themselves. That's the bear-baiting pit just behind the theatre.'

'Bear-baiting?' Jake asked.

'*C'est barbare.*' Topaz shook her head. 'They tie up a poor animal – having filed down its teeth – and set wild dogs on it, while everyone bets on the winner. And it's right next to one of the greatest theatres in all history. That's civilization for you . . . Don't ever get Charlie started on the subject!'

Nathan turned the map round. 'As far as I can

make out, it's one of those buildings there,' he said, nodding upstream towards a row of five stately houses that looked over the Thames. Light could be seen in most of the windows, and smoke came from at least two of the chimneys, but the *middle* one was completely dark.

They made their way through another maze of streets to a quiet road that ran along the backs of the mansions. It was lined with huge horse chestnut trees that seemed to swallow the sounds of the metropolis.

'It seems there's no one at home,' Nathan said as they approached the gated portico of the third house along, a grand red-brick building with two gabled towers facing the river at either end. The mullioned windows were large – particularly on the first floor – making the darkness inside all the more intriguing.

'Look,' said Topaz, 'a coat of arms.' Above them, half hidden amongst the ivy, was a stone emblem, recently carved: two dragons on either side of a shield. The latter was divided into four squares with a symbol in each: a ship, a trident, an eye – and an octopus. Jake's stomach clenched at the sight of Xi Xiang's symbol.

'Shall we . . .?' said Nathan, pulling himself up the wall onto the roof of the portico and jumping down the other side.

Topaz shook her head. 'I distinctly remember the commander putting me in charge,' she said, leaping after him. 'Jake? Are you coming?' she asked through the bars.

Jake was lost in thought, staring at the house, wondering what secrets it might contain, and whether he might find any clues about Philip. He came back to the present and quickly followed them over the wall.

They crept towards one of the ground-floor windows and squinted inside. They needed no further proof that the house was deserted: all the furniture was covered with dust sheets. It looked like a gathering of ghosts. They slipped round into an overgrown garden that led down to the river.

As Nathan examined the front door – a mammoth slab of oak – Jake followed a path towards the water, his feet crunching on the gravel. He soon came to a gate that led down to a little jetty, and heard a splashing close by; he realized that a rowing boat was heading towards him. It contained a single occupant: a girl, with her back to Jake. He beckoned to the others.

'There's someone coming,' he whispered. The three of them ducked down behind a hedge. They heard the boat thump against the jetty, and a moment later the girl came into view. She followed the path, a wooden bucket in her hand, unlocked the front door and disappeared into the house.

'Some kind of housekeeper, by the look of things,' Nathan suggested. 'Let's see what she knows.' He drew his sword, signalled to the others and tiptoed back towards the mansion.

Topaz looked at Jake, exasperated. '*Qu'est-ce qu'il a?* What is it that he can't understand about the fact that I'm in charge?'

They hurried after him, and saw that flickering light now illuminated the hall windows; again, they peered inside.

'What in God's name . . . !' Nathan exclaimed. The girl was standing on top of a set of steps; they could see her frightened face as she tipped the contents of her bucket – a mélange of shrimps and snapping crabs – through a funnel into a large fish tank containing a live octopus. The creature peeled its tentacles off the glass and started devouring its meal, drilling through a crab shell and sucking out the flesh.

'I hate those things,' Topaz muttered, shuddering.

'I think it looks rather sweet,' Nathan said with a shrug. 'Apparently they're fantastically intelligent. My aunt had one who used to play chess with her.'

Topaz ignored him and strode into the house, sword drawn. The girl saw her, lost her balance and toppled to the floor in fright, scattering the contents of her bucket.

'We're not going to hurt you,' Topaz reassured her, advancing with her sword up, 'providing you help us with what we need.' At this moment, the octopus smacked a tentacle against the glass, eyeing Topaz as if she might be its next meal.

'O-of course,' the girl stammered. 'I'll help you. Have I done something wrong?'

Topaz turned to Nathan and Jake. 'Would you sort out the seafood?' she said, gesticulating towards the wriggling things on the floor. The boys duly obeyed, gingerly picking up the crabs and prawns and replacing them in the bucket.

Topaz began her cross-examination: 'Is there anyone else in the house?' The girl shook her head.

'You're absolutely certain?' A vehement nod. 'What's your name?'

'I am Bess, miss.'

'And do you work here, Bess?'

'I come sometimes to feed the . . .' She motioned towards the octopus. From the look on her face, she hated the creature as much as Topaz did.

'*Sometimes?*'

'If the master is here, I do not come. Otherwise I am sent word and I come in the evening. I received word today.'

'And your last visit?'

'A week ago?'

'So we're to assume your master has been here in that time?'

The girl shrugged. 'I do not know. I have met him only once.'

'And have you any idea when he will be back? We noticed that the furniture has been covered, so perhaps it will be longer this time?'

'Perhaps, yes.'

'Topaz, behind you,' Nathan called over breezily.

She turned to find two of the octopus's arms swinging towards her, having slipped up the funnel. She caught her breath as one suddenly brushed

against her face. She swiped it away, only just resist-
ing the temptation to slice it in two with her sword.
'Will you please put it back?' she said, quickly
wiping the sticky residue off her cheek. 'The only
thing I hate more is eels.'

Nathan came to her aid, chuckling.

'I don't laugh at your ridiculous superstitions
about ghosts,' she snapped. 'Why should my dislike
of octopuses be funny?'

'Because ghosts are real. Octopuses are just . . .
fish with ambition.'

Jake was examining a large portrait at the foot of
the main staircase. 'Is this your master, Bess?' he
asked.

'I believe so,' she replied, trembling with fear.

The three agents stared at the painting.

'No doubt about it,' Topaz muttered grimly. 'It's
him . . .'

9 THE LAZULI SERPENT

The portrait showed two figures – one in the foreground, the other standing in his shadow behind. It was exquisitely painted, as fine as any old master Jake had seen on trips to the National Gallery.

'That's Xi Xiang?' he asked, pointing at the principal subject. His friends nodded in unison.

'The commander was right,' Nathan whispered. 'This is where he's been hiding – for some of the time, at any rate.'

Jake inspected the painting. He knew little about Xi Xiang physically – other than the astounding fact that he had three eyes! The portrait confirmed it. His right eye was normal, his left was slightly squeezed up into his brow, while below it, his third eye, blank and deformed like a rotten mussel, peered out of his cheek. Despite the disfigurement, or perhaps even because of it, Xi Xiang had an impish, gloating smile on his face.

His cheeks were rouged like a clown, and he wore a costume of turquoise, gold and crimson, emblazoned with motifs of sea dragons and fish. The long sleeves hung loosely, hiding his hands – though on closer inspection, Jake noticed a knife protruding from one of the cuffs.

His companion, standing behind, was a slight, stooped old woman whose stern gaze was just as arresting as his. She wore a black gown, and her hands were cupped together as if in prayer, though she was actually clutching an upright sword. Sticking out under her robe – the only flash of colour – was a pair of red slippers.

'Do you know who the woman is?' Jake asked.

'I've never seen a picture of her before,' Nathan replied, 'but I can guess. I believe it's Madame Fang, Xi's nanny.'

'His *what?*'

'His only friend in the world,' Topaz butted in. 'She's been his protector since he was born. The story goes that, when Xi was twelve, she helped him drown his own parents at a seaside picnic. Such a charming pair.'

Jake asked her, 'Didn't Xi Xiang work for the History Keepers when he was younger?'

'He did,' she replied, 'but no one knew anything of his past. He fooled them all, particularly Jupitus, who always stood by him.'

'So what's upstairs, Bess?' Nathan asked. 'More fish tanks?'

'I – I'm not allowed upstairs,' she stammered, 'but I believe they keep a study and living quarters.'

'I know this is a little unsociable of us,' Nathan said as he led her across the room to an adjoining pantry, 'but we must detain you for a short while.' He was about to lock her in when Jake called out.

'Wait!' He took out the picture of his family, half covering it with his hand to favour Philip, and showed it to Bess. 'What about him? Have you ever seen *him*?' he asked her. She had clearly never come across a photograph before, and was struck dumb. 'Look closely at him,' Jake said. She stared, almost as if she *had* recognized Philip – but then shook her head. 'Are you sure? Absolutely *sure*?'

'I am, sir,' she replied, but Jake suspected she was lying.

Nathan locked her in the pantry and the three of them walked up the creaking staircase, Topaz leading the way with a candelabra held high in one hand. They crossed the landing, and went through an archway into the main room of the house.

It was an Elizabethan gallery that ran the entire length of the building, with a series of large windows facing the river. By the entrance hung a lantern in the form of a sea creature. Nathan put a candle to it and it caught light with a soft *whoomph*. There came the sound of machinery ticking and whistling, and within seconds a whole succession of lights went on one by one.

'Respect where it's due,' said Nathan, gazing around. 'Taste-wise, Xi Xiang is not lacking.'

The room was decorated in a mixture of styles from east and west. The walls were panelled in dark oak, but the objects and furnishings – lacquer cabinets, golden screens, finely carved chairs – all had a Chinese feel. A vast mural covered the back wall – a seascape of swirling blues: turquoise, cobalt and ultramarine. In the centre of the room, dominating the space, stood a supersized globe. It all reminded Jake of his first glimpse of the London bureau – a place Xi Xiang would have visited in his time as a History Keeper.

'Interesting,' said Topaz, scanning the globe.

Thin red lines streamed across the oceans between the land masses, from South America, up through the Caribbean to America, then across the Atlantic to Europe. From here, they looped back down round Africa to Persia, traversing the Indian Ocean to Asia, before fanning out again across the Pacific to start the journey all over again.

'Trade routes,' she said, pointing to various spots on the map. 'Sugar, silver, silk, pepper, tobacco – the whole merry-go-round. Even slaves,' she added sombrely. Her finger lingered on the South China Sea, which had the greatest concentration of red; a whole network of converging lines. 'As we just saw, no exports are more popular than from *this* corner of the world.'

Jake went to examine the giant mural. Viewed close up, it was unsettling. In the heart of the ocean was a blue, quartz-like crystal, covered with intricate in-scriptions. It seemed to radiate some kind of magical power, as the seas raged and exploded all around it. At the edges of the scene there was destruction: ships sink-ing, sailors crying out, tidal waves engulfing cities.

'What *is* that thing?' he asked, pointing at the stone.

Topaz frowned as she studied it.

'My knowledge of Chinese mythology is rusty at

best,' Nathan commented, 'but isn't that the Lazuli Serpent?'

'The *what* serpent?' Jake asked.

'The *Lazuli* Serpent. It's a tide stone,' Topaz replied, though Jake was none the wiser. 'Tide stones have been part of Chinese folklore for thousands of years; they're mythical crystals that can control the oceans, producing giant sea monsters simply by coming in contact with water. There are large ones and small ones, each with varying degrees of power. The Lazuli Serpent is the most famous, the most dangerous, capable of harnessing the power of *all* the seas of the world. It is said that Qin Shi Huang, the first true emperor of China—'

'That's the one who started building the Great Wall,' Nathan chipped in, 'and insisted on being buried with an army of stone soldiers to keep him company.'

'– that he possessed it, but even Huang was so frightened of its might that he kept it locked in a jade casket, telling no one of its whereabouts.'

'But it's a myth,' Nathan butted in. 'Let's not forget that. No one in the history of the world has ever seen this stone. And that story is two thousand years old.'

As Jake gazed at the mural, his eye caught the glimmer of hinges and a handle, then a faint rectangle lost amongst the swirling colours: it was a door hidden in the wall. He turned the handle, and a panel opened out onto a small landing and a staircase.

'It must go up into one of the towers,' Jake said, remembering the outside of the building.

The agents drew their weapons before cautiously climbing the steps. At the top was a thick metal door that was slightly ajar. Nathan gently pushed it open with the tip of his blade, and they stepped into a small room that looked like a monk's cell: it had a single barred window, a bed of straw and a chamber pot. There was only one other object: a dusty painting in a smashed frame, facing the wall.

Jake turned it round, and in his shock, took a gulp of breath. 'Wh-wh-what? How . . .?' he stammered. It was a portrait – of Xi Xiang . . . and his brother, Philip.

They were dressed like battle heroes, in gleaming Chinese armour, and Xi's arm lay around Philip's shoulders. 'I – I don't understand . . .' Jake's hands were shaking.

Nathan and Topaz shared a look of concern. 'It's a painting,' Topaz reassured him. 'Many things can be captured in a painting – lies can be told.'

She tried to take it off Jake, but he clung onto it. Carefully he brushed the dust off his brother's face. Philip was a striking boy, with a square jaw, dimpled chin and the faint shadow of stubble. He was older and stronger than Jake, but they had the same curling dark hair and brown eyes. Those eyes stared right back at Jake. What was the story here? he puzzled, his mind frantic with quest-ions. Was Philip really in league with Xi? Or was he his prisoner?

He turned to look at the bed. The mattress was imprinted with the shape of its former occupant.

'Is – is this where he slept?'

'It's all right, Jake . . . it's all right,' Topaz whis-pered, holding onto him.

He shook himself free. 'Where is he now? Is he dead? Where is he?' Jake's voice echoed around the room. He fell to his knees and thrust his hand into the mattress, as if he might somehow find Philip there. 'Where is he?' he cried again, tossing the bedding aside. Nathan and Topaz tried in vain to calm him down. 'What did they do to him?' Jake demanded, half demented – then stopped as he saw something glinting amongst the straw: it was a watch, its glass smashed, its strap broken. Jake picked it up as if it were a priceless relic.

'I gave it to him,' he murmured. 'There was a stall in Greenwich market that sold old watches. I knew he'd like this one because it had a ship on it. He loved ships – I never fully understood why . . . until I met you lot, of course. He said he would never take it off.' He turned it over and received another surprise: a message was scratched in tiny letters on the back. He had to squint to make it out . . .

Tell family I love them. Find Lazuli Serpent – through the Ocean Door, C

'It's definitely written by him?' Topaz asked softly. Jake nodded, tracing his finger over the letters. 'Can I see?' She examined it carefully. 'Why did he sign it *C*? Did he have a nickname?'

'No.'

'But you're absolutely sure it's his?'

'A hundred per cent,' he said firmly. 'The Ocean Door . . . ? Do either of you know what that is?'

The other two looked at each other. 'Never heard of it,' Nathan confessed.

Jake slipped the watch into his pocket and stripped the painting from its frame. 'Bess must know more,' he said. 'Let's go.'

But when they got back downstairs and unlocked the pantry, Bess was gone. She had pulled a dresser aside and escaped out of a casement window.

Jake tore across the garden to the jetty. 'The boat's gone too,' he said as the others caught up with him.

BOOM! Suddenly there was an explosion on the other side of the river, and bright light illuminated their faces. A moment later, another blast shot a wave of heat across the water.

'What in God's name—' Nathan started to say.

Further upstream, a ship was on fire, flames engulfing the sails, sparks flickering into the dusky sky. There was pandemonium – the crew diving into the river to escape the inferno as people swarmed along the pier with buckets of water. All at once, in the hold of the stricken craft, another eruption catapulted the remaining crew into the air. Jake's ears popped and he shook his head to regain his hearing.

Almost instantly, the ship listed to one side and started to sink, its burning mast cracking in two and smacking down onto the Thames.

A fourth explosion echoed across the water – from a galleon moored close to London Bridge. Within moments, it too was ablaze. '*One* ship might be accidental,' Nathan said, 'but *two* must be a conspiracy.'

'And those aren't *any* old ships,' Topaz replied. 'You see the banners at the top of the mainsails? Red and white stripes, with the cross of St George? The emblem of the East India Company.'

They shut up the house and quickly retraced their steps back to the company's headquarters. A crowd of people had gathered, pushing their way inside; both English merchants and their foreign counterparts.

'I'm going in to find out what's going on,' Nathan said. 'Topaz, you'd better come with me – they'll be speaking every language under the sun.' He turned to Jake. 'Wait here for a moment, all right?' Jake nodded. 'We're going to find out what happened to Philip, if it's the last thing we do . . .' the American added as he shoved his way through.

Jake stood frozen on the spot as more and more people gathered. The thought of his brother locked in that tower had made him feel sick.

Someone barged past him – an old woman in a dark coat, carrying a bundle of papers. She wore a little cap with a black feather and a high collar that obscured her small head. She threw down the stack of papers and, drawing a knife, quickly severed the red ribbon that bound them, then ran off. The wind scattered the papers into the crowd. One flew directly towards Jake; he grabbed it and read the statement, inscribed in black ink:

YOUR SHIPS ARE DOOMED – YOUR CIVILIZATION TOO.

Jake looked again at the woman hurrying away, and saw a flash of red under her gown: red slippers. It was her, surely – the old woman in the portrait . . . Xi Xiang's nanny, Madame Fang. She rounded the corner and disappeared.

Jake didn't hesitate; adrenalin surging, he dashed up the road after her.

10 Into the Bear Pit

Jake turned the corner onto the wide thorough-fare that led to London Bridge. The street was swarming with traders and merrymakers, all being funnelled through the gatehouse. He scanned the sea of heads and found the distinctive black feathered cap.

He pushed and barged, weaving in and out, receiving angry shouts from those who were queuing patiently. On the bridge itself, things had slowed almost to a standstill. There was less than twelve feet between the shops on either side, and the travellers could only shuffle forward half a step at a time.

Then a bell rang out, and everything came to a complete halt. The drawbridge was going up, and Jake saw that his prey had already reached the other side. Now he would surely lose her. He struggled through the crowd, then ducked down and scrambled between the cartwheels and the horses' hooves.

The drawbridge was now halfway up: he leaped onto it, but immediately slipped back down again. The steward – a barrel of a man with a matted grey beard and blackened teeth – took him by the collar and threw him aside. Jake picked himself up, lunged forward, hooking his leg round the man's knee, and sent him careering back into a cart loaded with crates of wild fowl.

Jake saw that the drawbridge was now almost fully raised. At the front of the queue waiting to cross, four clergymen in a black carriage stared at him in astonishment. They gasped in unison as he vaulted from the carriage wheel up onto the roof, and launched himself towards the rising draw-bridge. He caught hold of it and swung round so that he hung over the churning river.

He realized that he was still too far from the other side – but a ship was now gliding towards the opening. As the mainmast sailed past, Jake took a leap of faith and managed to land on the crow's nest, before jumping towards the far side of the drawbridge. He caught hold of the tip and pulled himself over, tumbling down the other side and back onto the bridge.

Once more he searched for the black-feathered cap. There she was, passing under the southern arch! Jake jumped onto a cart and, using the queue of vehicles like stepping stones, leaped from one to the other until he reached the far side. Once through the arch, he turned and looked up. The severed heads of traitors stared back, the black tar gleaming in the evening light.

The south bank was thronging with people, but there were fewer buildings, and Jake caught sight of his target crossing a wide square, her steps marked by flashes of red.

She headed directly towards the octagonal building that Jake already knew well: the Globe. As she reached the forecourt, she suddenly stopped and half turned. Jake shrank back into the shadows. Did she know that he was behind her? But then a steward opened a door for her and she entered the theatre.

Jake had visited the replica of the Globe with his parents; the original was shabbier and more crooked, with the plaster coming away from the timber frame. A peeling poster was pinned to the wall near the entrance, the curly writing barely legible:

The King's Men Presente MACBETH
Entrance: One Pennie

The door was slightly ajar and Jake went in, eyes alert in case the old woman had stopped to wait for him. She was nowhere to be seen, and the performance had started. The theatre was packed – three tiers of galleries heaving with spectators, along with four hundred groundlings, their astonished faces gazing up from the pit. Someone grabbed Jake by the shoulder and his heart stopped – but it was just the steward holding out his hand for the entry fee. Jake fumbled in his pocket, found a penny and handed it over, then stepped cautiously down into the pit.

On stage, a female character, lit from below, moved back and forth in some agitation. She was dressed in the Jacobean style – a black dress with a white ruff – with a swag of tartan over her shoulders. Behind her the painted backdrop showed a castle set in the highlands of Scotland.

Jake slunk back against a pillar and cast his eyes around each gallery, working his way upwards, in search of the black feather cap. Everyone was craning forward, and there was a rustle of excitement as another character entered from the shadows at the back – a thick-set man, as jumpy as his partner. He remained in the gloom as he spoke.

'*I have done the deed,*' he whispered. '*Didst thou not hear a noise?*'

'*I heard the owl scream and the crickets cry,*' the woman answered without looking at him. Jake realized that she was actually being played – very convincingly – by a man. '*Did not you speak?*' she asked.

'*When?*'

'*Now.*'

'*As I descended?*'

'*Aye.*'

Jake remembered something of the play, having read it once in class at school. After being told by three witches that he will rule Scotland, Macbeth plots with his wife to murder the king.

Macbeth finally stepped into the light, and a shiver went round the audience. His hands were covered in blood. In one, he clutched two daggers, thick with gore. The pair continued in low voices.

'*This is a sorry sight*,' Macbeth said with a shudder.

'*A foolish thought to say a sorry sight.*'

'*Methought I heard a voice cry, "Sleep no more. Macbeth doth murder sleep," the innocent sleep.*'

In the crowd, some people started hissing, horrified by the unfolding drama.

'*Who was it that thus cried?*' Lady Macbeth said. '*Why, worthy thane, you do unbend your noble strength, to think so brainsickly of things. Go get some water, and wash this filthy witness from your hand.*' Suddenly she noticed his hands. '*Why did you bring these daggers from the place?*' she hissed. '*They must lie there . . . !*'

'*I'll go no more . . .*'

'*Give me the daggers: the sleeping and the dead are but as pictures.*' She seized the weapons and left the stage, her dress swishing and heels clicking, leaving her husband alone on stage.

As he watched her exit, Jake suddenly caught sight of his prey, ensconced in an individual stall at the end of the second tier. She was whispering in the ear of someone who was completely in shadow. This second person – a man, Jake thought – turned and left, leaving the old woman alone.

From backstage came a loud knocking, making everyone jump in their seats. '*Whence is that knocking?*' Macbeth called, his bloody hands trembling.

When Jake looked back at the compartment, the old woman was staring straight at him, her face as pale as a ghost. It was certainly the figure from the portrait: Madame Fang. She turned and darted away.

Stop her, he told himself. He *had* to stop her. He made his way round the rear of the pit under the galleries. Carefully he drew his sword and headed for the far door. As he left the theatre, something hard hit him on the side of the neck. He gasped, and caught a glimpse of Madame Fang karate-chopping again, this time sending him reeling back as she kicked his sword out of his hand. Despite her years, she was as agile as a teenager.

Now she drew a dagger from her coat, and Jake just managed to duck as she slashed at him. The blade caught his arm and he felt a sharp pain. She lunged again, but he had already rolled over, and the dagger stuck deep into the wall. A shout went up behind them as some people approached, and Madame Fang froze for a moment, then pulled her knife out of the timber and scurried off.

Jake watched as she disappeared into a neigh-bouring building that looked just like the Globe. He followed her inside, and immediately heard a roar of voices. The stench – of sweat, animals and beer – was overwhelming. He realized he was in an arena; the audience were stamping their feet, waiting for the games to begin. In the centre was a sandpit, surrounded by thick wooden walls, where a chained bear snarled as it strained on its leash. A stout man whose cheeks were ruddy from alcohol, the master of ceremonies, cupped his hand to his ear, daring the crowd to shout louder, working them into a frenzy, while behind him a pack of savage dogs barked in their cage, eager to attack.

Out of the corner of his eye, Jake saw Fang rush towards him, dagger glinting. Rage fired up inside him; he went to draw his sword, but his scabbard was empty. Lightning fast, he grabbed the woman's wrist, bashing it against the wall over and over until the dagger dropped to the floor. He made a lunge for it, but Fang twisted his arm behind his back, opened a door into the pit and pushed him inside. The bear lumbered over, teeth bared – until it was halted by its chain. Jake rolled clear as its giant paws thudded down into the sand. The master of ceremonies, unaware that someone had entered the arena behind him, pulled back the cage door, and two dogs charged in.

One went straight for the bear, but the other bounded towards Jake, sharp teeth snapping. It caught his shoulder, making him cry out with pain. Then, suddenly, a figure jumped down into the arena and struck the dog with the hilt of a sword. It padded on for a second and then dropped like a stone.

'Jake, it's me,' the person announced, holding out a hand.

A young man was standing over him; Jake recognized the face immediately – the rose-bud lips and almond eyes . . . but surely he was hallucinating . . .

'It's me, Yoyo.'

She pulled Jake to his feet and, as the second hound came rushing towards them, they vaulted over the wall. Jake gazed at Yoyo in confusion. She was dressed as a boy, in doublet and breeches, with a felt cap pulled down to her eyes.

'Where did you—' Jake started to say.

'I'll explain later,' she said. 'Let's go.'

'We have to—' He was out of breath, his mind a jumble.

'I know,' Yoyo replied, understanding perfectly. 'Madame Fang. She's gone back towards the bridge. We need to be quick.'

'You know her?' Jake asked as they pushed their way out of the building.

'My mother did. Madame Fang once tried to remove her legs at the knee – charming old woman.'

Despite everything, Jake was smiling. He was so thrilled to see Yoyo, he had forgotten about everything else. 'I like your outfit.'

'It's in keeping with the spirit of the age, no? If men can play women, why not the other way round? Look!' she said, pointing ahead.

The gatehouse at the southern end of the bridge was lit by torches and they could see Fang climbing it – her red slippers quickly finding their way up the tiny flight of stairs towards the grisly collection of severed heads at the top.

'Where's she going?' Jake puffed.

'She's not going anywhere . . .' Yoyo withdrew her dagger and sent it sailing into the air – a brilliant flash of steel in the night. To Jake's amazement, the old woman turned and caught the spinning dagger in her hand, before sending it flying back. Yoyo ducked quickly and charged up the steps onto the platform. The old woman was waiting for her, a black metal dagger in her hand. She sliced at her opponent, but Yoyo grabbed a stake and struck Fang with a severed head. Again and again she lunged with the gruesome weapon, until the flesh fell off and the dead eyes went flying, finally landing the decisive blow. Fang's dagger went spinning over the side.

Now the two of them fought with their bare hands, a blur of limbs jabbing, kicking and punching. Jake, trying not to breathe in the smell of rotting flesh, made it to the top just as Fang sent Yoyo tumbling backwards. The old woman spat at her, then turned and launched herself off the parapet, arms outstretched as she dived down into the Thames.

Unable to believe his eyes, Jake limped over and saw her surface upstream. Then he spotted a long metal tube emerging from under the dark water: could it be . . . a submarine?! As Madame Fang swam towards it, a hatch opened and someone helped her aboard. The vessel glided swiftly away up the Thames, bashing into ferries and overturning rowing boats.

There were shouts and screams from the banks

below and all along the bridge. People had seen the submarine and word spread: some came charging over to witness the extraordinary sight, while others ran for cover or fell to their knees in prayer. Horses bolted and carts overturned.

The craft gradually sank, crocodile-like, into the water; when it finally vanished a chorus of shrieks went up, as if the world were coming to an end.

11 Charlie Alone

At Point Zero, it was well past midnight. The castle was asleep, but Charlie Chieverley wasn't tired. He was tucked up in bed, trying to read a book about Alexander the Great's campaign in India. Even though it was a subject that usually fascinated him, he just couldn't concentrate: sadness sat like a stone in his stomach. He missed his friends terribly.

He pictured them in Jacobean London, Nathan fussing over his clothes as the others joked at his expense. *What secrets are they uncovering?* he wondered. *Are they any closer to finding Philip?* His thoughts changed tack again. *Are they all going hungry without me to cook for them? No doubt they're tucking into some dreadful hog roast. The Jacobeans are the worst: meat-mad.*

Charlie sighed, threw back the covers and hauled himself out of bed. He reached for his crutches and hobbled towards the door. Mr Drake opened one eye. 'I'm going down to the kitchen,' Charlie told him, 'to knock up a flan or something – that'll take my mind off things.'

He limped down the back stairs and along the passage that led to the kitchens. As he approached the open door, he heard a banging of pans, and stopped. 'Who on earth can be cooking at this time of night?' he wondered, peering inside.

On the far side of the room stood Oceane Noire, her face covered in flour, hair all over the place, clothes awry, mumbling to herself.

Charlie, intrigued – and just a little frightened – hobbled into the room, coughing to make his presence known.

Oceane was so engrossed, she didn't notice at first.

'*Bonsoir*, Mademoiselle Noire,' Charlie said in a clear voice, and she froze.

'Oh, it's you,' she sneered. '*Qu'est-ce que tu veux?*'

'I can't sleep,' Charlie replied, 'so I have come to make a flan.'

'*Ce n'est pas possible!* You can't,' she snapped. 'Can't you see I'm working here?'

'I'm sure there's room for two,' Charlie replied breezily, not to be deterred. As he crossed the room, he noticed her slip something – it looked like a small brown bottle – into a cupboard.

As Charlie selected ingredients for his flan and started to crack eggs into a bowl, he peered across to see what Oceane was doing. She had made a cake – a lumpy mess that she was now covering with gloopy chocolate icing.

'You're a woman after my own heart, mademoiselle,' Charlie said jovially, 'making a gateau for yourself in the middle of the night. Is it chocolate?'

'It's *bitter* chocolate,' she replied enigmatically, 'and it's not for me! Do you think I would keep my figure if I ate cakes all day long?'

Oceane was indeed as skinny as a rake; she had become even more so since Jupitus and Rose had announced their engagement.

'Oh, I see,' said Charlie. 'So who is the lucky recipient?'

Oceane's eyes glazed over. She poured the last of a bottle of red wine into her glass and took a slug.

'How's that little bird of yours?' she asked, changing the subject.

'He's much better, thank you. He'll be flying again by next week.'

'*C'est bien,*' she replied softly. 'Our pets are the only things we can truly rely on, aren't they?'

Charlie nodded solemnly. The lioness had tried to kill him, but he still felt sorry for her owner. He didn't like to think of any animal as bad, but Josephine had been an unusual case: even though she had grown up on the Mount, she simply didn't like humans, or any other animal. Perhaps it was something to do with having been kept in a circus when she was very young. He returned to the subject of the cake. 'So who is it for?' he persisted, nodding towards the brown mess.

Oceane's expression turned to acid again. 'It's for *them.* The lovebirds. *That man* and his British carpetbag.' She drained her glass and slid the cake onto a silver salver, then took a sharp knife, dropped it into her pocket, blade up, grabbed the cake and made for the door.

Charlie suddenly felt a flutter of panic. 'You're not going to give it to them now, are you?'

Oceane swung round and fixed him with a murderous glare. 'What is it to do with you?'

He gulped, looked down at the knife sticking out of her jacket. 'W-w-well, I – I imagine they'll be asleep by now.'

She gave him a twisted smile. 'Well, if they want to have their cake *and* eat it, they'll just have to wake up.' She turned and strode to the door.

'And besides,' Charlie went on, 'Rose and Mr Cole aren't even on speaking terms any more. I should leave them be.'

'Keep out of my business!' Oceane shrieked, and stormed away, slamming the door behind her. Charlie heard her clomp up the stairs.

He felt sick. He hobbled over to the cupboard and took out the brown jar she had just hidden. It was half full of powder, and Charlie recognized the label immediately – rat poison! He grabbed his crutches and limped after her.

'Miss Noire! Miss Noire!' he called. 'Whatever you're about to do, I beg you to think again.' But Oceane had disappeared. He started hopping up the stairs as fast as he could.

Five flights up, panting and wheezing, he finally made his way to the corridor where Rose and

Jupitus both had their suites. Their doors were open and they were both standing outside, Rose half asleep in a kaftan, Jupitus in dressing gown and slippers, with a look of thunder on his face.

'Don't eat the cake!' Charlie shouted as he flew towards them. 'Did you eat it – did either of you eat the cake?'

'Has everyone gone stark raving mad?' Jupitus yelled. 'It's nearly two o'clock in the morning. What are you all doing?'

'Just answer my question,' Charlie persisted. 'Did Oceane Noire just come up here?'

'Yes, she did,' Rose told him. 'She was thumping on my door, ranting about goodness knows what. We both came out and she said she had made us a surprise. Then she started mumbling to herself, invited us both to go to hell and tossed whatever it was into the bin there.'

Charlie turned and saw that the cake lay in pieces at the bottom, the knife thrown on top of it. 'So you didn't eat any of it?' he asked again, relieved.

'This is lunacy,' Jupitus hissed. 'I'm not listening to any more of it. Goodnight to you both.' He turned on his heel, went back into his room and slammed the door behind him.

Rose stared at him with loathing, before turning to Charlie with a smile. 'We didn't touch it, no. What's all this about?'

Suddenly Charlie didn't know what to say. Oceane had obviously seen sense at the last moment.

'You look much better, by the way,' Rose went on. 'You've got some colour in your cheeks.'

That was an understatement: Charlie had just hobbled up five flights of stairs! 'I'll get rid of this,' he said, picking up the rubbish bin and limping off. He stopped suddenly, another thought coming to him. 'Which way did Oceane go?'

Rose pointed along the passage. 'Up there, onto the battlements. I suppose she needed some air.'

Charlie wished her goodnight and headed out onto the terrace. He scanned the contours of the Mount, a dark collage of shapes and shadows. Finally he located Oceane on one of the upper levels. Was she about to throw herself off? He hid the rubbish bin behind a buttress and, reflecting that he would be happy if he never saw stairs again in his life, he limped up onto the terrace towards her.

He stopped when he saw that his guess had been correct. She had climbed up onto the parapet and was now standing swaying high above the sea. The summer wind made her dishevelled hair stream out behind her. She turned and looked at him, eyes smudged where her make-up had run. She no longer looked crazy – just desperate and dejected.

'Miss Noire' – Charlie's voice was calm – 'please don't do that.'

'*Pourquoi pas?*' she asked hoarsely.

'Because it's not really high enough and the chances are you won't die – you'll end up on crutches like me and it wouldn't suit you at all.'

'It wouldn't?' she growled. 'Why not?'

'You're much too pretty for crutches.'

She looked at him angrily. '*Ce n'est pas vrai!* If I was pretty, people would love me. But no one loves me.' She clenched her fists, and prepared to launch herself into space.

'You're the prettiest woman on the island. How can you deny it? When I first met you, I thought I had never seen anyone so beautiful.' Charlie was telling the truth . . . to a degree: there was no need to mention that he also thought she was mad as a box of frogs. 'Why don't we do a deal? There's a summer ball this coming weekend, over the bay in St Malo. It's a lavish affair, by all accounts, bound to be stuffed with aristocratic types – counts and dukes and so on . . . right up your boulevard. You'll meet one who'll sweep you off your feet. And if you don't, we'll come back here and I'll personally help you jump.'

Oceane looked at him, scrutinizing him carefully. 'Why are you helping me?' she asked.

Charlie sighed and let his shoulders drop. 'I don't know. I think perhaps . . . perhaps we're both a bit lonely.'

There was a long pause, and then Oceane stepped back from the edge.

12 NIGHTSHIP TO CHINA

After Madame Fang's dramatic exit into the Thames, Jake and Yoyo found a water taxi to take them across the river. Yoyo produced a gold coin and whistled for a ferryman as if she hailed one every day. Once on board, they discussed whether they should return to the East India Company or wait for the others on the *Thunder*. They agreed that it was best to head for the ship: Nathan and Topaz would return there – if they hadn't already done so.

As they glided across the water, Yoyo told Jake what had happened: she had escaped from the Mont St Michel less than an hour after he and the others had set sail. She had caused a diversion by setting off fireworks on the western battlements, before making her escape from the east of the island.

'I've often travelled solo through horizon points,'

she boasted. 'I calibrated my first Horizon Cup when I was three, and I'm the sharpest diamond in the eastern hemisphere.'

Jake didn't doubt it. 'Which boat did you come here in?'

'I borrowed the *Kingfisher*. I knew the commander kept an emergency supply of atomium aboard.'

'You took Galliana Goethe's yacht?' Jake exclaimed, startling the waterman. He went on in a whisper, 'That's not going to go down well at all.'

'*Borrowed*. And it's just a little skiff. It was the only choice I had,' Yoyo replied. 'It will look bad; but in the end she will thank me for it. I am vital to the success of this mission. No one will find Xi Xiang without me.'

Jake scrutinized his companion's almond eyes and alabaster face: whatever her shortcomings, her belief in her own worth was unshakeable. He swiftly brought her up to date on their mission, and showed her Philip's watch with the cryptic instruction to *find the Ocean Door*. But she had no idea what this might refer to either.

They arrived safely on the north bank, sought out the rickety pier where the *Thunder* was docked and, making doubly sure that no one had followed them, climbed aboard – to find the ship empty.

Jake took off his jacket, grimacing in pain. His shirt was blotched with blood from his wounds and he half slipped it off too. His shoulder had been scratched by the dog, but far worse was the cut on his arm from Fang's dagger.

'Let me see that,' Yoyo said.

'I don't think it's life-threatening,' Jake replied bravely. Yoyo inspected it: a deep gash.

'You'll survive,' she told him. 'But we need to clean it up. First-aid box?'

'The trunk there.' Jake nodded towards a wooden chest that doubled as a seat behind the helm.

Yoyo retrieved a leather case embossed with the emblem of a red cross and clicked it open. It contained a bundle of moustaches and beards. 'Interesting,' she commented.

'Oh, those are Charlie's,' Jake said, unable to resist a chuckle. 'He has a passion for disguises and likes to secrete them in odd places. Perhaps underneath . . .'

Below, Yoyo found two trays, the first filled with gleaming medical instruments, the second with vials of medicines and tinctures. 'I think it's best if we do this immediately,' she said, taking out a bottle and a pouch of waxy paper, which she tore open to reveal a swab. She doused it with drops from the bottle. 'This will sting,' she warned as she started to clean the wound.

The pain was intense, and Jake clenched his teeth to prevent himself from crying out. Once it was washed, Yoyo used another swab to anaesthetize the cut.

'When you say it's best we do it immediately . . .?' Jake began, but he trailed off when he saw her pick out a sharp needle and thread it from a roll of gut.

'Bite on this,' Yoyo said, passing Jake a chunk of leather. She wasted no time, leaning forward and piercing his skin with the needle. This time, he *did* cry out. 'Look for the others,' she told him, trying to distract him. 'Can you see them?'

Jake was panting as she laced up the gash; he scanned the busy quay and shook his head.

'What can you see?'

'Fisherman . . . selling crabs,' he moaned as he watched a man carrying baskets of live shellfish. 'Ah!' he cried out again.

'All done,' said Yoyo, tying the thread, snipping it and tossing the instruments to one side.

'Already?' Jake felt a sense of relief washing over him. As the worst of the pain subsided, he found himself giggling.

Yoyo took a length of clean bandage and smoothed it carefully around his arm. 'Have you ever had a girlfriend?' she asked.

Immediately Jake stopped laughing. There was silence as Yoyo tied the bandage. Suddenly his heart was pounding. On the pier, a lady bought some crabs from the fisherman.

'I'd expect you to have one. You've got the face for it. *Bel viso*, as Signor Gondolfino says.' Finally she cleaned up the scratches on his shoulders and packed up the first-aid case. 'Perhaps I could be your girlfriend.' It sounded more of a statement than a question. She put away the bundle of moustaches, but kept one back, placing it under her nose – to comic effect.

Jake had suddenly forgotten all about his wound. His throat was dry.

Yoyo was disappointed by his silence. 'Oh dear, bad suggestion.' She put the moustache away.

'No,' Jake said at last. 'I mean, *yes*. You could.'

He took a deep breath. 'That would be . . . Do you really mean it?' He lifted his shirt back over his shoulder, but kept his arm free.

'You're adorable.' Yoyo smiled, planting a kiss on his cheek. She lingered there for a moment. 'It hasn't been easy, getting your attention, I must say.'

'Hasn't it?' Jake had thought precisely the opposite.

'I've been following you around since the day I arrived.'

'Have you?' Jake was lost for words; he'd clearly misread everything.

'I'm starving. I'm going to pay a visit to your fisherman there and rustle something up.' Yoyo jumped down onto the pier and went over to inspect his catch, chatting amiably. Jake watched her, barely able to believe what had just happened . . . Yoyo had asked to be his girlfriend. Suddenly he flushed with pride. *She's been following me around since the day she arrived?* Then another thought struck him: Nathan. What would he tell him? He hated the thought of upsetting his friend.

Yoyo returned with an armful of crabs. 'Last catch of the day.'

'So, what you just said . . .' Jake began.

'Oh dear, you've changed your mind already?'

'No! But maybe – would you mind if it was our secret for a while?'

Yoyo chirped with delight. 'Absolutely not. I *love* secrets! They make everything even more exciting,' she whispered, and stepped down into the galley. There soon followed the sound of cracking crab shells.

After a while, Jake spied two familiar figures coming down the steps towards the ship.

'Jake, what happened?' Topaz exclaimed, vaulting up onto the deck. 'We searched everywhere for you. You're hurt,' she said, noticing the bandage.

'Listen, there have been developments—' Jake was about to tell them about Yoyo – and Madame Fang, of course – when his new girlfriend appeared from below decks with a tray of food and plates balanced on one hand. Not recognizing her in her boy's garb, Nathan and Topaz drew their swords.

'Relax . . .' Yoyo pushed Topaz's blade away with her finger and set down the tray. 'You'll give yourself a heart attack. Crab stir-fry, anyone?' she asked, lifting the lid off a silver salver. The food looked delicious – as good as anything that Charlie could rustle up: emerald-green vegetables tossed with chunks of pink crabmeat. She served up a portion. 'Jake first,' she said, handing it to him with a coquettish smile, 'as he's probably worked the hardest for it.'

Nathan sheathed his sword, unable to stop grinning; but Topaz kept hers clenched in her hand, blinking in disbelief. 'Excuse me . . .' She shook her head. 'What are you doing here?'

'Not that it's not nice to see you,' Nathan quickly put in. 'It's *very* nice to see you. I love, love, love what you're wearing. Tomboy chic – it's perfect, effortless, understated.'

Topaz shot him a sharp look before turning back to Yoyo. 'I asked what you were doing here,' she repeated impatiently.

'I don't think there is any need to take that tone, Miss St Honoré,' Yoyo replied with an insincere smile. 'For all you know, the commander sent me herself. Nathan, crab for you?' she asked, serving up a second portion.

'Well, yes, I wouldn't say no – smells delicious.'

'And *did* the commander send you?' Topaz persisted, still refusing to put down her weapon.

'Well, actually no,' Yoyo confessed, 'but she should have done. Crab, Miss St Honoré?'

'No,' the other deadpanned. '*Je n'aime pas les crustacés*. If you have not been given orders to accompany us, I must insist that you return to Point Zero immediately.'

'Sooo dramatic,' Yoyo chuckled, tucking into her food. 'You can insist all you like, but I don't believe you have the power to stop me travelling where I want to.'

'*Vraiment?*' Topaz squared up to her, her knuckles white on her sword hilt. 'While you work for the History Keepers and I am in command of this assignment, I have *every* right. How did you get here?'

There was an awkward silence, then Yoyo shot a glance at Jake before announcing coolly, 'I brought the commander's ship.'

'You did *what?*' Topaz let out a strangled laugh of astonishment.

Jake stood up to intervene. 'Maybe we should all calm down.' He had never seen Topaz so angry; her top lip was trembling.

'It's incredible,' Yoyo replied, her smile tight. 'You haven't even asked what happened to Jake. While you were up to goodness knows what, he was bravely pursuing Madame Fang.'

'Madame Fang?' Nathan exclaimed, choking on his stir-fry. 'She's here?'

'*Was* here,' Yoyo corrected him. 'She escaped the city over an hour ago, by submarine.'

'Submarine?' Nathan spluttered.

'As far as we can tell, Xi Xiang was with her,' Jake added.

'Xi Xiang?' Nathan echoed once more.

'*Pour l'amour de Dieu,* Nathan, stop repeating everything!' Topaz drew a deep breath and finally put away her sword. 'I'm sorry, Miss Yuting, perhaps we should start again. Jake, would you begin by telling us everything you know?'

He recounted the events of the last couple of hours: the sighting of Madame Fang outside the East India Company, the pursuit across London Bridge, her rendezvous with a man – presumed to be Xi Xiang – at the Globe Theatre, the episode in the bear-pit, the fight amongst the severed heads and, finally, the old woman's shock departure.

Nathan shook his head. 'Are you really trying to tell me that a seventy-year-old woman dived off London Bridge into the Thames?'

'As witnessed by about a thousand people on the south bank,' Yoyo confirmed. 'There is no limit to

Madame Fang's abilities; nor to her endurance. And with age, she becomes ever more resilient. She can survive underwater, walk through fire, glide across tightropes. She is barely human.'

'They must have locked up the house and then gone to plant the bombs on the East India Company ships,' Topaz surmised, trying to put all the pieces of the puzzle together.

'And what about you two?' Jake asked the others. 'Did you discover anything?'

'Yes,' Topaz said. 'That London is not the only city that has come under attack.' She pulled one of Madame Fang's handbills out of her pocket and set it down. '*Your ships are doomed. Your civilization too*. In the last few weeks, similar flyers have been left outside trading organizations in Amsterdam, Copenhagen, Cádiz, Marseilles and Genoa, each following an explosion either on a ship or in a warehouse.' She fished out another piece of paper. 'I managed to get this version, in Flemish, from a merchant with the *Dutch* East India Company.' She held it up for Jake and Yoyo to see. 'Different language, but the same writing, the same phrase.'

UW SCHEPEN ZIJN VERDOEMD – UW BESCHAVING OOK.

'Can I have a look?' Yoyo asked, taking the flyer from Topaz and carefully comparing the versions.

'Actually, the Dutch thought the British were responsible for the sabotage in Amsterdam last week,' Nathan chipped in. 'That's why they were in London – to investigate . . . This crab really is exceptional.' He turned to Yoyo and winked. 'Is there no end to your talents?'

Topaz tutted irritably and steered them back to the subject at hand. 'Which brings us to the question of where Xi Xiang has gone,' she said.

'I know this watermark,' said Yoyo. 'It's the same on both sheets. Look there . . .' The other three could just make out a faint imprint of Chinese characters set within the paper. 'It's obviously the insignia of Shen Pei-Pei.'

'Obviously,' Nathan agreed. 'Remind me – who's Shen Pei-Pei?'

'Reclusive millionaire of the era,' Topaz replied. 'Right about now, he owns half of Canton. He has a giant porcelain works there, a fish sauce empire – *and* a paper factory, the largest in southern China.

Where are we . . . 1612, so he must be almost eighty by now – though no one has seen him in decades.'

'Oh, *that* Shen Pei-Pei.' Nathan nodded. 'I was getting him confused with the other Shen Pei-Pei – the one who breeds those funny cats with no fur.'

'But the fact that this paper came from there tells us little,' Topaz pointed out. 'Xi Xiang may have simply bought it along with a million other Chinese.'

'No.' Yoyo tutted dismissively. 'You're missing the point: Shen Pei-Pei collects priceless relics – and a powerful tide stone would be the real prize of his collection.'

'The Lazuli Serpent?' Jake wondered out loud.

'Precisely. He allegedly keeps his jewels in a treasure house in his garden – a golden pagoda.'

Topaz thought quickly. 'We leave for Canton tonight. We'll take the Nightship.'

'The Nightship!' Nathan exclaimed. 'Absolutely not. I'm not doing that again. Last time I nearly detonated. And my hair fell out, remember?'

'That's an absurd exaggeration,' Topaz said. 'You moulted a little.'

Nathan eyeballed his sister. 'It fell out in clumps! I'm not doing it,' he insisted, stroking his lustrous mane as if it were a pet dog. 'I'm *nothing* without my hair.'

'If we don't take the Nightship,' Topaz replied, 'we'll lose days. We don't have a choice.'

'Besides,' Yoyo chipped in mischievously, 'you can get wonderful wigs. And that way, you could try different colours. Blond might suit you.'

'There is only *one* colour,' Nathan said indignantly, 'and that is *deep auburn*.' He emphasized his point by tossing his locks.

Jake was confused. 'I'm sorry . . . what is the Nightship?'

'The Nightship allows Keepers to cross to the other side of the world almost instantly,' Topaz explained. 'To a degree, you've done it before – *vaulted* over to the Mediterranean – but it's one thing to hop a few hundred miles to the Tyrrhenian Sea; to span the globe to southern China is another matter entirely, especially when you're maintaining the same date.'

'Maintaining the same date?' Jake was struggling to understand.

Yoyo stepped in. 'Maybe I could explain more clearly? To *vault* in the first place, we must enter the time flux. Usually the greater the number of years we are travelling backwards or forwards in time, the easier it is to hop from one part of the world to another. If we're keeping the *same* date – London 1612 to Canton 1612 – we essentially have to enter the time flux, go back a few hundred years, then immediately forward again – a journey that can have strange side effects. That's the Nightship. Obviously I'm simplifying.'

'It's much more civilized to set sail and take a few leisurely hops from sea to sea,' Nathan told Jake.

'More civilized,' Topaz pointed out, 'but more time-consuming.'

'Well, then, it has to be the Nightship,' Jake agreed. 'Time is what we don't have.' He looked around at the others. They were all diamonds, Valiants – young, powerful agents – and he suspected it would take all their focus to make this jump. An older agent would never risk it.

'We set off immediately,' Topaz said.

'And what about me, Miss St Honoré?' Yoyo asked. 'Would you still like me to go all the way back to Point Zero?' She looked at her rival with a twisted smile.

'I think she should come with us, Topaz,' Nathan said.

'I have to agree,' Jake added.

Topaz sighed. 'Miss Yuting . . .'

'Please – call me Yoyo.'

'I am in no doubt as to your capabilities. However, you are a loose cannon.' Topaz took a deep breath. 'That said, since we are going to Canton and you are an expert in that part of the world, I suppose there is some sense in taking you with us.'

'You won't regret it, I promise you,' Yoyo vowed.

'But you need to understand: I am in charge and you must obey my orders at all times. Is that clear? *Yoyo*?'

'As a bell.'

The two girls stared at each other. 'I will send a Meslith to the commander and explain the situation,' Topaz said grimly. 'She won't like it at all, but it can't be helped.' She held out her hand towards Yoyo and they shook on it. 'And please, call me Topaz.'

Before they set sail, the girls went to check that the *Kingfisher*, Galliana's yacht, was secure (they had no choice but to leave it in Jacobean London for the time being – until it could be picked up by someone from Point Zero) and to collect the rest of Yoyo's things. Suspecting that the mission was bound to go beyond London, Yoyo had brought quantities of money with her – Chinese currencies in particular. Topaz was so relieved to see it, she decided not to ask Yoyo whether, like the yacht, it had been stolen.

A short time later, with Jake at the helm, they cast off and started back downstream towards the North Sea.

Jake glanced over his shoulder at the city behind him. London, his home town; and he was leaving it once again, sailing into the unknown. As he surveyed the labyrinthine warren of streets, the million points of light that seemed to encase the city in a golden aura – so different from the London he'd grown up in – he realized it was the place that had shaped his life.

Sudden memories surfaced, long-forgotten moments in his life: the day he had first ridden a bike . . . his father letting go of the saddle on the crest of the hill in Greenwich Park . . . the green of the trees rushing towards him; the day he had begun school . . . the smell of his new uniform . . . the uncertain faces of his classmates; the birthday when it reached a hundred degrees . . . the neighbour's cat, panting on the pavement; and the blackest day of all – that November afternoon when his parents had told him that his brother would not be coming home.

Jake shuddered as he recalled being asked to sit on the sofa, his mother's face blotchy with tears, the coldness of the room, the radiator gurgling as the heating fired up. Jake had gone to bed that night in a daze, unable to take it in.

A week later, he had come back from school early and gone to Philip's room. The door was slightly ajar. The familiar sign declared:

Adventurer Within!

The room was colder than the rest of the house, and Jake could see his breath in front of him. He had inspected the shelf of medals and prizes. (Philip was a brilliant sportsman, as well as a bright pupil. Unusually for someone so talented, he was also popular. It was not just the shy kids he helped who looked up to him, but the tough ones too. Girls as well; even the loud, unruly ones became a little gentler in Philip's presence.)

Jake had turned and examined the rest of the

room: the bedside table with its pile of books telling of fascinating places and people from history; the bed itself, usually quite messy, the duvet now smoothed down and the pillows plumped up. The sight had made him realize, for the first time, that Philip was not coming home. Suddenly the cold had seemed unbearable and Jake had left the room. In three years, he had never gone back in . . .

Once they had cleared the Thames estuary and entered the North Sea, Topaz appeared on deck with four doses of atomium, which the agents drank swiftly. No one spoke; there was a serious atmosphere.

'Nathan, we need fresh eyes at the helm – would you take over from Jake now?' Topaz asked. 'We're using the north-north-east horizon point,' she added, nodding at the map. 'It will be less risky.'

Jake relinquished the wheel, turning to see the last of Britain's coast disappear behind him. There was a gust of wind from the east and he shivered with cold. *China*, he thought to himself. *I'm going to China.*

He looked round at the Constantor. The three rings that guided them to the horizon point were inching closer together. In the centre was a metal globe with engraved lines tracing the continents. Jake found the British Isles, and then Europe, Arabia, India, Siam, and finally China – the bulging cheek of Asia.

Keeping one hand on the wheel, Nathan reached down for the helmet he had placed at his feet and put it on. 'It might improve my chances, hair-wise,' he explained.

Jake looked round at Topaz. 'Should we be doing the same?'

Her hand made circles in the air beside her ear to indicate that Nathan was totally mad. 'It won't make the slightest difference,' she whispered to him. Then she smiled. 'I've never been to China either. I'm glad we are taking the trip together.' Her indigo gaze lingered on Jake a little longer than usual.

'Thirty seconds to horizon,' Nathan called.

Jake glanced again at the Constantor: the rings were all but touching. The ship began to shudder and Topaz clutched Jake's arm. Yoyo noticed and reached for his hand, squeezing it tight.

Nathan counted down: 'Ten, nine, eight, seven . . .'

The ship creaked and rumbled. As usual, a

whirlwind sprang up out of nowhere, encircling them. Colours flashed, and there was a sound like an explosion. Jake saw diamond shapes shooting in all directions as he flew out of his body. As his alter ego soared into the atmosphere, away from the curving earth, he wondered why the others had made such a fuss about the Nightship: it seemed like every other horizon point; in fact, it was smoother than usual. It wasn't until he had almost reached the zenith that he noticed the difference.

He began to spin head over heels – faster and faster; soon the earth was flashing by every fraction of a second. He wanted to be sick and found himself closing his eyes. Blind, the sensation was just as strange, but less nauseating. Eventually the spinning stopped, and Jake wondered if he had returned to himself on the *Thunder*. He opened his eyes and found himself suspended in the black void of space. Panic engulfed him as he realized that the Earth was nowhere to be seen. Had he travelled so far out of his body that he had lost his own planet? Terrified, he searched the heavens for the blue ball. Finally he realized that he had been turned upside down and that the Earth was hovering below his head.

In this topsy-turvy position, pulled by invisible

forces, he began to move forward, circling the globe, slowly at first, then at an astonishing speed. 'How?' he found himself crying out. 'How can I travel this fast?' He tried to make sense of it, while knowing it was pointless to do so: it was not he himself travelling but his alter ego. He was aware of three tiny shapes ahead of him. Then they were gone.

A second later, the apparitions began.

The journey from a horizon point was often accompanied by visions of the past – but these ones appeared to Jake upside down too. He saw snow-capped mountains and forests of bamboo bending in the wind. There were patchworks of fields, half under water, and wide, winding rivers. There were fortresses with roofs that curved up at the edges, curious pagodas, and palaces topped with golden tiles. He saw a wall that travelled into infinity, and an army marching across the frozen tundra.

He closed his eyes against the images, and soon felt himself falling, headfirst. He flew towards the ocean, towards a land he didn't recognize.

'China?' he said, craning to see as the Orient took shape beneath him.

Suddenly he spotted himself on the deck of the *Thunder*, standing with the others; in a flash he returned to his body. He stood there panting, his head whirling, then rushed over to the side and vomited. As he got his breath back, Nathan put his arm round him.

'You all right?'

He nodded. Nathan passed him a handkerchief, and Jake managed to croak, 'How's your hair?'

Nathan had already removed his helmet. He shook out his *deep auburn* locks and announced, 'We may all breathe a sigh of relief – it seems to have arrived in one piece.'

Jake looked out across the sea, a still expanse of cornflower blue disappearing towards a golden horizon. Only now did he notice that he was sweating. 'We've arrived all right?' he asked.

Yoyo smiled at him. 'Welcome to the South China Sea.'

13 Canton Time

'How much do you three know about China?' Yoyo asked, polishing the blade of her sword.

They were eating lunch as they sailed north from the horizon point towards the port of Canton.

'Shall I come straight out and admit it?' Nathan said with a theatrical flourish. 'Of course, I know the basics – the Great Wall and so on – but my knowledge is shamefully sketchy. Educate me!'

Topaz grimaced; Nathan's continual sucking up to Yoyo was starting to grate. He had been following her around like a puppy and cooing at everything she said.

'I know it's the longest continuous civilization in history.' Jake remembered a passage from his book about the travels of Marco Polo. 'Four thousand years and counting.'

'Spot on,' Yoyo told him. 'In four millennia, though it's had its ups and downs, our civilization has *never* fallen apart. The Romans lasted barely seven hundred years, the ancient Greeks even fewer. The Egyptians and the Mayans did better, but China wins the prize.'

'*Naturellement*,' Topaz commented with a tight smile.

'As for your western civilizations – the Ottomans, the Habsburgs, the Romanovs' – Yoyo looked at Topaz – 'the so-called French civilization . . . they were all over before they began.' She emphasized her point with a few clicks of her fingers.

Topaz bristled. 'Although, of course, that depends on how you define civilization,' she pointed out.

'France's heyday was fun – with a lot of powder and gaudy dressing-up – but ultimately it was all rather hollow and short-lived. *Non?*'

Nathan fell about laughing. 'You have to admit, that *does* have a ring of truth!'

Topaz was determined not to rise to the bait. 'Carry on, Yoyo. I'm fascinated.'

'So, you're asking, how on earth have we lasted so long? How have we been so absurdly successful?

How have we earned our title, the Middle Kingdom – as in, "the realm between heaven and earth"?'

'Yes, yes, tell us!' Nathan exclaimed.

'*Pour l'amour de Dieu*,' Topaz muttered under her breath.

'The answer is: our talent for invention – and *re*-invention – through the ages. Since 1700 BC the country has been ruled by a series of dynasties: all-powerful families, each one seeing in a new era of change. The Shang invented the Chinese alphabet and built the world's first navy. The Zhou followed with cast iron and mathematics. In 221 BC, the Emperor Qin – the first emperor – started on the Great Wall, the largest structure ever built: over four thousand miles long, the distance from London to Delhi.'

'The Emperor Qin,' Nathan piped up excitedly, 'was the one who buried himself with all those stone soldiers.'

'Not just soldiers,' Yoyo replied. 'An entire court: governors, cooks, musicians, slaves – thousands and thousands of them, all to look after him and run his empire in the afterlife.'

'I'll give them this,' Topaz quipped, 'they're not afraid to be grand.'

'And why should they be?' Yoyo answered. 'Modesty is for the rest of the world. After the Qin came the Han. Obviously, they invented paper, the compass, the seismograph – but, more importantly for all of us, they opened up the first global trade route. The Silk Road, as you probably know, wasn't just one road, but a whole network running through Asia, connecting the east to the west. The Romans couldn't get enough of that silk – this was the age of Julius Caesar, more or less; but even more importantly, *ideas* started going back and forth. It became an information superhighway.'

'Fascinating . . . fascinating,' Nathan gushed, running his hands through his hair.

'And we've barely scratched the surface.' Yoyo checked her reflection in her gleaming blade. 'During the Tang dynasty – AD 800, give or take – while the rest of the world was entering a dark age, we were scaling new heights. There was an explosion of art and culture. White porcelain was created, printing, gunpowder . . . There were huge advances in science, astronomy, geography.'

'What about Genghis Khan?' Jake asked. 'When was he?'

'He came after,' Yoyo told him. 'In the thirteenth

century he pushed the boundaries of the empire further than ever, from Europe in the west to Mongolia in the north. After Marco Polo visited the country and took his stories back, the whole world was clamouring for all things Chinese. The obsession grew and grew, and since the early 1500s, sea routes have been opening up between east and west.'

Yoyo sheathed her sword and looked at them seriously. 'Which brings us to now: the famous Ming dynasty. An age that is rich beyond all imaginings. The Great Wall is complete. Peking, the most populous place on earth, is filled with the golden palaces of the Forbidden City. And trade, the bringer of all this wealth – not just to China, but to all the world – is booming like never before—'

'And there ends the lesson,' Topaz couldn't resist putting in with a smile.

'Land!' Jake suddenly shouted, leaping to his feet. 'Land ahoy!'

They all turned to look at the horizon ahead, hazy in the midday heat. They pressed on, merging with a stream of ships heading to and from the mainland. Jake watched the other vessels with interest. There were many galleons from the west, setting off on their long journey home, their timbers creaking, their sails charged with wind, but it was the Chinese merchant ships – the junks – that intrigued him most. They were squarer than the western ships, the bulky sterns rising steeply out of the water – a sheer cliff of timber – and their sails looked like the fins of giant fish.

'That's Macao there . . .' Yoyo pointed towards a port just visible in the distance – a multitude of roofs nestling amongst undulating peaks. 'Almost a new city. It's a Portuguese trading post, admin-istered by the Chinese. In just a few decades – since world trade really began to explode – it's grown twenty-fold.'

They forged on along the coast into the giant delta of the Pearl River. The estuary was so huge that it was hours before the banks narrowed enough for them to see land on the other side. A sequence of tributaries flowed into the river mouth, each carrying away a portion of the ships. It was not until mid-afternoon that the *Thunder* finally reached the harbour of Canton itself.

The sun had got the better of Jake, and for the last hour he had been sitting under an awning, sweat dripping down his face. His discomfort was forgotten as the city came into view – like a mirage forming out of the sweltering heat. He stood up, gawping.

As in London, there were ships everywhere; the jungle of masts seemed to disappear to infinity. But where the other port had been rich and dark, Canton was a blaze of light and colour. The sea was a vivid turquoise, and the city itself looked golden, with its layers of yellow- and orange-tiled roofs. Adding to the magic, clusters of tropical palms sprouted between the buildings, and in the distance Jake could see elegant pagodas – slim towers rising in ever-narrowing tiers.

On one side of the river, in the grandest part of the port, the banks were teeming with people, mostly wearing conical *rice* hats to protect them from the sun. There was a carnival atmosphere, with people waving batons and jostling forward to get a better view of the river.

'How touching.' Nathan grinned. 'Our very own welcoming party.'

A cheer went up, and soon everyone was clapping and shouting. Nathan found himself waving back and tossing his glossy locks.

From behind came a blare of horns, so ear-splitting it made them all jump. They had been so busy looking ahead they hadn't noticed the vessel on their tail – a gargantuan ship that cast a shadow over the *Thunder* as she glided towards the dock. The horns were soon accompanied by pounding drums: *boom, boom, boom.*

The ship had seven masts, each with a fin-shaped sail of canary yellow. Along her many terraces was a series of grand pavilions decorated with golden carvings; on the prow a golden dragon, its jaw wide open, tongue reaching out. The decks teemed with soldiers, and a flotilla of at least twenty smaller vessels accompanied her.

'She's a flagship,' Yoyo commented, 'owned by the emperor and his family. It's illegal for any other craft to be decorated with royal yellow.' The colour was everywhere; Jake noticed a throne of lemon silk standing on the foredeck.

'A flagship?' Nathan asked. 'Sounds appealing.'

Yoyo was about to continue when Topaz butted in. 'They were made famous by Zheng He, the fifteenth-century explorer who went on many imperial missions across the globe – partly to explore the world, but also to blow China's trumpet, so to speak.' She turned to Yoyo. 'Am I right?'

'I suppose we *were* blowing our trumpet,' Yoyo replied, 'because we had a trumpet to blow. Navigationally speaking, the west was inept, stuck in the Middle Ages.'

Nathan laughed. 'She has a point there, Topaz: it did take us a while to get going on water – though I like to think we've made up for it now.'

His sister smiled back through gritted teeth.

'Anyway, as you can see,' Yoyo went on, 'a flagship like this, or a *treasure ship*, as they are sometimes known, is a remarkable craft by any standard. They can carry up to five hundred passengers – navigators, explorers, doctors, sailors, soldiers; they're really miniature cities, the royal court at sea.'

'So she's actually the emperor's ship?' Jake asked. 'Do you think he's aboard?'

Again Topaz cut Yoyo off before she could speak. 'Probably not Wan Li himself, as he rarely leaves Peking. But he has three sons and, judging by the armed guard, I would say that at least one of them must be there.'

'And what would they be doing here in Canton?' Jake wondered.

This time, before either girl could answer, Nathan held up his hand. 'Why don't we let Yoyo do the talking? She does seem to be the expert.'

'Thank you, Nathan,' she purred. 'Well, as you know, China is large – double the size of Europe; so the emperor or his family need to visit the provinces from time to time, for purposes of morale . . .' She turned to Topaz and added slyly, 'And for generally blowing their trumpets.'

As the imperial behemoth peeled off towards her mooring, the *Thunder* continued further into the port. Jake gazed at the multitude of quays, each buzzing with life: sailors and traders shouting, gulls screeching. The bright colours were repeated in the smocks of the dockworkers and the gaudy awnings of the many carts, carriages and litters that made their way through the tumult.

'If my memory serves me,' Yoyo announced, pointing further ahead, 'Pei-Pei's paper factory lies on that southern promontory there. Might I suggest we dock just short of it?'

Topaz turned to Nathan at the helm. 'You heard her: make for that quay.'

Jake reminded himself what they were doing here. Pei-Pei was a Cantonese millionaire who not only collected priceless tide stones – like the Lazuli Serpent – but also owned the factory that produced the paper for Madame Fang's flyers. The History Keepers hoped that by tracking him down, they might also discover the whereabouts of Xi Xiang.

They moored between a Chinese junk and a western galleon, both double the size of the *Thunder*.

There followed a debate about their clothes. Nathan suggested they go shopping immediately and buy appropriate *oriental* attire. 'There's some fantastic stuff to be had, in truly zinging colours,' he said enthusiastically. But Topaz vetoed the proposal, pointing out that Canton was full of Europeans and they wouldn't look out of place in their Jacobean costume.

'It's just no fun at all,' Nathan muttered to Jake as they disembarked. 'What's the point of coming to these places if we can't dress up?'

They set off along an alleyway between two warehouses. Away from the water, Jake was aware of the intense heat. The air was like soup.

'There's going to be a storm,' Topaz murmured as she looked up at the sky. Just half an hour ago it had been blue; now it was the colour of gunmetal.

Not far from the dockside they came across a long, low grey building with narrow barred windows.

'That's the paper factory.' Yoyo stopped in the shadows at the corner to assess it.

'Any reason why it's so heavily guarded?' Nathan asked, nodding towards the armed sentries at the entrance. 'How valuable *is* paper exactly?'

'Not as valuable as that,' Yoyo said. 'Let's see if we can get in at the back . . .' She set off, but halted almost immediately, remembering the chain of command. 'Sorry, Topaz – should we . . .?'

'Carry on,' the other girl replied. 'We'll follow your lead.'

They edged their way round the building, only to find the back even more impenetrable than the front: just a sheer, windowless wall.

'I dare say there's no way in through the roof?' Nathan asked. It was tiled and shaped in the Chinese style, curving up at the edges.

'There are air vents there.' Topaz pointed to a row of slits in the curve of the roof. 'At least we can *see* inside.' Without hesitation, she vaulted up onto an adjoining wall and leapfrogged onto the eave, keeping down so the guards wouldn't see her over the roof. She checked that the slates would bear her weight, then nodded to the others. In a flash, Yoyo was at her side. Jake followed, a little more clumsily. Nathan was about to join them when Topaz let out a soft whistle. 'You stay down there and keep your eyes on the guards.'

'No problem,' he muttered under his breath. 'You have fun. I'll just stay here and do the menial work.'

The other three crept along towards the vents; now Jake could see wisps of vapour curling out. They peeked in, and saw a large room below them.

Vats filled with a slurry of water and mashed-up wood bubbled over huge fires tended by men stripped to the waist. Further along, the boiled-down concoction was strained through porous screens. The residue was flattened by stone weights; finally, squares of damp, compressed paper were carried through into the adjoining space.

Topaz beckoned to the others, and they tiptoed across the roof, keeping their eyes on the activity below. The next chamber was a drying room, where workers were busy hanging up or taking down the parchment, some climbing bamboo ladders to utilize every bit of space. Finished sheets were stacked by the far wall.

Jake froze as a face suddenly stared up at him just below the vent. He clutched the hilt of his sword. But the man, an ancient hunchback with leathery skin, did not seem to notice him and simply felt along a sheet of parchment, mumbling to himself as he checked it. Jake realized that he was blind, his eyes milky white. At last he unhooked the sheet and made his way back down his ladder, leaving Jake to sigh with relief.

The three of them edged further along the roof, first over a hallway where two sentries guarded a metal door; then on to the next chamber. Here, the workers were fully clothed and had cotton gloves on. Several wore spectacles – tiny discs of glass held in gold wire frames – and were operating a pair of machines: cast-iron contraptions that clanked and thumped incessantly.

'Printing machines,' Topaz murmured.

Jake peered down with interest. He had seen such devices before, in the dungeons of Castle Schwarzheim, the mountain hideaway of Prince Zeldt, but these were far more elaborate, like the insides of a giant clock; they printed a page a second, each one covered with intricate writing.

'What's that?' Jake asked, watching as the sheets

were carried over to a workbench, carefully guillotined into smaller sections and stacked up in a metal casket. Then he realized: 'Money. They're making *money*.'

'As you may know, we invented the banknote,' Yoyo couldn't resist boasting, 'way back in the 1050s, while you were all still bartering with chickens.'

'Yoyo, we get the point,' Topaz sighed testily. 'We were late developers. Can we leave the subject now?'

'Are they printing it illegally?' Jake asked, trying to forestall another argument.

'Not necessarily,' Yoyo replied. 'The business of making money is franchised out by the government. This factory has an imperial seal, so it makes sense – and it explains the guards outside.'

'Someone's coming,' Jake said, hearing the bolts on the metal door being drawn back. They all watched as the door swung open and a young man swaggered in. He wore a light blue tunic, belted at the waist, with a sword swinging either side. Hanging from his lips was a toothpick, which he rolled from side to side. He made his presence known with a sharp whistle. An old bespectacled man – clearly the foreman – told him to wait.

'Give me your spyglass,' Topaz whispered to Yoyo. She opened it and peered at the new arrival. 'There's a mark on his tunic – an octopus! Xi Xiang's emblem. Can you see it?' She passed the telescope to Jake, but the man jumped up and went over to the metal casket of banknotes. The foreman took a key from a chain around his neck, locked the box and handed it to the man in blue. He fastened a chain around the youth's wrist and secured it to the casket. Finally he signed a piece of paper, stamped it with a seal, put it in the youth's free hand and dismissed him with a clap of his hands.

The young man winked at him, turned and strutted back to the door, knocking twice. The guards on the other side let him out, before slamming it shut behind him.

'After him,' Topaz declared. 'Quickly!'

They hurriedly retraced their steps back to Nathan.

'Anything?' he asked.

'It looks like one of Xi Xiang's men is taking a box of money somewhere,' Jake said. 'Let's go . . .'

14 Through the Ocean Door

The History Keepers crept back round to the front of the factory. The youth in the blue tunic was just emerging from the main entrance. He handed the sheet of paper to the guards, who examined it, patted him down, double-checked that the box was secured to his wrist, then sent him on his way. He crossed the street and boarded a rickshaw with an awning that was the same colour as his tunic. He snapped his fingers at the driver and they set off.

'Follow it!' Topaz commanded, crossing the street in pursuit. They hurried to the corner . . . and their faces fell.

'Rush hour!' Jake shook his head. They'd come to a wide boulevard. At this hour it was full of traffic: carts, carriages and litters – not to mention

hundreds of rickshaws – rattled past in both directions.

'There!' Topaz shouted, spotting a flash of blue in
the distance. Opening the telescope, she double-
checked it was the right vehicle. She could just see
the black money box on the seat. 'That's it.'

'Taxi!' Nathan shouted as an empty rickshaw
pulled to a halt.

'It's too small to take us all,' Yoyo said, flagging
another one down. She pulled Jake in beside her,
leaving Nathan to travel with his sister.

Topaz gave an order to the drivers in basic
Chinese, and they all trundled off.

Jake watched the Cantonese going about their
business, fanning themselves against the heat. They
were rushing home or shopping in the many stores
that advertised their wares on large banners. There
were apothecaries, calligraphers, tobacco shops,
spice and tea emporiums, pickle merchants, sandal-
makers, wood carvers and stonemasons. There were
stalls selling a host of different foods: chicken's feet,
white peaches, steamed dumplings and skewers of
meat. Festoons of paper lanterns hung between the
shops and across the street.

Accompanying the rumble of the city was a

cacophony of different music. Jake noticed a group on the sidewalk, ringing bells, plucking bamboo harps and bashing cymbals. And here and there locals gathered to play games: dice, chequers and chess.

Most of the people were Chinese, but as Topaz had pointed out, many were western. Canton was indeed as international a city as Jacobean London. The foreigners looked at home, having picked up the rhythms of the city, though some were sweating profusely in the tropical heat.

They followed the blue rickshaw as it wound its way up a slope, across an old bridge and into a shabbier district. Men trudged along, weighed down with yokes bearing heavy buckets, while bare-foot children and skinny dogs scavenged for food amongst piles of rubbish. Soon they found them-selves heading back towards the water past a succession of ramshackle wharves.

At the first, a number of horses was being herded down a ship's gangplank. Emerging from the hold after a long journey, they stumbled, their legs unsteady after being cooped up for so long.

'Probably from Persia – or at least the Middle East, judging by the ship,' Yoyo told Jake. 'As you may know, horses are not native to China, so we swap other wares for them. In fact – it's not too far-fetched to say – if it weren't for horses, world trade probably wouldn't even exist.'

As they passed the next wharf, Jake smelled an acrid stench that made him gag. The driver turned and smiled.

'Fish sauce factory,' Yoyo explained.

'Fermented rotting fish,' Topaz commented to her brother in the other rickshaw. 'It's not exactly haute cuisine.'

'I don't mind the aroma,' Nathan called back, for Yoyo's benefit. 'It has an earthy piquancy,' he added, remembering one of Charlie's phrases.

No sooner had the stink of fish faded than Jake smelled another aroma – spicy and woody, pleasant at first, but soon so overwhelming, it made him sneeze – once, twice, thrice . . . and a fourth time for luck. Workers were decanting velvety brown powder from a barrel and packing it into smaller cases. Soon Nathan and Topaz also started to sneeze; but Yoyo, who seemed impervious to it, was giggling.

'Nutmeg,' she told them.

Ahead of them, at the top of a slope, the blue

rickshaw stopped in front of a tumbledown building with a distinctive pink-tiled roof. It stood at the bottom of a rocky escarpment that marked the edge of the city; in fact, the building almost seemed part of it. The man in the blue tunic dismounted and, as his taxi started back towards the city, carried the money box up some steps, casually glanced around and went inside.

Topaz told the rickshaw drivers to stop. 'We go on by foot,' she said, handing over two silver coins to each driver. It was obviously much more than they were expecting: they thanked her profusely and helped the others out before turning to go back down the slope.

The History Keepers took in their seedy surroundings.

'Intriguing location,' Nathan deadpanned.

Jake looked up at the sky. Still obscured behind hazy cloud, a blur of sun was sinking towards the horizon. In the distance there was a crackle of thunder and the sky pulsed with lightning. They all turned to the building with the pink roof and, checking their weapons cautiously, walked towards it.

Close up, it was both larger and older than it had

appeared from a distance: a square edifice of crumbling stone overlooking both the city and the sea. There was music coming from inside – what sounded to Jake like a noisy jangle, along with drums thumping and high-pitched singing.

'Chinese opera,' Yoyo said. 'The building is probably a tea house.'

'Opera?' Nathan stopped dead.

Topaz couldn't help smiling. 'There is nothing Nathan loves more than the opera,' she teased.

For Yoyo's sake he tried to look excited. 'I do, I do – especially Chinese opera.' He thought about it for a moment. 'What exactly *is* Chinese opera?'

'Ancient tales told through music, dance and acrobatics. Entertainment for the people.'

'Wonderful! Wonderful! What are we waiting for?' Nathan exclaimed, before whispering to Jake, 'I'd rather be burned alive.'

Topaz saw a crooked sign above the entrance and stopped dead. The letters were half eaten away by the salt air, but she could just make them out. 'I don't believe it!' She turned to Yoyo. 'Does that say what I think it says?'

It was Yoyo's turn to catch her breath. She translated for the boys: '*The Ocean Door.*'

'Wh-what?' Jake stammered, his heart skipping a beat. He unbuckled his brother's watch from his wrist and examined the inscription once again:

Tell family I love them. Find Lazuli Serpent – through the Ocean Door, C

'The C was for Canton,' he said. 'Philip hadn't finished writing. So what's in there?'

Topaz cautiously peered inside. 'As Yoyo said, it's just a tea house. Why bring a casket of money here?' She turned and nodded for the others to follow.

They slipped through the shadow of the doorway into a large, noisy chamber. Dozens of people clustered around low tables, chatting as they sipped from little china cups. Many of them fluttered paper fans and some smoked thin white pipes, making the air hazy.

Topaz whispered to the others, 'See our man anywhere?' They all drew a blank: he had apparently vanished into thin air.

On a lopsided stage, a troupe of artistes were performing a Chinese opera – a curious display of exaggerated mime mixed with musical interludes. They were dressed in gaudy costumes – in turquoises, pinks and oranges. Some of them wore masks; others had their faces painted in black and white. The actresses all carried fans, which they moved in time to the music, and their elaborate headpieces jangled with jewels. Jake had never seen – or indeed heard – anything quite like it in his life.

'Wonderful!' Nathan repeated, doing his best to conceal his loathing. 'We've chanced upon entertainment gold!'

On one side of the room, staff bustled behind a bar, preparing tea: they selected dried leaves from a variety of jars and stirred them into steaming pots of water.

'Let's take a seat and see what's going on,' Topaz said, grabbing an empty table.

A man hobbled towards them holding a tray of skewers threaded with some unidentifiable food. Yoyo tossed a coin onto the tray and helped herself to a couple.

'What are those?' Nathan asked, half hiding behind his handkerchief.

'Fried beetles,' Yoyo replied, crunching into one with relish. 'High in protein and iron.'

'Why don't you try one?' Topaz suggested, mischievously passing them over.

Nathan pushed it away gingerly. 'I have a solemn rule: no bugs after sundown.'

Jake noticed that the waiter had a false leg – a piece of roughly shaped wood attached to his knee. His other, real leg looked frail, with black feet and curling toes. Wanting to help him out, Jake also threw a coin into the tray and took a skewer – though he didn't fancy insects either.

'What's the worst that could happen?' He grimaced as he bit into one. 'Quite tasty, actually – like a burned shrimp.'

'Jake is the only truly brave one amongst you,' Yoyo declared.

Nathan bristled. 'Excuse me, my good man' – he clicked his fingers – 'another portion here please.' He too paid up and bit into the beetle with a determined smile. 'Delicious! Heavenly! Never tasted the like!'

Looking around, Topaz suddenly noticed something odd. '*They* don't look like they belong here,' she said under her breath, nodding towards some new arrivals: four older men wearing silk robes and clutching pieces of paper. They seemed far more well-to-do than anyone else in the room; a few locals stared at them over the brims of their teacups as they conferred and took the next-door table.

A man with a long, thin moustache came out from behind the counter – the manager, Jake guessed – and approached them. The oldest of the customers perused the menu before placing his order, speaking very deliberately. The manager nodded, turned and went back to the counter.

Yoyo whispered to the others, 'He just ordered Jun Shan, but Jun Shan is not on the menu . . .'

'What is it?' Jake whispered back.

'Golden Needles, the rarest tea in China,' she replied.

The manager returned with a tray, poured out four cups of tea, bowed and took his leave. The four men had a hushed conversation before the eldest reached inside the pot, retrieved something and nodded at the others. They all stood up, filed across the room, round the back of the stage and out through a low door. Their cups of tea were left steaming on the table.

'What was in that teapot?' Jake wondered. There were shrugs all round.

'There's only one thing for it . . .' Topaz beckoned the manager over. 'Jun Shan. For four,' she said. He narrowed his eyes, scrutinizing each of them in turn – but returned with a teapot, filling four cups and leaving them to it. Topaz peered into the pot and saw something glistening at the bottom. Turning the vessel on its side so as not to scald her fingers, she reached in and pulled out a small jade disc. It was the size of a coin, with a rectangular hole in its centre and a motif of waves inscribed on it.

'Let's go,' she said. They all left the table and followed the route the other men had taken. The manager watched them suspiciously.

They emerged into an empty storeroom, lit by a single flickering lantern. The four men had disappeared; all they could see was just some old pieces of scenery leaning against the side walls.

'This building seems to just swallow everyone up,' Nathan commented wryly.

Jake's attention was drawn to a pair of painted backdrops – one of conical mountains rising through clouds, the other of a crumbling palace under the sea.

'Look at the back wall,' Topaz said. Jake did a double take. The mural was almost identical to the giant seascape they had seen in Xi Xiang's house in

London – though this one was faded and hard to make out.

'The Lazuli Serpent?' He pointed to a stone crystal in the centre that was engraved with strange markings.

They examined it more carefully and discovered a narrow slot in the wall just below the crystal. 'Is everyone thinking what I'm thinking?' Topaz asked, holding up the jade disc.

'Fire away, by all means!' Nathan suggested.

Topaz posted the coin into the slot and let it drop. For a moment there was silence, then the whirring of machinery: the central section of the mural clicked open to reveal a long stone passageway leading to what appeared to be a garden at the far end. They exchanged looks, then Topaz gave a signal. As they stepped cautiously along the corridor, the scent of flowers wafted through, along with the tinkling of fountains and the distant cries of peacocks.

At last they emerged from the clammy darkness. The transformation was astonishing – somehow they had come from a scruffy tea house in a rough part of town into the grounds of what appeared to be a palace. They were in a square cloister, bordered on all sides by a stone loggia covered with flowers. It was a relief to be away from the pungent odours of the city, but the air was stiller and the heat more intense than ever.

A gravel path crossed the centre of the square between two rectangular ponds full of huge white lily flowers. In the middle stood a bronze statue on a pedestal – a man with his arms held out as if to welcome them. Beyond him, an archway led to a larger courtyard. Above the cloister walls they could see the curved roofs of more buildings.

Jake wondered how such a place could lie hidden from the rest of the city. He looked back at the sheer wall – the other side of the stone ridge into which the Ocean Door had been built. It divided the gardens from the rest of the town, and they had just burrowed straight through it.

A sound of splashing came from one of the ponds and Jake peered down. Something was moving under the canopy of lily leaves. A glistening shape broke the surface, roiling and curling back in again.

'Eels!' Topaz recoiled at the sight. 'Is there a viler creature on this planet?'

'Well,' Nathan said in a quiet voice, 'do we investigate?'

Cautiously they headed along the path, stopping to examine the statue – a slim, elderly man dressed in traditional Chinese robes; his head was bent forward, half smiling. In the upturned palm of one hand he held a globe; in the other, a pair of scales.

'Look,' Topaz said, drawing their attention to an inscription in Chinese characters on the base of the pedestal.

'*Shen Pei-Pei*,' Yoyo translated. 'So this is certainly his place.'

'In which case,' Nathan pondered, 'are we to assume that's he's printing money for himself?'

'What about this treasure house of his . . . the golden pagoda?' Jake asked. 'Do you think it's here?'

Suddenly there was a rumble of thunder, much closer now, and the sky lit up like a flashbulb. For a moment they were all blinded. When their sight returned, they saw a man in a simple smock, short ragged trousers and a wide rice hat coming through the arch towards them, his bare feet crunching on the gravel. All four History Keepers reached for their sword hilts, but they soon realized that the man presented no threat: he was painfully thin and stooped and had a bad limp.

With a trembling hand he scooped something

out of a basket under his arm and tossed it into the ponds. The water bubbled as the eels came to feed, and he mumbled softly to them as they ate. Lost in his own world, he paid no attention to Jake and the others. Nathan threw Jake a quizzical look.

The man turned towards them, looking up from under his hat. Jake noticed a flash of something around his neck – a stone pendant. He spoke to them in Chinese, and Yoyo translated.

'He asked if we are here for the congress . . .' The stranger went on without waiting for a reply. 'He says we should proceed through the arch to the hall on the right – it has already begun.'

'Ask him if Pei-Pei is here?' Nathan said.

'Pei-Pei?' the man suddenly said, nodding his head and letting out a little cackle, before disappearing into the darkness again.

'He's madder than a wet hen in a sack,' Nathan murmured.

Jake looked up fearfully as another pulse of lightning split the sky.

'Come on.' Topaz led the way into the next, larger courtyard. On either side stood a grand build-ing, dark red in colour and topped with curving roofs clad in millions of golden tiles. 'Let's see what's going on in here.' She nodded towards the building on the right: the double doors were open, casting a soft pool of light across the courtyard, and they heard a rumble of chatter inside.

They tiptoed to the side of the building and, making sure their faces were in shadow, peered in.

It was a large room, lit by dozens of chandeliers, its cylindrical pillars painted red and gold with motifs of fire and water. Gathered along one side of a table was a group of forty or so people, all Chinese, mostly men, expensively dressed in embroidered silk gowns. Amongst them, Jake spotted the four they had seen in the tea house.

On the counter before them were models of ships: maquettes of junks and galleons, rendered in intricate detail. Some of the men were kneeling down to get a closer look at them, inside and out.

Then a gong sounded and everyone turned as a woman glided into the room. The chatter stopped. Jake recognized her immediately.

'Madame Fang . . .'

15 THE GOLDEN PAGODA

'That's her?' Topaz asked.

'No doubt about it.'

'I'll give her this,' Nathan said. 'Style-wise, she's audacious. Few people could get away with that assemblage.'

In London, Madame Fang had been in Jacobean costume – black gown and white ruff; now she looked like an empress. Despite the heat, she wore a court robe, embroidered with swirling flames and dragons, that hung down to her red lotus slippers (red shoes were obviously her trademark). Around her tiny neck was a necklace of jade and rubies; her tall headdress of peacock feathers and pearl droplets gently shook as she turned her head. Her face, though old, had a brittle beauty and her black eyes were utterly magnetic.

She welcomed her guests with a bow and started talking in a slow, measured tone. Jake hadn't yet heard her speak, and was surprised by how deep and smoky her voice was.

The girls craned their necks to hear and Yoyo started translating, in a whisper: '*I am here to talk to you about our enemies in the western world. They have come to our lands – the British, the Portuguese, the Dutch – set up their colonies here, appeared to be our allies, our partners.*' The old woman paused for dramatic effect. '*It is a trick – so they may take over our kingdoms.*'

'*Enemies? Take over their kingdoms?*' Nathan repeated indignantly. 'What's she talking about?'

'Sssh!' Yoyo put her finger to her lips to silence him and carried on: '*In two days' time, the west will declare war on us. In the weeks and months that follow, they will send their fleets to invade us, to enslave us—*'

'*Enslave us?* This is nonsense!' Nathan interrupted again, and this time Topaz put her hand over his mouth.

Yoyo continued paraphrasing Fang's speech, which was becoming more and more animated. '*We must defend ourselves! My master, the great Shen*

228

Pei-Pei, wishes to help you, to help his country.' She clapped her hands and a stream of servants filed into the room and distributed small golden caskets to all the guests. Inside each they found a thick wodge of banknotes tied with a ribbon. There were amazed murmurs at the sight. '*For each of you, we provide a fortune. Use it wisely. Build your ships of war. As for your ships that are already built, convert them for battle*.' Fang glanced at every face in the room in turn as she slowly raised her arms high. Her voice boomed like a drum. '*The war is coming! Be ready for your country!*'

Her speech finished, she bowed, stepped over towards the model ships and circulated imperiously amongst her guests.

'*The war is coming . . . be ready for your country?*' Topaz repeated. 'China has *never* had an interest in moving against the west; now less than ever. Yet Fang said war would be declared in two days' time. We need to find out why, and quickly.'

They went down an alley behind the building into the garden. They all saw the pagoda at once: six octagonal tiers rising up between tall Chinese pines.

'That's the treasure house?' Nathan asked.

It had perhaps once been splendid – it was, after

all, described as the *golden* pagoda – but it was now past its best. It was slightly lopsided, and the gilding had all but flaked off, leaving dark grey wood underneath. There were no lights on inside, adding to the ghostly feel. Only one window at the very top was open – wide open.

Looking carefully about them, they crossed the garden towards it, slipping in and out of the shadows.

As they drew close to the pagoda, they saw a moat around it, about ten feet across, the surface covered in lily pads. There was one tall door that evidently lowered like a drawbridge over the moat; two posts jutted out of the water to secure it when it was down. The door, covered with ivy and cobwebs, had clearly not been accessed in a while.

Jake wasn't convinced. 'Are we sure there isn't *another* golden pagoda?'

'There's only one way to find out,' Yoyo said. She took a few steps back and flew across the water, using one of the posts as a stepping stone to leap to the other side.

Topaz tutted in irritation. '*Qu'est-ce qu'elle a, cette fille?*'

'That was a great jump, if you don't mind me saying,' Nathan called over to Yoyo.

'Please don't encourage her,' his sister sighed.

Yoyo turned back to them. 'Well, as I am here, shall I look inside?'

'Be my guest,' Topaz said, tight-lipped.

Yoyo went over to a porthole window, which was secured with iron bars. She pulled herself up and peered inside. 'This must be it,' she said. 'There are lots of display cabinets, but I can't see inside them. Shall I try and get in?' She strained at the bars.

'Don't *do* anything!' Topaz hissed back, taking a dagger from her belt and peeling back the surface of lily leaves from the moat. Eels, a little fatter than the previous ones, seethed under the water. Topaz's heart sank, but she put on a brave face. 'Can everyone get across all right?'

'No problem,' Nathan said, taking a few steps back and leaping over.

'Jake?'

'Of course . . .' He shrugged, hiding his fear, then took a run-up and launched himself into the air. As he vaulted off the post, his foot skimmed the water; the eels surfaced and snapped at it – but he reached the other side unharmed, into the arms of Yoyo. He nodded back at Topaz.

She braced herself, and gave a grunt as she jumped. But her foot slipped on the post and she tumbled into the moat; the water erupted in a frenzy around her.

Terror stamped on her face, Topaz dragged herself up onto the bank. Three eels were still attached to her legs, letting out a curious whistle as they hung there, tails thrashing. Jake flew to her aid, expertly slicing his sword through all three creatures at once.

Worried that Fang and her guests would hear the commotion, the others helped him pull Topaz into the shadows. The three eel heads were still attached to her leg. As Jake picked them off, forcing their jaws open, she lay there panting, her trembling hands covering her mouth in horror. Jake had seen her look truly frightened only once before: the night on board the *Lindwurm* when he had tried to save her from Prince Zeldt, her own diabolical uncle, who had kidnapped her on his sister's orders.

'All right?' he asked.

Topaz got her breathing under control and gave him a smile. '*Petites créatures méchantes,*' she panted, pulling herself to her feet.

They took turns to peer through the round

window. Inside, the whole ground floor was laid out like a museum. The gilt-edged cabinets, like the pagoda itself, looked dusty and shabby. A spiral staircase led up to the next level.

'Jake, do you have Dr Chatterju's quill and ink?' Topaz asked.

'Of course.' He had been entrusted with them before leaving Point Zero, and handed them over.

She unscrewed the ink bottle, dipped in the quill and set it down next to the window bars. They took cover as it produced a cloud of smoke, making the metal burn and blister, before exploding with a flash of white.

Topaz gave one of the bars a forceful tug. It didn't budge, and she yanked it again, twice; finally it popped out of its casing. She removed the two adjacent rods, then hauled herself up through the opening and carefully let herself down on the other side. The floorboards creaked under her weight. Checking that it was safe, she motioned for the others to follow.

They went through one by one and set about examining the displays.

Topaz wiped the dust off a cabinet containing pieces of fine Chinese porcelain. The adjacent one was the same. 'It seems we're in the right place,' she said. 'Pei-Pei's collection. Let's not get distracted, though. We're after the Lazuli Serpent – and we all know what it looks like.'

'I have to ask . . .' Jake said. 'If this stone is so important, would it be kept here? No one's been in this place for ages.'

'I agree with Jake,' Yoyo said. 'It doesn't make sense.'

'And I agree with Yoyo; she's usually right,' Nathan added unhelpfully.

Topaz was beginning to lose patience. 'Well, now we're here, could we just *look*?' she asked testily.

The four agents carefully checked the cabinets, examining all the displays, but they uncovered nothing but more pieces of old porcelain.

Topaz turned to Yoyo. 'Am I right in saying that in these types of treasure houses the higher you go, the more valuable things become?'

'It's not a rule, but possibly,' she conceded.

Topaz nodded, then led the way up the spiral staircase to the next floor. Here there were more dusty cabinets; these held ancient robes, garments and headpieces. The next level housed some larger works of art, mostly soapstone sculptures, as well as a collection of bronzes of oriental deities and some lacquer ornaments, as did the third floor.

There were no crystals to be found, so they crept up to the last storey but one. 'This looks more promising,' Topaz said: the cabinets here were finely crafted – almost like works of art in themselves. A quick inspection of their contents showed they contained real treasure.

Jake had never seen such riches before. There were carved ivory figures and jade animals; ebony phoenixes and garnet dragons. There were golden artefacts – orbs, sceptres and crowns – encrusted with sapphires, emeralds, opals and tourmalines. His eye was drawn to one object in particular: an immense blue quartz engraved with a tableau of the ocean: a man had fallen out of his boat into the sea, his arms outstretched and his mouth wide open in a silent scream as a jellyfish curled round his limbs, dragging him down to the depths.

Meanwhile Nathan and Yoyo had come across a collection of dazzling jewellery.

'Look at that ring,' Nathan commented, pointing to an ornate gold band with an enormous diamond mounted in it.

'That's quite a piece of carbon,' Yoyo whistled,

leaning closer. 'It looks like an engagement ring, Tang dynasty. Someone certainly didn't want to take no for an answer.'

'If I gave you a ring like that, maybe you would marry me . . . ?' Nathan said, half in jest but sounding like he meant it. Jake peered round and Topaz shot him a glance.

'That's funny!' Yoyo snorted, moving along the display.

Nathan looked hurt. 'Funny?'

Yoyo giggled. 'I'm a little young to throw myself away, aren't I?'

Nathan shrugged. 'You're the same age as me. I don't know why it's so funny. I could list a hundred young ladies – from all parts of history, some of them of royal birth – who would jump at the chance of *throwing* themselves away on me.'

Yoyo turned and gave him a quizzical smile. 'You don't actually mean it, do you?'

There was a pause as they eyeballed each other. 'All right, not marriage as such, but perhaps – perhaps it wouldn't hurt if you paid me some attention . . . maybe laughed at my jokes . . . complimented me on my . . . ?' Nathan trailed off, his face flushing.

Topaz turned to Jake and shook her head in bewilderment as Yoyo started laughing, and Nathan's face fell.

'Why is it so funny?'

'Because . . .' Yoyo fought to get her breathing under control. 'I don't know. Because you're a bit of a buffoon, aren't you?' Nathan's eyes went wide and his shoulders slumped. Jake had never seen him look so crestfallen, and Yoyo sensed she had overstepped the mark. 'Sorry, that wasn't the right word . . .'

'*Comment oses-tu?* How dare you, Yoyo!' Topaz stepped forward, her eyes suddenly blazing. 'How dare you talk to my brother like that? He's worth ten of you.'

'I'm sorry, it's just my opinion. I'm entitled to my opinion, aren't I? I like Nathan – he's comical – but—'

'*Comical?*' Nathan gasped, his whole world crashing down around him.

'But all the clothes and the cologne and the fiddling with his hair. He's not to be taken seriously, is he?' Yoyo evidently thought she was making things better.

Topaz squared up to her. 'You will take that back. *Tout de suite!*'

'It's nothing to do with you,' Yoyo purred, pushing her out of the way.

The other girl stood her ground. '*Tu es impossible – j'en ai marre!*'

'You've had enough, have you?' Yoyo sneered back, her nose almost touching her rival's. 'Well, I've had enough too – of your snooty French attitude. Not to mention your so-called *leadership skills* which, at best, are amateurish and uninspired.'

'*Amateurish? Uninspired?!*' Topaz turned to the others, enraged. 'Am I hearing this right?'

'Come on, you two – it's the heat. It's – it's putting us under a lot of pressure.' Jake hadn't realized it until now, but it was true. He tried to get between the girls, but they paid no attention.

'*Comical?*' Nathan shook his head. 'How can I be boiled down to just *comical*?'

'What about you, *Yoyo*?' Topaz huffed. 'You're a liability – uncontrollable, selfish and plain dangerous.'

'Is that a fact?'

'Bona fide. Actually you're worse than that. You're a troublemaker, and a narcissist.'

'Ooh, big words, Miss St Honoré,' Yoyo said. 'You're scaring me now.'

'Arguing won't get us anywhere,' Jake tried again. 'Let's go up to the next floor.' As before, they ignored him.

'You want everyone to fall in love with you,' Topaz carried on, 'but no one ever will. Never, ever, ever. Because, despite all your so-called *qualities*, you add up to nothing.'

Yoyo's expression was hard. 'Jake, would you like to take my side here?'

Topaz laughed. '*He's* not going to take your side.'

'Really? Jake, would you like to tell them, or shall I?'

Nathan's eyes narrowed. 'Tell us what?'

Yoyo's announcement coincided with another loud peal of thunder outside as the storm approached. 'Jake is my boyfriend.'

Jake blushed as Topaz glared at him. 'We were going to say something . . .' he mumbled. 'W-we were just waiting for the right moment.' He stood awkwardly beside Yoyo, as if posing for their wedding photo. Then he looked sternly at Topaz. 'And I think it's best that you don't talk to Yoyo in that way.'

It was Topaz's turn to look crestfallen. '*Mon Dieu . . .*' she said, shaking her head, then pulled

239

herself together and forced a smile. 'I hope you are very happy together.'

Jake was upset. 'It would be nice, Topaz – as my friend – if you actually meant that, but you don't.'

'What do you want me to do?' she muttered. 'Dance for joy?'

'You're so ready to criticize,' Jake carried on, 'but you never stop and think how much you *hurt* people.' He summoned the courage to say it. 'How you hurt *me*.'

Topaz looked mortified. Even Nathan was surprised, suddenly seeing his friend in a new light.

Jake's words came out in a jumble – everything that had been locked inside for over a year. 'Twice I came to save you – first in Germany, then in ancient Rome – coming *this* close to death. All right, I didn't do much good in the end, but I think I made it pretty clear how I felt . . . how I felt about you. That I was in . . . That I—' He couldn't bring himself to say the word. 'In any case, you weren't interested. That's fine – I'm not a *he-man* like Lucius was – but I was hurt and you never even noticed. And that hurt me more.'

Topaz cast her eyes to the floor. Now Jake held

Yoyo's hand and squeezed it tight. 'So why shouldn't I have a girlfriend if I want?'

At that moment, they heard a soft thump above them, then the sound of something rolling across the floorboards. The History Keepers froze, and silently drew their weapons as Topaz led the way up the creaking staircase.

'Nothing here,' she called when she emerged into the room.

To their surprise, it was almost completely bare. There was no treasure – just a single high-backed armchair facing the open window. A number of tall candlesticks encircled it, all unlit. All were fitted with a single fat candle – except one. The candle had fallen onto the floor and rolled away. That's what had produced the sound.

'Look!' Jake exclaimed, suddenly noticing a pale, wrinkled hand clinging to the armrest – and then wisps of white hair sticking above the top of the chair.

'Pei-Pei?' Yoyo said under her breath, advancing towards the seated figure, sword drawn. 'Shen Pei-Pei?' As she reached it, her face fell and her sword went clanking to the floor. She gabbled something in Chinese.

Jake, Topaz and Nathan rushed over. It was a man – a dead man; long dead. The body was completely mummified, the crinkled skin yellow and waxy and the eyes gazing out of the window as lifeless as marbles. He was fully clothed in robes that had once been fine but were now tatty, with bugs crawling over them. Jake thought it must have been one of these that had knocked the candle over.

'I don't like this. I don't like this at all . . .' Nathan said, quivering with fear.

Behind them, they heard someone coming up the stairs. Yoyo quickly retrieved her sword, while the others swung round, blades raised. They were puzzled to see that it was the odd man they had met before, the eel-keeper. He carried a broomstick and started sweeping the floor, mumbling to himself as he did so. Noticing them at last, he nodded, saying something that even Yoyo couldn't understand, and they all looked at each other, spooked.

'Let's get out of here,' Topaz whispered, skirting round and heading for the stairs.

As he crept past, Jake looked round and noticed something odd under the man's hat: a strange growth on his cheek, with something shining in the centre of it. It looked like an eye staring back at him.

His blood ran cold. Three eyes! Xi Xiang had three eyes!

Just then the man let out a cry and brought his broom down on Jake, disarming him, before jabbing the butt into his windpipe. Jake went tumbling to the floor. The man moved swiftly on to Topaz, giving her a crack on the skull, then whipping the sword from her hand and sending it spinning across the room. Nathan and Yoyo advanced together, but the man had produced a jade bottle, and sprayed them with dark green liquid. They cried out in agony, clutching their faces.

The man threw off his hat, revealing his face for the first time, and let out a high-pitched giggle. He was skinny, with an impish face and crazy, spiked black hair. His lips were smudged with red lipstick and his cheeks with rouge. Suddenly five burly guards emerged at the top of the stairs, each holding a razor-sharp curved Dao sabre, and surrounded the astonished youngsters.

Xi Xiang – for there was no doubt that it was he – clapped his hands in joy. 'Do you think I'm a fool?' he sniggered. His voice was raspy and high-pitched at the same time. 'I saw you arrive! Dear me, the illustrious History Keepers' Secret Service.' He shook his head and pursed his lips. 'What imbeciles they produce nowadays.'

He inspected Nathan and Yoyo's faces. The skin where the liquid had struck looked raw; Nathan's eyes were streaming with tears. 'How do you like my squid venom? It has quite a bite, doesn't it?'

He turned and skipped across the room to the cadaver in the chair. 'And did you enjoy meeting my friend Pei-Pei? He loves the view from the window. Of course, the old man is not as chatty as he used to be' – Xi lifted the corpse's withered hand, waved it and let it drop again – 'but he would insist on drinking hemlock – after kindly bequeathing me his little palace.' Again Xi shrieked with laughter.

There were more footsteps, and Madame Fang appeared, coolly taking in the scene.

'Nanny, there you are. Have you seen what a clever boy I've been?' Xi Xiang said, gesturing to his captives. On seeing Jake, his smile dissolved and his lip quivered. 'And this is the Djones brother?' he asked quietly, glancing over his shoulder. Madame Fang nodded.

Xi turned up his nose in contempt. 'Yes, I can see it now. The same proud look in his eye.' He prodded Jake's cheek.

Jake had never seen anyone like Xi Xiang: he was in his forties, slightly stooped, but wiry and athletic. Under the badly applied make-up his face was mottled with acne and his eyes were chilling: two were beady and sharp, the third half formed and staring off at an odd angle.

'Where is he?' Jake croaked, his throat still sore from the blow with the broom. 'Where is Philip?' he repeated, eyes boring into his nemesis.

Xi stared back. 'Where *is* he?' He gave another cackle. 'Lost at sea! Like so many of my friends.'

Then he pushed past the guards and danced down the staircase. 'Tie them up. Bring them to the pool,' he ordered. 'I need to say goodbye to our guests.'

Madame Fang nodded at the men: they took sets of manacles from their belts and, one by one, cuffed the four History Keepers, the metal biting into their wrists.

16 THE TIGHTROPE

'The hospitality's shocking here,' Nathan dead-panned over his pain as the sentries forced them down the stairs. 'I shall be writing a stern letter of complaint.'

As they descended floor by floor, Jake tried to steady his breathing. 'Are you all right?' he asked Yoyo and Nathan. Their faces were still red, their eyes bloodshot.

'I think squid poison might be the least of our problems,' Yoyo replied grimly as they were marched out of the pagoda, over the bridge and round the quadrangle.

At last they went through a pair of iron gates fashioned in the shape of jellyfish, and into yet another courtyard. There was a pond here, bigger than the others and empty of vegetation – presumably the *pool* Xi had referred to.

Bordering it was a succession of striking statues: Chinese stone warriors, helmeted and breast-plated, frozen in time, all staring fixedly out as if protecting the pool. Each had a different weapon: a spear, a double-edged Jian sword; sickle, dagger, axe, javelin, crossbow, and many more.

Jake looked down into the water. The pool was deep and, like the others, contained eels – he could see them twisting in the murk beneath the surface; however, these were as thick as a human neck and over six feet long. They moved slowly, endlessly circling their stone prison. They had tiny eyes on their flattened heads, brown backs, yellow stomachs and a pair of tiny fins – defunct features from their primordial origins. Jake saw some lighter shapes at the bottom of the pool, and it took a moment for him to realize with horror that they were bones.

With a gleeful clap of his hands, Xi Xiang emerged through the gateway, Madame Fang at his side. Behind them, two soldiers carried a wooden throne, another a small table, some caskets and other paraphernalia. At the rear, more guards accompanied a fifth prisoner – the young man in the blue tunic whom they had followed from the paper factory. The cocky air was gone: he'd been roughed up, given a black eye, and his clothes were spattered with blood.

Xi had thrown a long cape over his peasant disguise. It was encrusted with jewels and trailed along the ground behind him. He wore a matching crown, set at a jaunty angle like some lunatic king. '*Electrophorus electricus*,' he squealed, flicking a limp wrist towards the pool. 'Electric eels. Have any of you met one of these ingenious creatures before? What a punch they can pack, with their six hundred volts. They can incapacitate an alligator.' He turned to Jake with a mock grimace. 'Imagine what they can do to a child . . .'

Jake glared at him, but Xi simply clicked his fingers at two of the guards. They set to work, opening a large box, unpacking a coil of thick wire, casting it across the pool and tightening it on either side like a tennis net.

'After a hard day's work planning the destruction of humanity,' Xi sighed, 'there is nothing I like more than to relax with a little light entertainment – and tightrope walking is such fun!' He clapped his hands, and the chair and table were put in position, with the caskets on the table. Xi pursed his lips, swished his cape to one side and sat down. 'He can go first,' he said, pointing at the youth in the blue tunic. 'Teach him to be more careful next time – if there is a next time for him, of course, for my little pets are . . . hungry!'

He sucked his thumb, watching eagerly as the guards seized the youth and pushed him towards the tightrope. Madame Fang held up her blade to make sure he stayed there. The young man turned round, pleading for mercy.

Xi removed his thumb from his mouth to announce, 'If he reaches the other side, he can walk free.'

The young man trembled as he looked down at the eels gathering below. The water lit up with pulses of electricity as the creatures bumped into each other, reacting in fear to the people around them. He put his foot onto the wire and tested its strength.

'Wait!' Xi jumped to his feet. The youth turned, hoping for a reprieve. 'It's too easy. Use this as a blindfold.' He whipped off his scarf and passed it to Madame Fang, who tied it around the man's head. 'Tight as you can; we don't want him peeking.'

When Xi sat down again, Jake studied the pendant hanging from a leather thong around his neck. It was a cylinder of blue crystal, the length of an index finger, engraved with complicated inscriptions. With a jolt, Jake realized what it was. 'The Lazuli Serpent,' he whispered in Topaz's ear.

She turned and squinted over at it, and her eyes widened.

The terrified youth teetered onto the tightrope and set off across the pool.

'Tolerable . . . tolerable,' Xi commented, chewing on his thumb in anticipation. The young man decided that speed might save him, and suddenly accelerated, but then he lost his balance and plunged down, slapping onto the water. He cried out as six eels converged on him, delivering a succession of electric shocks, making the pool crackle and his limbs jolt in every direction. But he was still conscious when the fish opened their powerful jaws, pulling off chunks of flesh. His blindfold slipped and Jake saw the terror in his eye; then it glazed over as his heart stilled. The eels continued to feed, and pulses of light shot through the water, which had turned red with blood.

Xi Xiang stood up again, his two good eyes gleaming; even the third, deformed slit shone with delight.

Finally the water was still again. Xi clapped his hands together and, looking round, asked, 'So who's next?'

Jake stepped forward, his face rigid. 'If you tell me what happened to Philip, I will go.'

For a while Xi did not move. Then he tilted his head back, brought up a ball of phlegm and spat it on the ground.

'I gave that boy everything he desired,' he proclaimed. 'Treated him like my own son. But all the time, he was double crossing me, repaying me with betrayal. *Betrayal!*' he repeated shrilly, so that the word echoed around the walls.

Despite everything, Jake stood tall. This surely confirmed that Philip had been working not *for* Xi, but *against* him; that he had not been a traitor to the service.

Xi ran his finger around the edge of his third eye. 'He was sent, by *your* people, on that absurd mission to Vienna – when was it: 1689? The Habsburg–Ottoman War; a glorious opportunity for Zeldt to meddle in world affairs.' He sniggered. 'And for myself, naturally – it's amazing how sometimes we all wash up in the same dirty corners of history.' His smile hardened. 'But imagine sending a fifteen-year-old boy off alone? To assassinate Zeldt?' He let out a strangled laugh. 'Fifteen years old? He was still a child! And they call *me* barbaric!' Xi paused for a moment before continuing. 'So he failed – obviously; and that witch Mina Schlitz shot him in the neck with a blunderbuss, left him for dead on the banks of the Danube, swilling around with all the muck from the sewers, prey for the Ottoman forces.'

Jake started. Mina Schlitz! He had run into the young assassin on his first mission, and remembered the whip she used to strangle her enemies. So she had used a *blunderbuss* on his brother . . .

'I saved him, carried him away on my back – Schlitz and Zeldt are no more friends of mine than you lot are – I took him to my lodgings, gave him my bed, sat with him day after day. When he woke from his coma, he didn't know who he was. I nursed him back to health, and gradually he started to remember . . .' A tear rolled down Xi's cheek. 'I would have let him return to his precious organization. I *liked* your brother, you see. He had character. He was strong' – he pointed to his head – 'here, where it counts – not the usual idiots they train up at Point Zero.' He spat out the name as if it were poison. 'Yes, I would have let him return, even *I*. But he convinced me – in that sly way of his – that he did not *want* to go back. *They haven't sent anyone to find me – why should I care about them?* he said. I believed him.'

Xi clicked his fingers at one of his men. 'I'm dry.' The minion stepped forward and opened one of the caskets on the table. It contained a jumble of cosmetics. Xi searched around and retrieved a little tube. His eye on Jake, he turned the tube until a purple-brown lipstick, the colour of a bruise, emerged. He applied it right round his mouth, chucked it back in the box, took out some rouge and brushed it onto his cheeks; then he opened the second casket, which was full of white talc. He padded a cloud of it onto his face to seal the make-up.

'I took Pip – that's what I called him; Philip didn't suit him . . . I took him to London. I gave him the keys to my mansion, showered him with gifts, educated him in the arts, introduced him to the wonders of literature. We *haunted* the play-houses. We were dazzled by Richard Burbage as Hamlet. We met Shakespeare, Jonson, Marlowe. I chaperoned him to Rome, to the studio of Caravaggio himself.' Again Xi's voice became shrill.

There were flickers of lightning every few seconds now as the storm gathered overhead. 'Yes, *we* were painted by the greatest artist of the day. I gave him all this, loved him like a father. And how does he repay me?'

Xi struck Jake across the face, making his cheek sting. 'Of course Nanny told me all along that he was not to be trusted; that the Djoneses were devious.' He turned to Madame Fang, frowning. 'But I didn't listen to you, did I?' He looked back at Jake with an expression of pure hatred. 'You see, all the time Pip Djones was double-crossing me, waiting for his moment to strike. But *I* struck first. I tortured him – with knives, with water, with needles. I didn't want to kill him – that would have been too easy; I needed him to suffer – so I locked him in a place where he will never see light! No, he will *never* see light again. He will never see his precious secret service. Or his family. Or another human being. Ever again!' His voice echoed around the walls. 'He will die cold, dark and alone.'

All at once, rain started to patter down – huge, steaming drops of it – quickly becoming a downpour. Madame Fang motioned for a servant to hold an umbrella over her and Xi. Within moments, the rain was battering the pool, making Xi laugh with delight, while the eels retreated into the murky depths.

Jake eyeballed him. 'Tell me where Philip is?' he repeated, almost shouting to be heard over the deluge.

'I'm bored of this game,' Xi said. 'Bring me the helmet.' One of the guards was carrying something that looked like a medieval instrument of torture, and he gave a nod. Two soldiers held Jake while the third forced the helmet over his head.

'Leave him,' Topaz cried, struggling to help him, but Madame Fang forced her back again. Yoyo pleaded in her native tongue, but received only a thump in reply.

Jake's head was suddenly in clammy darkness; he could hear nothing but his own breathing. The helmet was lined with rubber, and the collar was fastened tight around his neck.

Xi Xiang stared at Jake through the visor. 'I apologize for this,' he purred, 'but you see, when I take your remains back home, dismembered, to show your brother, he needs to see who it is.' He patted the metal casing. 'This should keep your face in one piece – more or less.'

'You loathsome, spineless—' Nathan snarled.

Even in the midst of his terror, the phrase jolted Jake: *When I take your remains back home? Back home!* So Xi had *another* place? Was that where Philip was?

'*Laissez-le tranquille!*' Topaz pleaded, eyes streaming with tears. '*Pour l'amour de Dieu . . .*' Madame Fang gave her another slap.

Xi Xiang turned to his henchmen. 'Lower him, headfirst. Slowly . . . we want to enjoy it.'

Jake was dragged over to the side of the pool, his head forced down into the water. Eels attacked the metal casing with the force of battering rams, making his skull ring. Pulses of electricity fizzed around; only the rubber collar kept him safe from the shocks. But for how long? The men prepared to push Jake's shoulders into the water too – at which point the eels would surely finish him off. He could see only a churning maelstrom of movement, and red eyes darting towards him. As he braced himself for the worst, snapshots of his family appeared before his eyes – his mum and dad, then Philip, starving in a dark dungeon.

Xi Xiang was shaking with laughter, so much so that tears streamed down his face. And Nathan suddenly spotted his opportunity . . .

He cupped his manacled hands together, grabbed the casket of talc and threw it at Xi, blinding him; then he grabbed the jade bottle from Xi's belt, opened it, and threw the contents at the two guards holding Jake. He reached for his friend, and at the same time pushed the first man into the pool. With a high kick, Yoyo dealt with the other, and the eels immediately set upon them.

Taking advantage of the confusion, Topaz swung round and struck another guard in the jaw with her manacles. As Madame Fang came for her, drawing her sword, Topaz dodged, snapped a stone spear off one of the statues and turned to do battle. They fought around the edge of the pond, metal sparking against stone in the pounding rain.

Nathan and Yoyo followed Topaz's lead, snapping weapons off the other statues and taking on the remaining guards.

Jake was struggling with the clasp on his helmet, made slippery by the rain. Suddenly Xi Xiang, teeth clenched, came into view through his visor. He was covered in white paste, and the lipstick around his mouth was smudged. He drew a dagger, but Jake head-butted him with the helmet. A vivid red gash appeared across Xi's forehead and blood streamed down over his eyes.

He let out a shrill cry and stabbed at Jake, catching his shoulder. But Jake had finally managed to pull off the helmet – with which he proceeded to bash his opponent's skull, harder and harder. Dazed, Xi tottered backwards. Jake took him by the collar.

'*Where is he?*' he shouted, half demented. '*Where is Philip?*'

Xi hawked up another gob of phlegm and spat it in Jake's face. Then his mouth fell open and he lost consciousness.

Meanwhile Nathan and Yoyo had overcome the last of the guards: he fell to the ground, breaking his neck with a snap. Nathan snatched the key from the man's belt and started to unlock his handcuffs, while Yoyo collected up the weapons and rushed to Topaz's aid, tossing her a sword.

'*Merci bien,*' she cried, swapping her stone weapon to her left hand, while catching the sword in her right. She attacked Fang with renewed vigour, Yoyo engaging her from the other side. Even with two young agents coming at her at once, the old woman was a fighting machine, lightning-quick on her feet, eyes pin-sharp, always anticipating the next move. But in the end they were too much for her: they pinned her to the wall and disarmed her.

Fang hissed at them through the warm rain. 'There's no escape,' she taunted.

'Why will war be declared in two days' time?' Topaz demanded, the tip of her sword piercing the old woman's wizened neck. 'What's happening? *Tell me!*'

Fang gave a peculiar smile and stamped her heel. A fresh blade that had been attached to her knee sprang out and she jabbed it into Topaz's thigh, knocking Yoyo out of the way at the same time. She jumped onto the tightrope and danced across the pool in three steps, before climbing onto one of the statues and throwing herself into the air. The History Keepers watched, open-mouthed, as she caught hold of the eave and somersaulted onto the roof. Topaz launched her sword towards her, and the others followed suit with the extra weapons they had to hand, but Fang was too swift. She scurried away over the tiles, disappearing in the haze of torrential rain.

A moment later, there was a blare of hunting horns. Through the archway Nathan saw a platoon of guards heading towards them. He ran back to the metal gates and pulled them shut, but there was no way to lock them. The soldiers advanced, weapons drawn.

'Up here!' Topaz called to the others. She had pulled Xi Xiang's throne over to the wall and used it to scramble up onto the roof. She helped Yoyo up after her.

'Let's go!' Nathan shouted at Jake.

'Wait!' He ran back to Xi's comatose body, grabbed hold of the blue pendant – the Lazuli Serpent – and yanked it off.

'Quickly!' the others called. 'Let's go!' The soldiers were rapidly approaching.

For a moment Jake froze. A stray sword was lying on the ground and he grabbed it and held it up in both hands. With one blow he could kill his enemy. He made to thrust downwards – but stopped just short. *Philip* . . . If he killed Xi, he might never find his brother.

As the guards stormed through the gates, Jake turned and ran, leaping onto the back of the throne and then up to the roof. Drenched to the skin, the four of them set off across the palace roofs, the steaming rain pounding down around them.

17 THE DRAGON BAZOOKA

'This way – back to the Ocean Door,' Topaz called, pointing towards the rocky outcrop that divided the palace from the rest of the city. The golden tiles were slippery underfoot and they had to take care. Horns were sounding everywhere now, and hundreds of soldiers emerged from every doorway.

'Here . . .' Nathan said, passing the key to Topaz. She unfastened her manacles, throwing them off, and handed it to Yoyo – who did the same before giving the key to Jake.

Having freed themselves, they continued to the main square – to find a volley of arrows whistling towards them through the curtains of rain. 'Down!' Topaz cried out. They ducked just in time, hearing the clatter of missiles against the roof.

A second volley of arrows, followed by a third, *rat-tat-tatted* onto the tiles. The History Keepers doubled back, stumbling across the maze of rooftops, until they reached the jagged hill. They climbed the slope, and suddenly the vista of Canton opened out before them again. Constellations of lights marked out the port, with its thousands of ships and warehouses. The river, swollen by the downpour, was a fat black snake twisting through it.

They clambered down towards the Ocean Door and onto the roof of the teahouse. The Chinese opera was still playing below and the roof shook with the beats of the drums. They slid down it, lowered themselves one by one over the edge and jumped to the ground.

'Quickly!' Topaz shouted again, leading the way along the track towards the port. They reached the first of the warehouses and turned to see if they were being followed. Above them, there was another blare of horns, and a door – a vast black rectangle – appeared in the side of the rock itself. They heard the pounding of hooves, and suddenly soldiers on horseback came galloping through the opening. In seconds they were thundering down the slope, led by Madame Fang on a white stallion.

The four agents turned and ran into the warehouse. The workers shouted at them to stop, but they paid no attention. They found themselves in a colossal storeroom, stacked from floor to ceiling with millions of pieces of porcelain. They headed along the central aisle, which led out onto the dock.

Suddenly they heard hoofbeats, and Fang swept in on her white charger. Jake did a double take: she looked more formidable than ever in a silver breastplate, gleaming helmet, a giant steel sabre in her hand. As she scanned the room, her horse flared his nostrils and tossed his head. On seeing Jake and his friends, she called out to the cavalry outside.

Fang led them across the room, crashing into the stacks of china. Screaming dock-workers fled for cover.

Just as the agents approached the exit, a large pile of crates collapsed in front of them, the porcelain shattering in their path. As they climbed over the debris, Jake glanced back and saw stack after stack of white china toppling to the floor in billows of dust. Spearheading the destruction, Fang still held her sword up, black eyes fixed on Jake.

The History Keepers crunched their way through onto the docks, gazing around at the network of pontoons and wooden gantries. They followed a path along the water's edge, but came to a dead end and had to turn back.

'This way!' Nathan shouted, leading them up a gangplank onto a large trading junk, where sailors were lowering crates of tea into the hold. They yelled in alarm as the strangers flew past, jumping over the rail onto the next vessel along. But a moment later, Fang had galloped aboard, followed swiftly by her soldiers, the horses' hooves rapping like war drums on the deck. This time the sailors dived into the hold as horsemen careered around in pursuit of their prey.

Jake and the others hurtled from one deck to another, flying past bemused sailors, weaving in and out of sails. Fang and her men pursued them relentlessly, leaping over the ships' rails. Some horses stopped dead, daunted by the gap between the vessels, or got entangled in rigging; some carried on even when they had lost their riders – a surging tide of them, froth dripping from their mouths, sweat mixing with the rain.

When the four agents reached the end of the line

of ships, Nathan led the way down onto the shore. They rattled along a pontoon and dashed inside another warehouse, realizing that it was the spice depot they had passed earlier. The air fizzed with peppery odours as the workers filled kegs with rich-coloured powders.

'Arm yourselves!' Topaz ordered, holding her nose as she took hold of one of the casks.

'You'll have to excuse us . . .' Nathan advanced towards a girl who was fixing labels on the barrels. 'We have a situation,' he added, taking hold of one and inspecting its contents. 'Nutmeg? Great for the complexion.'

Just then, the doors flew open and Fang and her men galloped in. The youngsters started hurling the casks at them: many hit their mark, knocking the soldiers out of their saddles. The air was thick with spices and pepper, blinding the riders, and making them cough and sneeze. The horses whinnied and reared up, or simply bolted, out of control.

In the confusion, the agents escaped, following the zigzagging path of rickety pontoons, and ran into a third storehouse. They were immediately overpowered by the stench of fish sauce – at least ten open vats of it, each one full to the brim with festering brown gloop, alive with flies.

'When they follow us in,' Topaz panted, barely able to speak, 'overturn the barrels.' Quickly they took up positions behind the vats; the putrid aroma shot up Jake's nose and coated the back of his throat, making him gag.

Once more, Madame Fang was the first to appear. Her horse was tiring, but she was still full of energy – though her cavalry was now drastically depleted.

Topaz gave the word: 'Now!' All at once, they overturned their barrels, sending the contents sweeping across in a tidal wave of fetid gunge, followed by swarms of flies, the noxious gases overpowering. Neighing in terror, many of the horses refused to go on.

Jake saw one last opportunity to stop their pursuers. Empty barrels had been stacked up, ten high, against the wall, with a wooden lever keeping them in place. He warned the others to stand clear, and then released them. A landslide of barrels juddered across the floor, knocking some of the horses over like skittles. They slipped and skidded on the wet floor, trying to regain their footing as their riders scrambled out of the way of the flailing hooves.

'Let's go!' Topaz shouted, and the others followed her out of the back door.

'The horses – see over there!' Yoyo shouted, remembering the herd they had passed earlier on their way to the Ocean Door. They headed for a fenced enclosure, where a group of young mares was feeding. Jake threw open the gates, and they each picked a horse, vaulted up, dug their heels in and took off out of the pen.

The wranglers, who were eating their dinner nearby, shouted in alarm, and three of them gave chase. One caught up with Topaz and grabbed hold of her leg.

'*Je suis desolée*,' she said, aiming a kick and sending him cartwheeling back down the track.

The History Keepers tore up the slope away from the wharves. 'Whoever gets to the *Thunder* first,' Nathan yelled, 'start the engine.' He looked round. 'And we still haven't lost *her*.'

Jake glanced over his shoulder. Fang was in pursuit once again, whipping her horse, but there were now only two soldiers behind her.

The four agents crested the hill and tore down

into the main part of the city. The streets were teeming with Cantonese, most sheltering from the rain under the awnings of bars and tea houses that had come alive after nightfall. Those in the middle of the road had to jump clear as the horses galloped past.

Finally they made it back to their ship. Leaving the mares on the quayside, they sprang aboard. Immediately Nathan went below decks and fired up the engine. Normally they'd at least make a show of raising the sails, but this was an emergency, and no one could hear the motor in the torrential rain anyway. Within moments, the *Thunder* had edged away from the pier and they breathed a sigh of relief.

But Madame Fang was not finished with them.

Jake saw her charging across the quay, sweeping aside anything in her path. He assumed she would stop at the dockside, as their ship was now several yards from the shore and the gap was widening. But she hurtled on, shouting her defiance. Jake's eyes went wide as her stallion leaped across the chasm. The horse let out a whinny as his front leg caught on the rail, so that he thumped down onto the deck, hooves skidding. Fang was sent tumbling off.

Unruffled, she picked herself up and reached for

a weapon attached to her saddle – a golden bazooka crafted in the shape of a dragon. Before the History Keepers even realized what was going on, she had primed the mechanism and fired. A jet of flames shot out, setting fire to the rigging. She was about to let off a second shot when Topaz leaped up onto the mainsail, took hold of a rope, swung round and struck her on the back of the head. The bazooka flew out of her grasp and she toppled over the side of the ship. For a moment she clung to the rail, but Yoyo slashed downwards with her sword, leaving her no choice but to let go.

Even now she wasn't ready to give up, swimming after the ship, but it was moving too fast now.

Meanwhile the white stallion got to his feet. Whinnying and snorting, he dashed to and fro, looking for his mistress. Suddenly he heard her cries and swung round, almost knocking the wheel from its casing. The mighty beast reared up and launched himself over the side. Jake watched in awe as the animal smacked down into the water and started swimming towards Fang; she managed to climb on his back, and they headed towards the shore.

'Go!' Topaz shouted to Nathan at the helm, and the *Thunder* roared off across the bay at full speed;

the port of Canton, with its millions of lanterns, quickly receded behind them.

Once they had put out the fire, Jake studied the dragon-shaped bazooka that Fang had left behind. It seemed familiar, and he remembered with a start where he had seen it before: it was the weapon that Philip had drawn . . . He ripped open the pouch with the bundle of his brother's things, took out the diagrams that Galliana had given him and checked the design against the weapon lying on the deck . . . They were identical.

18 A NIGHT ON THE TOWN

Charlie waited for Oceane on the pier. He was smartly dressed, his crutches at his side and Mr Drake perched on his shoulder. Three nights earlier he had agreed to take her to the summer ball in St Malo; he was braced for a difficult night ahead.

Oceane had a terrible reputation: she was spoiled, pompous, self-obsessed and dependably rude. She was not much of a spy either. (In the past, she had only undertaken missions that offered opportunities for adding to her collection of jewellery. People only put up with her out of respect for her late parents, who had both been great Keepers and wonderful characters.) But Charlie was determined to try and cheer her up after the death of Josephine – he could sympathize with *anyone* who lost a beloved pet.

He looked at his pocket watch. It was almost nine o'clock. 'She's an hour late. The party will be over by the time we get there!' he said, shaking his head at Mr Drake.

Just then, he heard the sound of pattering footsteps. Oceane floated down the steps towards them in a gown of blue chiffon, with long white gloves, and flowers in her hair. A pearl necklace and an ivory bag completed her elegant outfit. Charlie didn't know anything about fashion, but he was certain that she looked breathtaking.

'I've decided it's a bad idea,' she announced coolly before she had even got to the bottom of the stairs. She might have looked the part, but her attitude was sourer than ever. 'I'm not coming. *Désolée*.' She turned on her little gold heel and started up the steps again.

'*Non*, Mademoiselle Noire,' Charlie called after her. 'Permission is not granted for you to return to your rooms and be miserable for the rest of your life. Do you wish to die a lonely spinster with nothing but your jewellery for company?'

'That sounds perfect,' she replied, without breaking step. 'Jewels are the only thing that can really be depended on.'

'You wouldn't have dressed up like that if you weren't desperate to go.'

She ignored him, so he took a sheet of paper out of his pocket and started reading out names: 'Charles St Jean, le Vicomte de Rennes, Michel-Pierre Rousseau, from the house of Nantes, Alain Fourgère the Second, le Comte de Breton.'

Oceane stopped in her tracks and swung round. 'Who are those people?'

'This is a good one: Frédéric-Xavier Montjac, Duc de Bretagne, and his little brother, Alençon. Actually Alençon's only seventeen. But they have a cousin who has the largest vineyard in Normandy.'

'*Arrête! Arrête!*' Oceane exclaimed, sweeping back down. 'Are you trying to tell me that those people will be guests at the ball?'

'Those, and many more like them.'

She put her nose in the air and thought about her options. 'Is that the ship you're proposing to take me in?' she said, pointing at a yacht bobbing by the pier. 'It's hardly Cleopatra's barge.'

'I have champagne on ice and asparagus tartlets at the ready. I know how you love asparagus. It's just half an hour across the bay.'

Oceane pursed her lips. 'Well, I suppose they'll

be crying out for women of my class. I wouldn't like to let them down.' She threw her head back, strode over to the boat and stepped down. It didn't cross her mind to help Charlie, so he hobbled aboard and started the engine.

From a window high up in the Mount, Rose Djones stood watching them.

'Charlie Chieverley needs his head examined,' she commented to Galliana. 'If I went out for an evening with Oceane Noire, only one of us would come back alive.' She was in Galliana's study, a half-eaten cake in her hand. She polished it off and licked her fingers. 'I'm so happy that rum babas are back on the menu – now that Jupitus isn't.'

'Are you two still not talking?' Galliana asked. She was busy at her desk, poring over maps of China with a magnifying glass.

'What is there to say?' Rose shrugged. 'He's a cold fish, and that's that. Thank goodness that ring never made it onto my finger.'

Galliana studied her old friend.

Rose let out a little sigh and turned away from the window. 'Apologies. Selfish of me to be chatter-ing away when you've got far more important things on your mind.' She squeezed herself onto the commander's seat and switched her attention to the maps. 'Do you think they've found Xi yet?' she asked.

Galliana took a deep breath; her lip trembled and a tear pricked her eye.

'Oh, my darling,' Rose said. 'What is it?'

'I should never have sent them in the first place,' Galliana cried. 'Better that he commits his crimes than I lose more people I love. I should have stopped them from going to China, insisted they return.'

'It's what we do. It's what we're *here* for. We are the History Keepers.' Rose tried to hide her shock; she hadn't seen Galliana cry in decades.

The commander shook her head. 'I should be protecting them, not sending them to . . . to . . . Xi is so utterly evil, Rose, so black-hearted. The others have humanity, *some* humanity. Not he. He is a fiend.'

Rose felt a shiver go down her spine. She opened her carpetbag, took out an old tissue and started dabbing her friend's face. 'Come on – if you don't perk up, I'll have to take you to that ball in St Malo and make you dance a polka.'

'It's not invented yet,' Galliana retorted, the glimmer of a smile on her face.

'That's more like it. We can't have the venerable commander of the History Keepers' Secret Service blubbing away like Marie-Antoinette.'

There was a knock on the door, and Fredrik Isaksen put his head round, smiling roguishly. 'Here you all are,' he said. 'There's the beginnings of a startling sunset outside. I wondered if either of you would like to come and view it? I have a bottle open – a very confident Margaux from 1787.' He pretended that he was speaking to both of them; but his Lothario eyes were fixed on Rose.

'Rose, darling,' Galliana said, 'why don't you go with Fredrik while I finish up here?' Seeing that her friend was about to protest, she whispered in her ear, 'Go – it will do you good.'

Rose squeezed her hand. 'Five more minutes with these maps, then come and find us.' She picked up her carpetbag and turned to leave.

Fredrik held the door open for her, eyes twinkling. 'May I be so bold as to say how beautiful you look tonight?' he purred. 'Vermillion is your colour.'

'You may be as bold as you like, Fredrik,' she said, winking at Galliana.

Then her grin dropped: Jupitus was coming down the corridor towards them. He ignored Rose at first; but as he passed, he bowed slightly and said stiffly, 'Fredrik . . . Miss Djones.'

Rose, irritated, watched him retreat. Then she took her companion by the arm and said in a loud voice, 'Let's go and see that sunset, then.'

'Mmm. Let me think . . . My ideal man?' Oceane munched an asparagus tartlet as she pondered. She was seated on deck, a silver tray of goodies at her side. Charlie was at the helm, navigating across the flat summer sea with Mr Drake. 'He'd be idiotically wealthy. Impeccable manners, naturally. Discreet, respectful, gracious. And I don't like nose hair or big feet.'

'And I suppose you want someone who loves you . . .' Charlie offered. 'Who likes you the way you are . . . That's the important thing, isn't it?'

Oceane screwed up her face. 'That sounds a little vulgar, doesn't it?'

'Maybe I'll have one of those tartlets now,' he said, changing the subject.

'Oh dear, I didn't know you'd be eating too,' Oceane said carelessly. 'I polished them off.'

Charlie smiled bravely and wondered what on earth he was doing on this expedition. What were his friends up to at this moment? He had always wanted to go to China; such a fascinating culture, so full of surprises. 'St Malo ahead,' he said.

Oceane turned and squinted at it. The city walls glowed in the sunset. A hexagon of stout ramparts protected a pyramid of dark grey buildings, with the cathedral at the apex.

Charlie docked in the harbour, and Oceane swanned ashore without a thought for her companion. He managed to hail a carriage, and they zigzagged their way up through the warren of narrow streets, alighting outside a grand-looking hall.

'*Mon Dieu*,' Oceane gasped, clasping her pearls at the sight of dozens of smart young men chatting on the terrace. 'What a brave new world this is.' The driver opened the door for her. 'I shall see you in there,' she sang to Charlie. 'Wish me luck.'

Before he had even managed to alight from the carriage, she had swept off, making sure that all male eyes were upon her. Charlie paid off the cabbie before looking at his parrot. 'Why did I ever think I could change her? She is ungrateful and beyond redemption.'

He hobbled into the hall, and couldn't help

smiling at the scene he found inside. It was a proper ball. The room glittered with candlelight from two enormous chandeliers, and at least two hundred revellers were dressed in all their finery: the men straight-backed and dark-suited; the women visions of silk and fluttering fans. Many took part in a lively dance; others chatted and gossiped around the edge. A twenty-piece orchestra – the musicians immaculately turned out in golden coats and breeches – played at the far end.

'Oh goody, a buffet!' Charlie said to himself, spying a long table on the other side of the room. Taking his chances with his crutches, he made his way across the dance floor, helped himself to a plate and started piling it up with delicacies.

'I like your parrot,' a voice said in his ear. It was a young girl with dark eyes and ringlets. 'Is he tame?'

Charlie was going to tell her that actually he was a rescue parrot and quite temperamental, but the girl had already reached out to stroke the bird's head. To Charlie's amazement, Mr Drake didn't squawk and flap his wings; instead, he began to chuckle, before hopping onto the girl's shoulder and nuzzling her cheek.

'Hell's bells and Bathsheba, I've never seen him

do that before,' Charlie said. 'Can I get you something to eat? The mousse looks quite special.'

'Anything as long as it's not meat,' the girl whispered. 'Though don't tell my brothers that . . .' She nodded at three red-cheeked youths behind her. 'They're pig farmers. *Je m'appelle Ambre. Enchantée.*'

'Charlie . . .' The word got stuck in his throat and he blushed.

Suddenly he caught sight of Oceane talking to a distinguished-looking man in uniform. He had a neat beard, a sash over his shoulder and a row of medals pinned to his chest. Though Oceane was fluttering her eyelashes and smiling, it seemed to Charlie that the man wasn't interested. The band started up again, and she held out her hand, signalling that she would like to dance, but he merely turned away, leaving her hand suspended in mid-air. Her face fell in mortification as a group of young girls giggled behind their fans, and she retreated to a corner. Never in his life had Charlie seen anyone look so lonely and dejected.

'Would you excuse me for a second?' he said to Ambre.

He quickly limped round to Oceane. He expected a tirade about how rude everyone was, and was taken aback when she smiled at him and said: 'Thank you so much for bringing me, Charlie.'

'*Thank you?*' he repeated. He wondered if she was being sarcastic. She wasn't.

'I know I have my little ways; that I'm not the friendliest woman in the world. But I am grateful when people show me kindness. And no one has ever shown me kindness like you have this week. I will never forget it.'

'Oh. Well . . . I . . .' Charlie was lost for words. 'It's my pleasure, Mademoiselle Noire. I wasn't sure if you were enjoying yourself.'

'Of course, of course, *c'est une fête merveilleuse.* It's been an age since I came to a ball like this. The orchestra and the dancing . . . and *so* many tall men. It all makes me feel weak with happiness.'

Just then a man approached, bowing his head at Oceane. '*S'il vous plaît, mademoiselle . . . ?*' he began in a deep voice. Oceane looked him up and down. He was no taller than she was, thick-set, with a strong face and deep-set eyes. His suit was a little too small for him, and less fine than some of the others on show, but he had a warm smile.

'Tell him you'd love to dance,' Charlie whispered in Oceane's ear.

'Would I? I don't think he's my sort.'

With a nudge, Charlie pushed her forward. The man smiled, bowed and led her off onto the dance floor. She in turn shot Charlie a stern look.

Despite his size, the man was light on his feet, and very courteous. Smiling all the time, he spoke to Oceane as they twirled around. At first she was grim-faced, but soon she began to open up, smiling and finally laughing. In all his years at Point Zero, Charlie had never seen her laugh, except at someone else's expense.

He was starting to feel very proud when Oceane suddenly stopped and left the dance floor; her partner stood there, baffled. 'What happened?' Charlie asked as she strode back towards him, picking up a flute of champagne on the way.

'*C'est un charlatan*,' she said, knocking it back. 'He shouldn't be here, pretending to be something he isn't.'

'What do you mean, a charlatan?'

'*Il est pêcheur d'huîtres*. He's an oyster farmer.'

'You can't just leave someone standing on the dance floor like that.' The poor man was looking over at them, not sure what to do next.

'We would be wasting our time, both of us.

I think I can do better than an oyster farmer.'

Finally Charlie lost his temper. 'You can't do better . . . No, mademoiselle, I'm afraid not. Perhaps I don't understand the ways of the world – I'm just a fifteen-year-old boy, after all – but I would speculate that he is probably worth ten of you.' Mr Drake squawked in agreement, while Oceane reeled in shock. 'He looks like a nice man. With a nice smile. And a nice suit, with a flower in his buttonhole. He has a solid job. Besides, you love oysters. What could be better? Now go back and dance with him. It is not a request, mademoiselle, it is an order.'

Oceane looked at him, frozen, her mouth gaping. So Charlie prodded her with one of his crutches and goaded her back over to the oyster fisherman. '*Bonsoir – je m'appelle Charlie,*' he said to the man. '*Et vous?*'

'Jacques,' he replied, mystified. 'Monsieur Jacques Vernet.'

'A good, dependable name. *Mon amie voudrait continuer à danser. D'accord?*' Charlie said, taking Jacques' large hand and joining it with Oceane's. '*Vous êtes un beau couple.*'

The music started again, and Charlie motioned for them to get going – they were both rooted to the spot. '*Dansez!*' he repeated. 'Who knows what tomorrow will bring?'

Eventually Jacques grinned uncertainly, and led Oceane across the floor. Soon she was laughing again, this time at the top of her voice.

After the sun had set and their bottle of Margaux had been polished off – amidst many fond remembrances of old times – Fredrik Isaksen suggested to Rose that they wait for the stars to come out.

'It's such a clear evening,' he purred, 'it's bound to be a wondrous show. Shall I fetch us some blankets? We can make ourselves a den.'

Rose looked at him sadly. 'Fredrik, you are probably the most handsome man who has ever suggested making a den with me; but I will have to say no. I'm out of sorts tonight.'

His smile did not falter. 'Of course, Rose, I understand.' He took her hand and kissed it.

She went back to her room with a heavy heart. As she passed Jupitus's door, she saw a sliver of light underneath and heard soft music. She knelt down and looked through the keyhole. She could just see Jupitus in his dressing gown and slippers, sitting motionless on his ottoman. Suddenly she felt a surge of bravado and made to knock – but stopped, paralysed, then turned and plodded away down the corridor to her room.

She put on her nightdress, got into bed, blew out her candle and pulled the covers up to her nose. She hadn't closed the curtains and could see the stars beginning to come out. Suddenly the words that Galliana had spoken before came back to her:

He's so utterly evil, Rose, so black-hearted. The others have humanity, some humanity. Not he. He is a fiend.

Suddenly the spectre of Xi Xiang seemed to hover in the gloom in front of her. Yesterday she had gone to inspect a picture of him in the library of faces (oddly, she had never met him in person), and now remembered his rouged cheeks and the horrible third eye sullenly watching, whatever the rest of his face was doing. Apparently he had a high-pitched laugh. She felt a cold clamp of terror and screwed up her eyes, but Xi's image remained, staring at her in the darkness.

'Jake?' she said out loud. 'Come back to us soon. Please come back.' And then she burrowed under her covers and sobbed.

19 SOUTH BY SOUTHEAST

Jake and the others didn't set a course – they just wanted to get away from Canton as quickly as possible; to flee Madame Fang and the horrors of Xi Xiang's palace. Their engine set at full throttle, they headed due east, back along the Pearl River, overtaking ships as they went.

It was an uneasy journey: the eye of the storm seemed to track their passage, stalking them. Occasionally the rain would subside and the water grow calmer, only for it to start again moments later with renewed vigour; the wind pummelled the sea and the ship listed dangerously, timbers creaking, sails flapping.

This was bad enough, but the fear of pursuit was worse. No matter that Fang had been left bobbing in the harbour; they knew that she might already have commandeered a ship to hunt them down. Nothing seemed beyond her. With that in mind, while Topaz took the helm, Jake, Yoyo and Nathan stood watch under a dripping awning at the stern, keeping an eye on the vessels behind them – just dim shapes in the gloom. Once there was clear water behind, they felt safer.

'How are you feeling?' Jake asked the other two. Their faces were still red from Xi Xiang's squid serum, and Nathan's eyes were very sore and inflamed.

'As long as my hair doesn't fall out,' he said with a shrug, 'I'll be all right.' He turned pointedly to Yoyo, remembering their argument. 'Shallow or not, it's a fact: fifty per cent of my personality is wrapped up in my hair. Anyway' – he swept his hand around – 'there's no point in us *all* being here, so I'll leave you two lovebirds alone.' He retreated to the prow.

Jake watched him sadly, then turned to Yoyo. 'How are *you*?'

'I'm fine,' she said, putting on a brave smile. 'Apart from the fact that everyone seems to hate me.' She stared down at the wash left behind the ship and heaved a sigh. 'I'm going to go and make us something to eat. See if I can cheer everyone up.'

She turned and headed down the steps into the galley. Standing at the helm, Topaz watched her go, but she didn't speak. Moments later they heard the sound of chopping.

Jake looked at Fang's golden bazooka again. He tested its weight, it was very heavy. He inspected the craftsmanship, running his finger along the outline of the dragon and gently probing the trigger, which was fashioned like a claw. He wondered if Philip had ever fired it himself. He studied the sketch of the other gun – the slim revolver – did this also exist? he wondered. And if so, who had it?

Next he unfurled the canvas from Xi's house in London, and examined the picture again. There was Philip staring back at him, with Xi Xiang at his side. Had this indeed been painted in Rome by Caravaggio? There was no signature at the bottom, but it was evidently the work of a master.

Jake scrutinized his brother's dark eyes and square jaw. In Jacobean London, the image had upset him; even though he'd been amazed and relieved to see that Philip had survived after all, he couldn't comprehend the connection with Xi. Now, of course, he understood everything – Xi himself had explained it: Philip had got close to him as part of his mission – to spy on him. He was a double agent.

But this still left the biggest question unanswered: where was Philip now?

Xi's words came back to Jake: *I didn't want to kill him – that would have been too easy; I needed him to suffer – so I locked him in a place where he will never see light! No, he will never see light again.* The last phrase was the most chilling of all: *He will die cold, dark and alone.*

But where was that? Xi had said Philip was *back home.* Where was home? Jake finally took the Lazuli Serpent out of his pocket, wiped it on his sleeve and examined it. In the lantern light he saw that it had a faint blue aura, but otherwise it didn't look particularly special: it was just a cylinder of blue stone. Its sides were inscribed with swirls and lines, but none of them made any sense to him. Whichever way he turned it, they didn't create a proper picture. It didn't look like writing either. As he peered closer, though, he noticed a tiny dent in the stone – and a symbol: a hallmark. All at once he realized that it was an octopus.

Yoyo came up with four bowls of food and passed

them round. They all ate in silence, Topaz remaining at the helm. They made their way back past the distant lights of Macao.

Eventually the rain subsided to a patter and then stopped completely. Suddenly the air felt clean and fresh; the stifling humidity had gone. As the sea became calmer, their passage was easier. They headed southwest, hugging the coastline, a dense jungle of trees and palms.

It was two a.m. when they came across a deep inlet; a tiny fishing village nestled at the end of it. A couple of ships – each roughly the size of the *Thunder* – were moored there.

'We'll dock here until dawn,' Topaz said. She cut the engine and they glided into the bay. As they approached the shore, she called to Jake and Yoyo to drop anchor. They released the latch and let the chain unravel, clinking and rattling until it stopped with a thud. The ship slipped forward a fraction more, until it was held by the weight, and they quickly furled the sails.

All was silent as four pairs of eyes examined the inlet. Nothing stirred. Rising up on three sides were sheer walls of rock, covered in thick vegetation. Behind them was the ocean. Far in the distance, ships continued to and from the ports of China, a never-ending stream of world trade. Cutting through the stillness came the sound of squawking, and a flock of parrots flew up from the trees before disappearing inland. Jake thought of Charlie.

'We're safe here, are we?' Yoyo asked, sounding uncertain.

'We need to plan our route,' Topaz replied curtly. 'We can't just wander about aimlessly. May I see that crystal now?'

Jake gave it to her and they all sat down. When Nathan came into the light, Topaz did a double take. His eyes were even more bloodshot and his face had a sickly purple hue.

'You look dreadful,' she said. 'Are you sure you're all right?'

'I'm fine,' he muttered. 'But thanks for the vote of confidence.'

'You don't have to be proud,' Yoyo said. 'If you're not well, Nathan, it's better that you tell us.' She turned to the others to explain. 'Squid venom can be very dangerous; some people are affected more than others.'

'There's nothing wrong with me!' Nathan hissed.

'And I hardly need *your* sympathy, *Miss Yuting*. Now let's look at that blasted stone.'

There was silence as Topaz passed it over and he inspected it, blinking his sore eyes. The other three eyeballed each other.

'These markings don't mean anything,' Nathan said impatiently. 'What is that?' he asked, noticing the motif.

'It's an octopus,' Jake replied.

Nathan was having trouble focusing, so he gave the stone back to his sister. Yoyo leaned over her shoulder and the two girls studied it together.

'The lines have been meticulously drawn,' Topaz said, 'so they must have some significance.'

'Maybe there is another piece to the puzzle?' Yoyo ventured. 'A companion stone perhaps?'

Topaz passed the crystal back to Jake, reached over to a little shelf below the wheel and took out the map of China they had used to navigate their way to Canton. She traced her finger around the crinkly coastline. Below lay the expanse of the South China Sea, crisscrossed with the faint lines of east–west trade routes. 'All we know is this: *apparently*, the west is about to declare war on China. Why? How? Where? We have until tomorrow to find out. I'm going to send a report to Point Zero.'

She took the Meslith machine out of the trunk, sat down away from the others, and started typing. Pulses of electric light from the aerial flashed on her face.

'If no one objects,' Nathan said, clambering to his feet, 'I'm going to have a little lie down.'

Topaz, Yoyo and Jake replied in unison as he shuffled down the steps: 'Of course not. It's a good idea. Let us know if you feel any worse.'

'Wake me if my hair falls out—' Nathan stopped. 'On second thoughts, it's probably best not to know.' He went into the cabin and stretched himself out on his bunk, carefully arranging his hair on one side of the pillow as if it were a sick pet.

The other three sat in silence. The only sounds were Topaz tapping on the Meslith and the far-off lapping of water against the shore. Yoyo tucked herself against a bundle of rope, and her eyelids drooped. 'Maybe I'll have a little rest too . . .' she mumbled. A moment later, she was fast asleep.

Jake and Topaz couldn't see one another – the mast was between them – but they were acutely aware of each other. They had argued for the first time since they had met. The words Jake had spoken were still turning around in his head: *You're so ready to criticize, but you never stop and think how you have hurt people. How you have hurt me.* He hadn't even realized that he'd been bottling up his feelings about Topaz, about the past. They were best friends and had spent most of the last year going on madcap expeditions around the island; it was odd that this had come out now. He didn't know whether to apologize or not.

The sound of a mandolin floated across the bay, playing a slow and haunting tune. Jake looked around, trying to make out where it was coming from. Topaz did the same, and caught his eye. They peered across the bay and saw the silhouette of a man leaning against the prow of a far-off ship, gently plucking the strings. They listened for a while, until Jake started to feel drowsy too; he stifled a yawn.

'You rest for a while,' Topaz said. 'I'm wide awake. I'll keep watch.' A tear beaded in the corner of her eye and she wiped it away.

Jake didn't reply. He yawned again, suddenly feeling exhausted. He took out the Lazuli Serpent and looked at the curious lines. Then he lay down and fell into a slumber, the blue crystal clutched in his hand.

He woke with a start, just as day was breaking, his mind full of images – of strange lands and crinkly coastlines. He sat up and looked around, shaking his head to banish the vestiges of his dream. Yoyo was still asleep, curled up amongst the ropes.

'Morning,' Topaz said brightly, coming up from the cabin.

'How's Nathan?' Jake asked.

'Flat out, still. His breathing, it's . . . strange.' Topaz did an imitation, inhaling with an odd shudder. She poured a cup of water from the barrel. 'Here,' she said, handing it to him. He swigged it back, picking up the Lazuli Serpent, which had dropped onto the deck beside him. In an instant, he remembered his dream: the flashes of maps and coastlines. They meant something to him, but he wasn't sure what at first. The cogs of his mind turned – and suddenly it came to him.

'It's a map,' he said, studying the stone intently. 'It's a *map*!'

Topaz was nonplussed. But Jake opened the trunk where they kept paper for the Meslith machine and pulled out a blank sheet. He set it down and placed the jade cylinder on top of it. He started to roll it firmly across the page – then back again, repeating the motion until he had marked the page with an embossed design. Then he took a stick of charcoal from the trunk and gently rubbed it over the paper – until a black-and-white image material-ized. He held it up for Topaz to see. The Lazuli Serpent had indeed printed what looked like a map: a corrugated coastline with islands of all shapes and sizes dotted along it.

Jake grabbed the map they had been looking at last night, checking the drawing against it. 'There! Look!' he said, indicating one section. It exactly matched the map made from the stone. 'The mark of the octopus, Xi Xiang's emblem,' he said, 'points to this place – *here*. It must be *home* – as Xi called it – his own island.'

Topaz took both pieces of paper and compared them, realizing that he was right. She studied the little island, paying particular attention to its co-ordinates, and let out a gasp. '*C'est extraordinaire . . . Partons tout de suite!*'

'How long will it take?'

'Eight hours – seven, if we make good time.'

Without waking the others, they hauled up the heavy anchor. Jake looked at the sky: it was going to be scorching, but it was less humid than it had been the day before.

As there was little wind, they had no choice but to start up the engine; Jake – who took the helm – was careful to keep it to a low purr so as not to attract attention. On the other ships, sailors were stirring, and fishermen were getting their nets ready on the shore. He steered the *Thunder* towards the open sea and they followed the coast once more, picking up a breeze. Their mission suddenly had a purpose. Could they stop Xi in his tracks? And was Philip on that island? Would he see his brother again before the day was out?

They sailed south-southeast, into the heart of the tropics. The coastline soon became more dramatic. Vast empty beaches of virgin sand stretched out in front of rolling green hills. There were forests of palm trees, and soaring escarpments of purple rock. And then islands started to appear, jewels set in the sapphire sea. It looked like paradise.

Every once in a while they checked the map against the coastline, charting their progress. Jake glanced over at Yoyo, while Topaz went down to check on Nathan, bathing his fevered brow with a cold cloth. However, the pair of them slept soundly through the morning and into the afternoon.

Yoyo was the first to stir. Her eyes opened and she stared blankly at the horizon. Then she sat up, clutching her head and blinking. She looked much better, Jake thought; her cheeks were no longer blotchy and red.

'Jake had a breakthrough,' Topaz told her, explaining about the Lazuli Serpent. 'We're heading for Xi's island. We'll be there by evening.'

Nathan didn't stir until late afternoon. He tottered up the steps, holding onto the rail, a blanket wrapped round him. There was a hectic flush to his cheeks and he was shivering.

'How are you feeling?' the other three asked in unison.

'Cold?' he said, his voice cracking. 'But it's not cold, is it?'

His companions looked at each other. It was almost forty degrees.

'Where are we going?' he asked, staring around at the tropical scenery.

Topaz told him about the map inscribed on the

crystal, but Nathan barely took it in. He was finding it hard to breathe and his teeth chattered. 'Why is it so absurdly cold?'

'We need to get him to a doctor,' Jake said quietly to the other two, the mission forgotten: he was worried about his friend.

Topaz looked down at the map. 'There's a port here – at Zhanjiang. It's not far from our final destination. We head there first. Agreed?' she said decisively.

Jake and Yoyo nodded.

'Doctors are not to be trusted!' Nathan blurted out, hearing their whispers. 'They'd kill you sooner than cure you.' He staggered towards them, looking from one to the other, as if he only half recognized them, then said slowly, 'Did you know, I am comical?'

Yoyo bent her head in shame, regretting her words. 'Why don't you lie down again, Nathan,' she said quietly, reaching out to him.

He shook her hand off. 'You're not to be trusted either.' Suddenly his eyes rolled back in their sockets and his legs gave way. The others just managed to catch him as he fell. They laid him down under the awning; Topaz dabbed his forehead with cold water. His eyes flickered open for a moment, then closed again.

'Head for Zhanjiang immediately!' Topaz called to Jake in alarm.

Jake was already at the wheel, setting their course and ramping up the speed, his stomach hollow with anxiety.

They arrived an hour later. Yoyo explained that Zhanjiang had been important during the Song dynasty of the eleventh century, due to its deep natural harbour, but had now declined. It was a compact town, set between hills and sea, ten times quieter than Canton.

As the sun sank towards the horizon, they made their way into the main port; they passed a number of dry docks where ships were being built, some just timber skeletons, others almost complete. One stood out: a five-masted junk of pristine bleached timber. The officials inspecting the bulging hull looked minuscule next to it. Jake remembered the meeting at Xi's palace in Canton and wondered whether these boat-builders had been present. Maybe this was one of the warships that Fang was commissioning? He steered the *Thunder* into the harbour and docked.

Nathan was barely conscious, and it took all three of them to carry him ashore. Topaz and Jake took a shoulder each as Yoyo rushed along the pier to speak to a group of fishermen.

'There's a doctor at the top of the street,' she said, pointing.

They peered up the steep incline. Jake took most of Nathan's weight, and they started to climb.

The city of Canton had been cosmopolitan and the youngsters had blended in. Here, the townsfolk eyed them suspiciously. As they passed a tea house, the customers turned and looked at them, muttering under their breath. A man with a white beard and spindly moustache emerged and pursued them up the street, calling after them. In his crumpled white gown and white cap, he looked like a wizard, and Jake saw that one of his eyes was much paler than the other. As he spoke, he rattled a container of sticks inscribed with Chinese letters.

'What's he want?' Jake wondered.

'He wants to tell our fortune,' Yoyo explained, before turning and informing the man that they didn't need his services.

He paid no attention, darting in front of them, shaking his jar of sticks and touching their clothes.

Yoyo grew impatient and waved him away. Suddenly his voice changed and became so deep and sinister that Jake and Topaz stopped and turned round. The fortune-teller repeated the phrase again, this time running his finger across his throat.

'What is he saying?' Topaz asked, unnerved.

'Nothing . . .' Yoyo shook her head and tried to hurry them on.

Then the man spoke in English, his thin lips trembling as he formed the words: '*One of you will die.*'

Jake caught his breath in shock. Yoyo shooed the man away, and they continued up to the top of the hill, where they found a square timber building. In the dying light, they saw a placard bearing a red symbol.

Luckily the doctor was an amiable man. He was just packing up for the day, but when he saw the state Nathan was in, he told them to lay him on the timber bed in the centre of the dim room.

Putting on his spectacles, he lit a lantern and brought it over to the patient. He checked Nathan's pulse in various places, feeling the glands under his jaw and examining his tongue. As he did so, Yoyo spoke to him in Chinese, telling him about the squid venom.

At length, the doctor took a deep breath and selected a couple of jars from among the hundreds that lined the wall, mixed together a quantity of powder from each, added some water and stirred it together. He asked the others to hold Nathan's head up as he carefully poured the concoction into his mouth, then checked his temperature. He spoke to Yoyo, and she translated.

'He says Nathan has reacted badly to the venom, that it has paralysed his insides, making it hard for him to breathe.'

Topaz reached for Nathan's hand and squeezed it tight. 'Will he be all right? Can the doctor do anything?'

'He says that if we had come even an hour later, it might have been too late, but he will try and stabilize him.'

Jake couldn't stop thinking about the fortune-teller's prophecy. *One of you will die . . .* He wished they'd got help sooner. Finally the doctor suggested they leave him to work in peace; he lit more lamps and set out bottles on the workbench.

'Topaz,' Yoyo said softly, 'let me stay with him.

You two need to get to the island. Time is running out.'

Topaz was about to protest, but she knew that Yoyo was right. Someone had to remain, and as she knew the language, she was better able to look after Nathan.

'I promise to take good care of him,' Yoyo said, squeezing Topaz's hand. The other girl nodded and blinked away a tear. Suddenly, amazingly, Topaz hugged her old adversary.

'We'll leave the *Thunder* where she is,' Topaz told her. 'She'll be noticed on the island. We'll use the rowing boat, with Dr Chatterju's outboard motor. And before we leave, we'll send a Meslith to the commander.' She kissed Nathan on his forehead, whispered something in his ear and left the room.

Jake looked at his friend with a lump in his throat. 'Good luck, old boy,' he said, mimicking Nathan's Charleston drawl. He took out the makeshift map from the Lazuli Serpent and gave it to Yoyo. 'If we don't come back, you know where to find us,' he said with an uncertain smile.

Suddenly Yoyo threw her arms around him. 'I'll miss you so much,' she declared passionately.

Jake was taken aback. 'W-w-well, please be careful,' he stammered, peeling himself away before hurrying after Topaz.

Yoyo went to the door and watched them leave. She suddenly felt as if she might be sick.

Jake and Topaz ran back to the *Thunder*. Topaz quickly typed out the Meslith to Commander Goethe as Jake untied the rowing boat and lowered it into the water, then got out the casket containing Chatterju's outboard motor.

Topaz locked up the Meslith machine, collected some weapons together – the arrow gun that Chatterju had given them, a regular crossbow, along with swords and daggers – and piled them into a sack. She grabbed some bread, cheese and a bottle of ginger ale for the journey.

'What about the bazooka?' Jake asked. 'Should we take that?'

Topaz attempted to lift it. 'It weighs more than I do,' she said, giving up. 'It would probably sink us!'

She covered it with some blankets, and she and Jake climbed down the ladder into the boat. Taking an oar each, they set off, away from the lights of Zhanjiang. Once they were clear of the harbour,

Jake took out the motor, remembering how the rudder, engine and propeller were all connected in one ingenious mechanism, positioned it over the stern and clamped it in place. He yanked the cord to fire it up; it gave a little chug and was silent again. After a few more attempts, it finally engaged. He took hold of the rudder, put it in gear and they took off across the dark sea.

Night was not far off.

20 The Staircase under the Sea

They followed the map, using the stars to navigate their way due south, the tropical breeze rustling their hair. The faint line of white behind them marked their course across the smooth sea. It was warm and still, and the moon soon rose over the horizon, turning the ocean ultramarine; as rich as lazuli itself. Jake glanced at Topaz. She was quiet, her eyes steely, concentrating on the sea ahead. The words they'd had in the golden pagoda had still not been discussed. But for Jake, it didn't matter; he was happy to be alone with her.

He felt a stirring in his heart. Suddenly he thought of his life in London before meeting the History Keepers: the drudgery of school; the grey winters and aimless summers. He wondered what he would be doing now (whenever *now* was) . . .

Poring over algebra or writing an essay on urban sprawl?

Instead, here he was in Ming dynasty China, voyaging across a tropical sea, an incredible girl at his side: two adventurers from different eras of history on a mission together – a crucial assignment to protect the fabric of the past. Certainly there was danger to come, but excitement too.

'Jake,' Topaz said softly, 'there is something I need to tell you.' He braced himself, certain that she was going to talk about their argument. But: 'It's about Philip – his whereabouts.'

Jake's stomach flipped. 'What about him?'

'Well over a year ago, the commander received a Meslith from an unknown sender. She suspected it was from Philip.'

Jake scrutinized Topaz's indigo eyes. 'What did it say?'

'There were no words. It consisted of just four numbers. The commander believed they were longitude co-ordinates. As you know, when someone is describing a precise place in history, they write numbers of longitude, latitude and date – in that order. The Meslith may have been a call for help.'

Silence; just the whine of the outboard motor. Jake felt a stab of betrayal. 'And no one thought to tell me?'

'There was no proof; and no one wanted to give you false hope.'

'But the co-ordinates . . . they were incomplete? That's what you're trying to say?'

Topaz held up the map of the South China Sea. 'You see the longitude of the island we are travelling to . . . it's exactly the same.'

'So Philip might be there?' Jake said.

'*C'est possible.*' She reached out to touch his hand. 'Though of course, you have to prepare yourself for . . . the *possibility* that—' She didn't need to finish the sentence.

'Could I have a drink, please?'

Topaz opened the flask of ginger ale and passed it to him. He drank and gave it back. Then they shared out the food and ate in silence.

Gradually they drew near to a group of islands. Topaz examined them, comparing them to the marks on the map. 'We're getting close,' she said, standing to get a proper look. 'It's the furthest one.'

Finally Jake cut the engine and they took up their oars once more. He had never seen the sea so calm.

'There,' he said, turning to catch a glimpse of their destination for the first time. 'Xi's island . . .'

They both stopped rowing. The island reared up out of the sea, sharp and pointed, the peak slightly crooked, like a witch's hat. With the moon behind it, it looked as dark as charcoal. Beyond was nothing but endless sea.

'It's like Point Zero,' Topaz said. 'Or rather, like its evil cousin.' It looked eerie and uninviting.

They continued rowing and then stopped again a couple of hundred yards from the island. 'Let's leave the boat there,' Topaz said, pointing to a stack of rocks that jutted out of the sea. 'We'll have to swim the rest – if we don't want to be seen. Agreed?'

Jake nodded, and managed to secure the rope around a finger of stone. They took off their shoes and packed them, along with their weapons, into a sack, which Jake slung over his shoulder; then they lowered themselves into the water. It was as warm as a bath.

They swam towards the island. There was no sign of life – no hint of green; just facets of rock twisting up to the lopsided peak. Jake wondered if he had somehow misunderstood the map on the Lazuli Serpent, but he didn't say anything.

Suddenly the sea, hitherto so calm, grew choppy. Jake choked on a mouthful of salty water.

'Something's coming,' Topaz said, feeling the vibration in the water. They both turned, but the horizon behind them was clear. Still the waves built up, crashing against the rocky shore ahead.

Then they saw it: a shape rising out of the sea – a length of glistening grey metal.

Jake recognized it immediately. 'It's Xi's submarine,' he shouted to Topaz, who was a little way ahead. He had last seen it disappearing below the Thames by London Bridge. It surfaced, heading towards them on a direct collision course. 'Swim!' he shouted.

They tried to get out of its path, but suddenly, from the island, they heard a deep rasp of metal: a secret entrance appeared in the sheer wall of mountain in front of them; a pair of stone doors creaked open to reveal a mammoth cavity. A soft light from within illuminated the curved hull of the submarine. Jake swam furiously, but it struck him a glancing blow as it swept past, and he sank beneath the water.

Dizzy and spluttering, he swam back to the surface. Topaz was calling, but he couldn't hear what she was saying. Then he realized that she was pointing to the great doors – they were closing. Jake quickly swam through the opening after her. The metal hinges – hidden behind the façade of rock – groaned and creaked as the doors edged together. Jake swam faster, and felt them brush against him, about to cut him in two; but Topaz yanked him through just before they snapped shut.

They both took a gulp of air and slipped underwater. Using the harbour walls to guide them, they felt their way along, then surfaced for a quick peek. They were in a dimly lit cavern that rose to a sharp point high above their heads.

Further along, Xi's submarine was drawing towards a gantry. They saw that its shining steel plates were emblazoned with the symbol of the blood-red octopus. With a clang of metal, a large hatch opened and figures emerged – four soldiers, who lined up along the gantry. They stood to attention, swaying, clearly ill, their eyes bloodshot; they looked like Nathan had. One of them could barely stand.

Next came Madame Fang; *she* looked more energetic than ever in her silver breastplate; her grey hair was pulled up in a tight bun, her face imperious, but she bowed as the last figure emerged.

Although he could not see his face, Jake knew it was Xi. He wore full armour fashioned from linked bronze plates; huge gold epaulettes stood out from his shoulders. A tail of golden hair cascaded down from his pointed bronze helmet, which he removed with his chainmail gloves to inspect the harbour; his two good eyes swept one way, his third lingering another. His rouged face no longer looked impish and playful; his expression was stony. He strode along the gantry, armour rattling, and disappeared through an archway, lit up by the glow they had seen from outside. As Fang followed, one of the soldiers fell to his knees and vomited; she turned and shouted at the others, who pulled him to his feet and hurried after her. The little harbour was deserted once again.

Jake looked back at the double doors through which they had entered; he wondered if they should escape this place now, before it was too late. But he knew that turning back was not an option. If Philip was there somewhere, that was enough reason to go on.

'All right?' Topaz asked him.

He nodded. 'Let's go.'

They levered themselves out of the water and headed through the archway; here a stairwell led down, deep into the earth. Jake's ears popped as they descended, gas lamps lighting their way. After two flights, they came to a landing. The walls were decorated with panoramas of epic scenes from Chinese history. There were armies crossing rivers, climbing mountains and cutting down forests. In each, a leader in full imperial dress led his troops.

'It's Qin Shi Huang, the first emperor,' Topaz gasped. 'Look at the dates.' She pointed to numerals in the corner of each panel. '211 BC. That was a year before he died.'

'That's the emperor who had the army of stone soldiers buried with him, isn't it? The first owner of the Lazuli Serpent?' Jake asked.

But Topaz had seen something else. '*Ce – ce n'est pas possible*,' she stammered. She was pointing to the end of the landing, where another, much grander flight of steps dropped in a succession of curving tiers.

'It goes right under the sea . . .' Jake said in amazement. It was the grandest staircase he had ever seen; diamond-shaped windows let in a dim, bluish light. He went down a few steps to look through one, and saw, far below, on the sea bed . . . a palace.

It was night-time now, but the huge building was floodlit, and there was a soft glow coming from its many windows. Jake could see the wall of the stone staircase, which spiralled round the base of the mountain. The palace itself was both stately and forbidding; it was built in the oriental tradition, with tiers of curving roofs. Other small buildings were linked by tunnels along the sea floor. There were even marine gardens of giant seaweeds. Most striking of all, the entire building had a blue hue, as if its millions of tiles were made of lapis.

Suddenly Jake realized what it was: 'The Lazuli Serpent . . .' he said. 'This is it. On a huge scale.'

Topaz let out a sigh of wonder.

Since he had first met the History Keepers, Jake had come across a number of secret staircases. On his first encounter in London, he had wound his way down below the Monument. There had been the one concealed under Prince Zeldt's laboratory in Venice; another below the Forum in ancient Rome. But this, he thought, was the most extraordinary by far.

Halfway down, ahead of them, they saw a soldier in ancient armour; then, as they followed the curve of the staircase, another, and another . . . They stopped and drew their weapons.

'The guards from before?' Jake whispered.

Topaz shook her head. 'I think they're made of stone.' She peered round the corner; the figures remained utterly still. Finally she primed her crossbow gun and loosed an arrow. It struck the first soldier with a clang, before clattering to the floor.

She and Jake went to investigate. There were six amazingly lifelike warriors, bearing real weapons. Their poses were realistic too, as if they were chatting to each other, while keeping their eyes on intruders.

The pair edged round them and continued down. The pressure in their ears grew painful as they descended, and they had to swallow repeatedly to clear them.

Finally, at the foot of the stairs, they came to a vaulted hallway lined with doors – all shut but for the huge central portal. This led into a large room. As Jake and Topaz peered in, they saw, not far from the doorway, four dead bodies lying on the floor – the guards from the submarine.

Jake didn't notice at first – it was gloomy and they were piled on top of each other – but the men had had their heads removed.

21 THE END OF SEAS

They froze, staring at the decapitated corpses in horror. Jake looked back up the curving stairwell, and wondered again if they should leave now . . .

Topaz peered round the doorway. 'More statues – dozens of them.' Holding her arrow gun in one hand, she unsheathed her sword with the other and stepped inside. Jake armed himself too and followed.

'What is this place?' he murmured.

It was a high-ceilinged, circular chamber, full of lifelike stone figures, their glass eyes glinting. One group stood together on a raised tier, as if gossiping, eyes trained on a point in the centre. On the other side of the room, twelve serious-looking men sat at a long table, all gazing ahead.

Between the two groups, on a dais, sat a man who was more finely dressed than all the rest. He too looked down sternly at the same central point of the chamber. A series of frescoes decorated the walls.

'It's a court,' Topaz said. 'A law court.' She pointed to the various groups of people. 'Spectators, jury, judge. In one of Yoyo's books it said that in Chinese mythology, when someone dies, they are tried in the *hell court*. If their sins cannot be for-given, they are punished.' She indicated the frescoes on either side of the judge. In one, the dead were being beheaded; in another, they were being forced to climb trees made of knives that sliced into their hands and feet.

Speechless, Jake tiptoed around the space. He looked up into the granite face of the judge, then crept past the spectators. The statues were incredibly lifelike: one old man had his ear cocked as he strained to hear; the young girl next to him had her mouth open in a slight smile; the stout woman behind her looked frightened, and the man next to her had a cruel sneer. Further along, another man had his hands over his face. There was some-thing familiar about his golden epaulettes, Jake thought.

Then the statue lowered its arms and let out a shrieking laugh.

Xi Xiang!

Without pausing to think, Jake raised his crossbow and fired. Xi ducked and the arrow struck the wall. On his hands and knees, Xi raced between the stone figures; Topaz swung round and discharged the remainder of the arrows from her gun, but her missiles merely pinged off the statues.

Unsure what was in store for them, she and Jake turned and ran, but their exit was blocked by a pale, bare-chested giant of a man, armed with blood-stained machetes. As they careered the other way, a net came down from the ceiling; it was pulled tight, sweeping them off their feet so that they cracked their skulls on the marble floor. They were winched up off the ground, caught like wild beasts. With their arms pinned to their sides, they couldn't raise their weapons to defend themselves.

Xi snatched one of the huge man's machetes and thrust it through the net, catching Jake under the jaw. Fresh blood dripped from the blade. 'Take their weapons,' he ordered.

The man stepped forward, cut a hole in the net and reached inside. Jake shrank away from his foetid breath. All their weapons were collected up – except for one broken arrowhead that Jake had managed to conceal in his palm.

Suddenly, behind the judge's dais, Jake caught sight of Madame Fang. She stood there waiting while Xi reapplied his lipstick. Jake glared at him, teeth clenched, nose snarling.

'So,' Xi said finally, 'welcome to our great first emperor's secret palace. If anyone was in any doubt that the Chinese were the cleverest people in history, they need only come here.' He swept his hand around the room. 'It's eighteen hundred years old and built under the sea – and it still survives, as if it went up only yesterday!' He came closer and grinned at Topaz. 'You're quite clever, aren't you? Cleverer than that halfwit next to you. Did you know that Qin had built this palace?' Topaz made no reply. 'Half a million people were washed away during its construction; some exploded from the pressure, eyes popping out . . . such a pleasure to watch. But what do half a million slaves matter, when this splendour is the result?'

Jake struggled uselessly against the ropes.

'I am in awe of the great Qin,' Xi carried on. 'I still honour his traditions.' He nodded to the decapitated guards. 'Mere mortals aren't allowed in – though these four were kind enough to convey me here. No, no, what if they were to speak of its location . . . ? We're a compact group here: Nanny, myself – and our trusty eunuch, of course.' Xi patted the giant's arm fondly as he whispered to his captives, 'He's my executioner, but don't expect much in the way of conversation – I had his tongue removed.' He cackled again. 'Yes, just us three. And ten thousand statues, of course.'

Xi sliced his sword through the rope that held them aloft and they crashed to the floor.

'Bring them . . .' Xi strode off towards another set of doors, throwing them open. Madame Fang followed him into a wide, stately corridor.

The eunuch carelessly dragged Jake and Topaz across the floor in their wake, heads and limbs bumping into walls and doorways as they went. As they proceeded, lights came on as if by magic in an endless series of shell-shaped sconces. Jake scanned every inch of space, looking for clues as to where Philip might be.

They passed hundreds more statues – an entire imperial court. Stone soldiers guarded every entrance; pages, squires and attendants went about their duties, frozen in time. They passed a room where the empress and her ladies-in-waiting were being dressed by their maids; in another a motionless dance was taking place.

At last they came to a doorway from where steps led down into the largest chamber yet. Xi waited at the foot of them. 'Qin built this palace to control the seas, just as he controlled the land,' he purred, running his tongue around his mouth. 'But I'm going to do it *so* much better.'

Jake and Topaz were kicked down the stairs, *thump, thump, thump*, and Fang closed the door behind them.

'Where is he? Where's my little one?' Xi rushed over to an enormous glass tank in the middle of the room and took out an octopus. He put it around his neck like a scarf, and the tentacles clamped onto his face. 'You missed me, didn't you? And your sister? Next time I'll bring her back from London, I promise. Careful of Daddy's make-up,' he said as the octopus's suckers brushed over his lips. He held it and kissed it on its beaky mouth, then put it back in the tank. He turned to his prisoners. 'Let's make things a little more comfortable,' he said, producing a knife and ripping open the net so that Jake and

Topaz spilled out onto the floor. 'If you try and escape, fish will eat you – it's as simple as that.' He clapped his hands in delight and did a pirouette. 'So what do you think of the place?' When they made no response, Xi kicked Jake hard in the stomach. 'Get up, History Keeper,' he sneered.

Eyes blazing, Jake got to his feet, still clutching the arrowhead. Topaz stood up next to him, while the eunuch watched over them, a machete in each hand.

Looking around, they realized that they were in Xi Xiang's war room. In front of them, four colossal arched windows looked out across the dark sea bed. Along one wall, from floor to ceiling, there was an ancient mirror framed by a frieze of snaking sea creatures. In front of this, a row of empty cages fixed to the floor looked like something from a medieval torture chamber.

The tank that housed the octopus was the size of a small swimming pool. Stone islands shaped like the continents – Asia, Africa, Europe, the Americas – rose clear of the water in the centre. It was a map of the world. Hundreds of minuscule galleons bobbed on the surface, scale models of ships complete with masts, sails and rigging. Some had fallen onto the floor and been flattened underfoot.

Between the pool and the four windows stood another throne, this one so encrusted with jewels it looked like a big toy. Next to it there was a control panel, fitted with various buttons and levers. Jake started when he saw the golden revolver lying casually beside it: Philip's other gun – exactly as depicted in his drawing, with its curving dragon shape and long, slender barrel.

'Shall we light up the sea?' Xi said, pulling one of the levers on the control panel. More floodlights, much brighter ones, began to illuminate the ocean floor, coming on one after another, stretching for miles into the distance and bringing the underwater world to life. It was rich with vivid colours of emerald, coral and amethyst, and alive with swirling schools of fish.

'Ingenious, isn't it? Light and power provided by natural gas from the sea. In a moment, Nanny is going to give us a little show out there. It concerns one of these,' he said, pointing to the model ships in the pool.

Xi continued his tour of the room. 'And that, behind you, is Qin's looking glass. The world has no idea that the mirror was his invention too – the

324

vulgar Romans always laid claim to it. Look at it!'
He took Jake by the shoulders and propelled him
towards it, whispering in his ear, 'They say that
when you look into it, you can see your past.' He
pushed Jake's face into the glass. 'What can you see,
you uncouth boy? Can you see your trivial life? The
tribulations of your sad story?' The third eye
blinked slowly at Jake and his voice grew quieter
still, his tongue darting like a lizard's between his
teeth. '*Can you see your brother?*'

Jake lashed out at Xi's neck with the arrowhead.
Xi cried out as he lunged again, this time aiming for
his deformed eye. Xi swung round and kicked Jake
hard between the legs, while the giant grabbed him
around the neck with his fat white fingers and
Madame Fang took hold of Topaz. Xi kicked the
boy over and over again.

'Cage them!' he spat, throwing off his armoured
tunic and inspecting his wound. Jake and Topaz
were forced into separate cages.

'Nanny, it's time,' Xi said, clicking his fingers
at her.

Jake's heart pounded as he braced himself for the
worst, but Fang merely nodded, climbed the stairs,
unlocked the door and left. Xi returned to the pool,

scooped up his octopus and sat on his throne, sulking as his pet stroked his face with its tentacles. Gradually he grew calmer and sank down into his seat.

Fifteen minutes passed as he gazed out at the underwater view; then he leaned forward. 'Here she is,' he said.

The windows darkened as a vast shape approached, blocking the view entirely. At first Jake couldn't make it out, but then he realized what it was: a giant squid. The egg-shaped body glowed with light, its eight limbs undulating as it moved. Jake shook his head. How could Xi control such a thing? It defied all logic. Then he saw that the beast was man-made, forged in steel. Its tentacles were lengths of jointed metal, attached to a glass cockpit in the centre.

'Isn't Nanny the cleverest girl on earth!' Xi shrieked excitedly, jumping up and waving at the driver in control of the beast. His pet octopus gestured with its tentacles in agreement. The mechanical squid drew closer until its outline filled all four windows. Fang's shadow nodded back at her commander, then guided the machine out to sea again. It motored south towards the deep part of the ocean.

'Lower the lights,' Xi ordered, and the mute giant turned a dial until the lanterns around the room grew dim.

Now the underwater vista came into sharper focus. In the distance they saw the hull of a ship bound for China. Gradually, Fang ascended towards the surface to intercept it.

Jake and Topaz watched as the two shapes came together, the squid's tentacles enveloping the vessel. For a while the two moved as one, before they separated again, the destroyer's tentacles folding up as it came away.

The ship floundered on, slowly sinking, turning onto its side as it went. Its three sails spread out, ghostlike, as they were dragged underwater. Tiny shapes flowed out of the sinking vessel, and Jake suddenly realized that these were people. The destruction of the ship looked unreal, graceful almost, but he could imagine the cries of the sailors as they were sucked down into the vortex. As the ship hit the sea bed, the hull split silently in two. The mechanical squid lingered for a while, hovering above its conquest, before turning and gliding back towards the palace.

Topaz, who had been watching in horror, started

mumbling curses, rattling her cage in fury. '*Vous êtes le diable. Vous allez souffrir d'une mort inimaginable.*'

Xi wasn't listening. He clapped his thin hands in joy and did a waltz around the room with his octopus. Then he went to the window, giggling and talking to himself as he watched his monster return.

As it approached, Jake saw that there was a corpse skewered on one of its tentacles: a sailor from the ship, mouth wide open, eyes frozen.

The beast carried on towards a docking bay at the side of the palace, and a few minutes later there was a distant clanking of metal. After another pause, footsteps approached, and Fang stepped into the room.

Xi got down on his knees and kissed her hand. 'No one murders like Nanny does!'

He went over to the pool, set his pet down in the South Pacific and waggled his finger over the fleet of miniature ships, looking for one in particular. Finally he found it and threw it on the floor, stamping it underfoot. It scrunched like a beetle and he shrieked with laughter.

Jake looked around at the other flattened maquettes – at least ten of them – and realized they must *all* be ships that Xi had sunk. This was horrific enough, but a hundred more craft remained bobbing in the pool.

Xi's master plan was now clear: he had an underwater palace beneath the busiest trade routes the world had ever known. In this region of the South China Sea, in the seventeenth century, vessels crisscrossed from Europe to Asia and from Asia to the New World and back again in an endless loop; vessels from Britain, Holland, Spain, Arabia, Indonesia, India, Japan, Brazil and hundreds more countries . . . The fortunes of the entire world, present and future, were tied up in this ceaseless movement.

Topaz shook her head. 'You're going to destroy all those?' she said, looking at the pool. '*C'est ça?*'

Xi giggled. 'I would happily sink every last one – but I don't think it'll be necessary.' His lips tightened and his good eyes narrowed as the third one opened wide. He spoke in a whisper. 'Very soon everyone will start doing our job for us – by destroying each other. And I have a feeling that the catalyst will be this ship here . . .'

He turned back to the pool and selected another model; one of the largest. Even in miniature, Jake recognized its distinct yellow sails: it was the

Chinese emperor's flagship, which they had seen in
Canton.

'Tomorrow morning at eight a.m., the imperial
fleet sets off on its vulgar tour of neighbouring
lands, showing off their big ships,' Xi added. 'But
their voyage is already doomed. The sovereign's
favourite son will perish, along with all the royal
court.' He paused to appreciate his cleverness. 'A
letter – composed by me, of course, but apparently
written and signed by all the European trading
nations – will arrive in Peking, claiming responsi-
bility in retaliation for their own losses. War will
break out – world war, east versus west.' Again he
lowered his voice to a whisper. 'It will be the *end of
seas*. The end of everything.'

Now Jake and Topaz had put all the pieces of the
puzzle together: the destruction of the galleons in
London and Amsterdam; the commission to build
warships in China – followed by a mammoth battle
waged by the most powerful factions of the day.
They knew enough history to understand that it
would result not just in terrible loss of life and the
cessation of trade; it would also stop the exchange of
ideas. Kingdoms would become isolated, paranoid.
Progress would stall.

Jake suddenly remembered the mural of the Lazuli Serpent in London: an ancient tide stone at the bottom of the sea, a crystal so dreadful that it could destroy the world.

'Anyway' – Xi clapped his hands and turned back to his prisoners – 'that's enough talking. Let's get you two eaten, shall we?' He skipped over to the control panel and pushed a button. A trapdoor beneath Topaz flipped open and she let out a little gasp as she dropped through the hole.

'Noooo!' Jake cried. Topaz called back, but her voice grew more distant as she was carried away. There was the sound of splashing, followed by a far-off scream.

'No palace would be complete without a maze,' Xi tittered, 'and a *water* maze is even more thrilling. Brace yourselves for a truly gory drama.'

He pushed another button and the floor gave way beneath Jake, but he clung onto the bars, his feet dangling. Below him, he could see nothing but darkness.

'Really?' Xi said, coming over as Jake's hands slipped. 'That's *so* touching; he doesn't want to leave us. We understand: we *are* rather fun, aren't we? But we're busy now, Jake Djones . . . *so* much to do.

Nanny will be setting off again in no time, and she abhors killing on an empty stomach.' Still smiling, he kicked Jake's whitened knuckles. 'Say goodbye,' he said, nodding at Jake's reflection in the mirror, then jabbed his heel hard into Jake's fingers. There was a nasty crack, but still he clung on, every sinew stretching.

Xi stopped smiling. 'You're being stupid now. Don't you need to go and find your friend?' He was about to kick out again – but Jake took a deep breath, let go of the bars and fell into the void.

22 Water Torture

He plunged into darkness. Soon his feet hit a sloping wall. He slid down the slimy stone, then plummeted through the air, catching a glimpse of a cavernous space before he finally struck water – hard.

It was hot – he swallowed a mouthful – and he felt creatures moving around him: fish slipping through his shirt and his trousers, biting with sharp little teeth. He shot up, breaking the surface, hearing himself scream. He tried to reach a ledge above him, but it was too high. He felt a sharp pain in his heel and looked down to see a long brown fish like a pike. Jake launched himself upwards again, and this time he caught hold of the ledge and pulled himself up onto a rocky shelf.

He stood there panting, his bites stinging, and

looked around, eyes slowly growing accustomed to the gloom. He was at the intersection of three cavernous tunnels that led in different directions, rising or falling and twisting and turning. Spread out along them were many more pools, all different sizes and shapes. Water dripped everywhere.

'Topaz!' he cried out. 'Topaz, can you hear me?' His voice echoed into distant, unseen spaces. This hell he was in, this *maze*, as Xi had called it, seemed to be as large as the palace itself. 'Topaz!' he called again.

Finally a reply came, so far away that he could barely hear it: 'Jake?' He tried to work out which passage it was coming from. 'Jake . . . I'm trapped.'

'I'm going to try and find you,' he shouted back, selecting the widest of the three tunnels. He edged round the side of another pool that disappeared into a chamber beyond. This one was stuffed with fat, round fish covered in sharp spikes. Sensing his presence, one of them suddenly puffed up to its full size.

Jake called out to Topaz again, to check that he was going the right way. 'Here . . .' There was a tremble in her voice. He quickened his pace, vaulting up and down steps, over the ponds if he could, but wading or swimming through them where he had no choice. He quickly became used to the many sharp-toothed creatures.

He came to another intersection of three tunnels and called out again. Topaz's voice echoed back to him, closer now, as if she was in a deep chamber. Jake took a passage that led directly to a wide pool that blocked his path completely. On the steps leading down into it sprawled a human skeleton, one hand reaching out. The upper half was intact – but everything from the knees down was missing.

Jake looked into the pool. It was perfectly still; nothing stirred. But was it safe to go in?

He picked up the thigh-bone of the skeleton and carefully poked it into the water. The surface bubbled and seethed as a school of plump little fishes flocked around, trying to bite it. Jake quickly pulled it out, but a couple of fish were still clinging on. He shook them free, their jaws still snapping ferociously. *Piranhas* . . . Jake had seen them before, and he knew that they worked as a pack, stripping flesh from anything that lived. He flicked them back into the water. Realizing that it might be a useful weapon, he kept hold of the thigh-bone, wielding it like a sword. 'Better than nothing,' he said to himself, taking the largest of the arm bones as well, and stuffing them both into his belt.

Suddenly there was a rumble from above. Jake looked up and saw one of the decapitated guards dropping down a narrow chute and crashing into the pool. Another corpse followed soon after; then the third and fourth. As the fish set upon them, making the water boil, four heads followed, one gliding by with its eyes fixed on Jake. In they dropped, *plop, plop, plop, plop.*

He turned, ran back to the intersection and saw that the next passage twisted round in a similar direction to the first. He went along it, calling again to Topaz. 'Are you still there?'

'Not going anywhere,' her voice came back; but then she let out a little scream.

'What happened?'

'There are jellyfish,' she replied. 'I'm trying to keep away.'

'Jellyfish,' Jake sighed to himself. 'Of course there are.' He followed the path up and down steps, across more pools – until he came to a dead end. He thumped the wall in anger.

'Topaz?'

'I think you're closer now,' her reply came.

Jake swung round. It seemed like she was directly beneath him. 'Say something again . . .'

'If I'd known there was going to be swimming, I would have packed my bathing suit,' she joked through her terror.

To one side, a pool led under the wall, with just a few inches of space above it. Her voice was carrying through this slither of air from the other side. There was nothing for it: Jake tested the water with the thigh-bone and, finding no piranhas or other predators, took a deep breath and slipped in.

He found that he could touch the bottom with his toes while keeping his mouth just above the water level. He waded forward into the darkness, heading for a sliver of light at the far end. He was halfway along when the surface rippled and something gently skimmed his waist. He froze, gripping the thigh-bone tightly. Whatever it was, it was thick and long. Jake edged forward a little, and this time it slid between his legs and curled round the back of his knee. This was no eel, snapping aimlessly; this was a sea snake, a python.

'Jake? Are you still there?' Topaz's voice sounded urgent.

He dared not answer, or even move. The snake coiled round, gently breaking the surface, then retreated. Jake knew that snakes were more frightened of people than the other way round (except, of course, for Prince Zeldt's black mambas), so he decided to carry on.

He was a yard from the light at the end of the pool when there was another disturbance. This time, the snake encircled his chest and back, tightening its grip. The effect was dreadful, instantaneous: the air was pushed out of Jake's lungs. He tried to thump the creature with the femur, but it had no effect. Its neck was against his ribcage, and he dropped his makeshift weapon, grabbed the snake in both hands and squeezed. It simply coiled tighter, its grip like a vice, making the blood thump in his head.

Jake tried in vain to take a breath. Then a fragment of memory came back to him: *Constrictors do not have poisonous fangs – you can open their jaws and break them.* Jake slid his hands along the scaly head, felt for the mouth and tried to prise it open. At first it didn't budge, but desperation made him strong. He edged it apart, slipping his fingers between the jaws. Now it fought back, trying to close its mouth while thrashing to and fro with the end of its tail. Jake kept up the pressure, opening the jaw wider and wider, but the python continued to crush him.

He swore and yanked harder still; he heard the jaw bones snap, and suddenly the beast's grip loosened and it dropped away, dead. He reached down and retrieved the thigh-bone, then pulled himself out of the pool, his hands shaking from the ordeal. He found himself at the far end of the passageway that had been blocked by the piranhas.

'I'm coming,' he panted to Topaz. 'Where are you?'

'Here.'

Jake stopped and turned round. In the wall behind him was a rectangular hole, and he looked through it. Below him was a square well, just three yards wide, but extending deep into the ground. At the bottom, huddled in a corner in the semi-darkness, Topaz was standing shoulder-deep in water.

'How did you get down there?' Jake asked, trying to make light of things.

'Just thought I'd drop in . . .' She indicated a chute that curved up into darkness – all the way to

Xi's war room. Then, suddenly, she exclaimed: 'They're coming back.' Two little umbrellas of ghostly light drifted towards her, trailing ragged tentacles. 'Cubozoa. Box jellyfish,' she said. 'They can kill you with one sting. You have to find some way to pull me out. Probably a stupid question, but have you come across any rope in your travels?'

Jake turned round, edged himself through the hole and dropped down into the water.

'What are you doing?' Topaz cried.

'Helping you.' She shook her head, on the verge of tears. 'I'll give you a hand up. If I can get you on my shoulders, you can reach the opening.'

'But how will you get out?'

'It won't be a problem. Besides, we don't want to stay in here too long,' Jake jested, masking his profound terror. 'As Nathan would be the first to point out, too much water's bad for the skin.'

'Jake, careful!' Tendrils from one of the jellyfish were sidling back towards them.

'I have weapons . . .' Jake held up the two bones. 'Can we kill them with these?'

'I don't know. Hitting them might make things worse. Best to lift them out of the water until they suffocate – or maybe you could pass them through that hole there.'

Jake turned to see the tiny aperture in the rock, level with his head. 'You're a genius, Miss St Honoré,' he said. Using the longer bone, he pushed the nearest jellyfish away. Then, staying clear of the long tentacles, he slipped the end of the femur under its body and raised it up. Its body was no larger than an orange, and he suddenly noticed its eyes. 'Can they see?'

'They're the only ones of their species that have true eyes.'

Carefully he squeezed the fish through the opening. It dropped down, and there was a splash on the other side. He did the same with its mate, then turned back to Topaz. 'Alone at last,' he said with a smile.

Topaz's lip was trembling. She shook her head before speaking. 'Why do you always save me?'

'What?'

'Time after time, you come and save me. After everything I've done.'

'You mean . . . our argument? I wondered when you'd mention that. I shouldn't have said what I did—'

341

'No! *Il faut que tu ne me parles plus!* You should never speak to me again. I'm sorry, Jake, so sorry.' She wiped her eyes and nose. 'And with Yoyo too. I've been a monster to her . . .'

'Well, Yoyo can give as good as she gets—'

'*J'étais envieux.* I was jealous. So jealous. She was getting all your attention.'

'Jealous of Yoyo?'

'You said before that you weren't a *he-man* like Lucius . . . Jake, you are braver than any person I have met. And I . . .' She shook her head. 'And I – it's not much good me telling you here, in this dungeon below the ocean, where we'll probably die – *mais tu sais que je t'adore*, Jake.'

There was silence. He blinked. *I adore you, Jake.* That's what Topaz had just said. They both stood there, not moving, each in one corner of the well.

There came a hollow click from above, followed by the sound of grinding stone. Jake and Topaz looked up. The ceiling of the well was slowly heading towards them. As it came down, it began to block the doorway at the top.

'We have to get out of here, *now!*' Jake exclaimed. He waded over to Topaz. 'Climb on my shoulders.'

'Jake, this won't work.'

'Do it! Quickly!'

He gave her a leg up and she jumped and twisted onto his shoulders. Then, steadying herself against the wall, she got to her feet.

'Careful,' he said, gently hoisting her.

Topaz felt her way up the wall until she found the edge of the opening. From here, she could pull herself out – though the ceiling had already half blocked their escape.

'What are you waiting for?' Jake thundered. 'Go!'

'How will *you* get out?'

'You can lift me – reach down and pull me up.'

Topaz shook her head. She knew it was impossible.

'Go!' Jake shouted. 'It's an order.'

Topaz let go of the ledge and jumped back into the water. 'I'm in command, remember?'

'I'm not going to tell you again. Climb back up and get out of here!'

'*Non*, Jake Djones! *Jamais*. I'm staying. We find another way out . . . or we die together.'

The ceiling edged its way down. Soon, there was only a sliver of a gap left; then it was gone. They were locked in a box. A stone box at the bottom of the sea. They would drown, suffocate or be crushed to death – it was hard to know which would come first.

'Give me one of those bones,' Topaz said. Jake handed over the largest, and she started bashing away at the hole through which Jake had thrown the jellyfish. He started to help her, and the edges crumbled a little, but the wall was a foot thick.

The roof continued to descend, inching its way towards them. They were out of time . . .

Then Jake had a flash of inspiration. He took hold of the bones and wedged them in the opening. As the ceiling came down towards them, it stopped. The mechanism whirred as it tried to push on, and the bones creaked under the strain.

Jake and Topaz looked at each other. They had bought some time, but they were still trapped. Jake suddenly thought of the memorial stone in the shadow of the willow tree on the Mont St Michel – the black marble statue of the hourglass. He saw his name freshly carved on it, next to Topaz's. He saw mourners standing before it, his parents and Aunt Rose at the front, tears streaming.

'Do you remember when we first met?' he asked Topaz. 'Underneath the Monument, on the day of the storm. I'd never seen weather like it in London. It was a hurricane. You came from the British

Museum and started telling me about Tutankhamun, talking like you'd known me all my life . . .' He took a deep breath. 'But actually, that moment was the *start* of my life. I would rather die here with you now than live until I was ninety and never have met you.'

There was a splintering sound as the femur shattered. The ceiling shunted down, and snapped the arm-bone in two; the slab of stone came nearer.

Jake and Topaz held onto each other. Soon the gap was so small, they had to angle their heads back to breathe. Then their chins were below the waterline. There was just an inch left, enough space for their noses and mouths – when the ceiling suddenly stopped. For a moment they took long, trembling breaths.

Miraculously, the slab of stone began to rise, and they watched in amazement as the opening appeared again. A pair of sturdy boots was standing in it. They belonged to a tall, slim figure in shining battle armour – man or woman, it was impossible to tell – armed with two rapiers and a length of rope and holding a helmet. The fingers were slim and elegant. Long grey hair came into view, swept across one shoulder.

Then the face . . .

'C-Commander Goethe,' Jake stammered.

Galliana smiled down at them. 'All in one piece?' she asked, and threw down the rope.

Jake and Topaz looked at each other, unable to stop smiling. It felt like a dream. 'You first, this time,' Topaz said.

Jake took hold of the end, and climbed up the wall. 'Good evening, Commander,' he said, once they were face to face. 'Well timed.' Even now, having been saved from certain death, Jake was still a little shy of her. The commander tossed back the rope for Topaz and they pulled her up together.

'Here . . .' Galliana took out a flask and passed it over. They drank greedily. *Fresh water.*

'How did you get here?' Topaz asked. It was extraordinary to see the commander away from Point Zero, let alone here, in China, in an undersea palace.

'Answers later,' Galliana replied. 'First, a question: is Xi planning to attack the imperial Chinese navy? It set off from Macao early this morning, a fleet of at least forty vessels.'

'Yes,' Jake replied. 'They mean to target the

emperor's flagship. They've got a submarine in the form of a giant squid.'

'Then we need to leave; time is against us!' Galliana turned and headed off along the tunnel, Jake and Topaz following behind. She navigated her way confidently through the maze – up steps, down passages, through holes and half-hidden entrances, never once needing to cross one of the diabolical pools.

'In answer to your question,' she called over her shoulder, 'you remember that Xi Xiang once worked for the secret service? He was my lieutenant before Jupitus. We once discovered a map together, in a secret vault in Peking's Forbidden City – of Qin Shi Huang's underwater palace.' She patted a roll of parchment in her belt. 'He kept it, but I made a copy first. Of course, at the time, we had no idea where it was. Well, I found out yesterday, and came immediately. Every chamber and passageway is marked. I'd almost forgotten what it was like to travel back two hundred years.' She smiled at them. 'It feels good.'

At length she came to a corner and stopped, getting her bearings. She passed her hand over the wall and, finding a ridge, gave it a sharp nudge. A hidden doorway opened, and she ushered Jake and Topaz through.

They looked up and saw that they were at the base of a giant shaft, around which a staircase rose, part stone, part patched up with decaying timber.

'This is the *fire exit*, so to speak,' Galliana explained. 'Some of it is rotten, so I advise you to stick closely to the sides.' She led the way upwards, round and round. At one point, Jake looked down and felt his head spin, but Topaz slipped her hand into his and they carried on.

Finally they felt a fresh breeze and heard the soft hiss of the ocean. Moonlight shone through a hole above them. They emerged into a rocky crater. Galliana guided them over the edge, and suddenly they saw the sea, a sheet of dark silver below. They were on the other side of Xi's island. A small ship bobbed just off shore, a Chinese dhow with green sails, and Jake recognized her from the harbour at Point Zero. Her name was inscribed in green letters on the prow: the *Lantern*.

'I picked up some friends on the way,' Galliana told them. 'And some weapons.'

Then a familiar voice drawled, 'I knew they'd be safe. In my experience, fortune-tellers are not to be trusted.' It was Nathan, now dressed in Chinese clothes, with Yoyo at his side. They came over and all four youngsters wrapped their arms around each other.

'Better already?' Jake asked, hardly believing his eyes.

'I woke up, suddenly feeling like my old self again. A little shaky, of course, but that doctor is a miracle worker – and very generous with it. Look how he kitted me out. Taste-wise, he is not lacking.' He showed off his new outfit, an embroidered silk tunic, belted at the waist, baggy trousers, boots and a conical rice hat.

'Great silhouette!' Jake agreed, knowing that his friend had been desperate to dress up since first arriving in Canton. Jake's eyes found Yoyo's. She looked bashful. The last time he had seen her, she had declared passionately: *I'll miss you so much!* 'It's good to see you again, Yoyo,' he found himself saying, rather formally. 'I hope Nathan wasn't too much trouble.'

Galliana interrupted, saving him further embarrassment. 'The plan is this,' she said, pointing at the ship. 'The four of you are to take the *Lantern* and head northeast until you intercept the imperial fleet. You must find the captain and warn him of the danger. They must turn back; failing that, they must prepare their cannons for an attack – *all* their cannons. Is that understood?'

They looked at each other, hesitant. 'Commander, with all due respect,' Nathan began, 'if we try to intercept the imperial fleet, aren't they likely to just blow us out of the water?'

'Well then,' Galliana said brusquely, 'you will have to use your heads. You are History Keepers, remember? Who has the Lazuli Serpent?'

'I do.' Yoyo took it out of her pocket and held it up.

'You may need it as a bargaining tool: they will recognize the stone. So, take your stations, everybody – immediately!' She clapped her hands to emphasize her point.

Nathan led the way, wading through the water and climbing the ladder up onto the deck of the *Lantern.*

Jake hung back, confused. 'Commander, are you to remain here?'

She looked at him, and there was a light in her eye that he hadn't seen before. 'I plan to return once more' – she pointed back to the staircase – 'to do what I should have done many years ago: kill Xi Xiang.' A whole arsenal of weapons was set out beside her, including the golden bazooka from the *Thunder*. Piece by piece, she slung them over her shoulder or fitted them to her belt.

Jake looked round at the *Lantern*, then back to Galliana. 'Please, Commander, let me come with you?'

She shook her head firmly. 'You have all suffered enough. Xi Xiang is my business now.'

'But there is a chance that Philip—'

'I know, I know,' she replied in a softer tone. 'And if he is there, alive, I will free him. Now go and join your friends; your mission is with them.'

'But, Commander—'

She put her finger to his mouth. 'Jake, I will not let any of you back into this infernal place. It is my order and it is final.'

He turned reluctantly, splashed through the water and climbed aboard the *Lantern*. Topaz helped him up as Yoyo and Nathan raised the anchor, then took the helm and started the engine.

Jake watched Galliana, laden with firearms, disappear into the shaft that led down into the island.

Topaz stood by his side and reached for his hand. Suddenly he turned and kissed her. 'Forgive me,' was all he said as he jumped up onto the rail and dived into the sea.

He swam back to the shore, ignoring the shouts as he leaped across the rocks and disappeared down the staircase in pursuit of the commander. On the deck of the *Lantern* his friends looked at each other in shock and amazement.

'Jake Djones' – Nathan cheered – 'you're my shining example, my hero, you put us all in the shade!'

Jake tore down the steps until he caught up with Galliana. She had stopped to wait for him, her expression stern.

'I didn't think there was much chance of you leaving me,' she announced coolly. She passed him an arrow gun, slightly bulkier than Topaz's, as well as a rapier and a dagger. She had a similar stock of arms, along with a belt of knives. 'Let's go.'

'Can I take my brother's bazooka?'

Galliana unslung it from her shoulder and handed it over. Jake had forgotten how heavy it was: the weight of a small canon. He strapped it across his back.

They both headed back down the staircase towards the palace. The oppressive smell of dampness wafted up into Jake's nostrils, and he shivered.

23 The Flagship

The three others followed the trade route, first north and then east in the direction of Macao. Less than an hour after leaving Xi's island, they spied the Chinese fleet approaching, the sun rising behind them.

Dozens of vessels were sailing in a spearhead formation around the emperor's huge ship. Its mass of yellow sails was so bright it was like a second sun.

'Am I just imagining it,' Nathan said, 'or are there more ships than there were in Canton?'

'At least triple the number,' Yoyo replied. 'It's one thing impressing your own people; but now they're heading for foreign shores and wish to display their might.'

'And may one ask what all those boats are for?' Nathan asked. 'I like a decent entourage as much as the next man, but aren't they taking things a little too far?'

'Obviously the main vessel, the flagship we saw in Canton, is the command centre,' Yoyo explained. 'It houses not only the imperial suite and the rooms of the empress, but also the captain, the navigators, map-makers, translators, doctors and so on.'

'And no doubt the royal wardrobe?' Nathan chipped in. 'That must be high on their list of priorities. We all know the three essentials of vacationing abroad: options, options, options.'

The two girls looked at each other and rolled their eyes. Yoyo continued: 'Then you have ships carrying the horses; supply vessels for food, water tankers, troop transport and repair ships full of timber. There are boats carrying *tribute* gifts – silk, porcelain and ivory – and finally there are the patrol boats, which are much smaller and have oars as well as sails, so they can nip from one craft to another.'

'Then we need to get to a patrol boat first,' Topaz said decisively, her eye fixed on the horizon. 'They're hardly going to allow us onto the emperor's flagship without a formal invitation.'

'Good plan.' Nathan nodded. 'A patrol ship it is.'

They surveyed the approaching fleet in silence. It

was one thing talking about it when it was at a distance; but the closer it got, the more terrifying it became. The *Lantern* was just a speck in the ocean, the Chinese fleet ploughing unstoppably towards them: forty ships carving their way through the waves, a thousand sails groaning, a million ropes creaking.

'Any ideas?' Nathan asked the others, with a gulp.

'Cut the engine,' Topaz ordered. 'Yoyo, are there torches in the trunk there?' Yoyo looked through the box by the helm and produced one, along with a flint lighter. Topaz took them from her, lit the tar-covered torch and used it to set light to the mainsail. It caught immediately.

Nathan held his hands up in disbelief. 'Have you lost your mind?'

'Topaz is right,' Yoyo replied. 'We are in their path, and we need to send out an SOS, give them a reason to stop – while showing ourselves to be vulnerable.'

'And what if they don't stop? What if they have better things to do? We'll burn to death or drown while we're about it.'

'Shut up, Nathan,' the two girls sighed in unison.

He looked from one to the other suspiciously.

'And when did you two become such good friends anyway?'

They shared a sly smile. 'Nathan,' Yoyo remarked, 'your coat seems to be—'

He looked round. The back of his new silk tunic had caught fire too. He tore it off and stamped on it. 'Ruined already and we'd barely been introduced,' he muttered under his breath.

The flames spread across the sails and licked up the mast, producing a cloud of black smoke that carried towards the oncoming fleet. Topaz opened her telescope, her eye on the wide rectangular prow of the flagship. She noticed a solitary figure dressed in gold and blue, standing dead centre, returning her gaze through his own telescope.

'Is it just me, or is this getting out of control?' Nathan asked; the inferno had now engulfed the stern, giving off an intense heat. They edged away towards the prow, and Topaz wondered if she'd been a little hasty.

Suddenly they saw one of the patrol boats shooting forward from the pack, heading towards them, oars splashing furiously. As it drew close, the bearded captain shouted over to them in Chinese. His tone was gruff: he clearly resented having to stop for the burning vessel. After a hurried exchange with Yoyo, he barked some orders to his crew: the oars on one side of the boat were drawn in and they came close enough for the youngsters to jump aboard.

With machine-like efficiency, the oars were replaced and the boat swerved round, just as the fleet arrived. The smaller boats dodged past the *Lantern*, but the flagship thumped straight into it, reducing it to matchsticks.

'There she goes,' Nathan groaned under his breath, as the *Lantern* disappeared for good. He looked around and, meeting twenty pairs of unfriendly eyes, tried one of his winning smiles. 'British built,' he commented. 'Rather shoddy . . .'

Yoyo and Topaz wasted no time explaining to the captain that the fleet was in peril; that an enemy from below would attack at any moment – *a monster from the deep*. The captain stared at them in disbelief. When they insisted on speaking to the commander of the fleet or, better still, to one of the royal party, he let out an incredulous snigger. He told his crew, and they all laughed too.

At this, Yoyo produced the Lazuli Serpent and told him what it was. She tried to put it in his hand, but he was superstitious about it and shrank back, shaking his head.

'The Lazuli Serpent?' he said in Chinese, peering from one youngster to the other. They nodded in unison. He looked them up and down, then burst out laughing again, his crew joining in.

'We don't seem to be getting our point across,' Nathan observed with a tight smile.

Topaz gazed across the sea, searching for any signs of Madame Fang's monster. Over on the flagship, she saw the figure still standing in the prow, observing them through his telescope.

Yoyo made another determined attempt to make the captain understand the danger they were in, but he and his crew now seemed to find everything funny. Exasperated, she suddenly twisted the captain's arm into a half-nelson, unsheathed her dagger and held it to his neck, threatening to cut his throat if he did not take her seriously. The laughter stopped dead, and there was a rattle as everyone drew their weapons at once. Then stalemate . . . hands clasping hilts, eyes darting back and forth.

All at once there was the blast of a horn, and a beam of light struck the captain's face, flashing on and off. Someone on the flagship was tilting a mirror to and fro, sending a signal. The captain said something to Yoyo and she put down her weapon, whereupon he shouted out a series of orders, and the crew quickly returned to their oars. The boat swung round again, weaving her way through the flotilla.

'It seems someone wants to speak to us,' Yoyo explained to the others.

Topaz looked up once more at the prow of the flagship, but the figure had gone.

The patrol boat drew alongside, and the captain cupped his hands round his mouth and called out in a booming voice. A cargo door opened in the hull of the huge ship; inside stood a group of guards, along with a thin man in a black tunic. After some discussion, a wooden pontoon was positioned between the two craft and the History Keepers were pushed onto it.

For a second they froze as the ocean flew by beneath their feet, but the man in black shouted at them to hurry and they jumped aboard. Then the plank was whipped away behind them and the cargo door slammed shut.

The three of them turned to stare at the stern-looking man. He had beady eyes and a thin black moustache. He ordered the guards to confiscate all their weapons.

'I suppose there's no chance of a receipt?' Nathan asked dryly. 'I am rather attached to that sword.'

The dour man snapped another command and headed off along the corridor, while the History Keepers were forced to follow on behind.

They moved into the heart of the ship, up steps and along passages, from deck to deck: through the crew's quarters, with its warren of compartments, up to the cannon decks – vast, low-ceilinged chambers that smelled of sulphur. On either side stood rows of guns, while in the middle lay thousands of weapons: swords, rifles, axes, lances, along with piles of armour. Nathan looked around, trying to take it all in.

They came at last to a heavy door. The thin man took a key from a chain on his belt, unlocked it and led them into a long, red room. The walls were panelled in silk and it was laid out with gold furniture.

'The imperial quarters, I presume,' Nathan commented, peeking into an opulent suite of rooms. Inside, he saw a group of ladies-in-waiting, all silk and powder, with lips like rosebuds. They peered back at him, and when he flashed his smile and did an elaborate bow, knocking his head on the doorframe, they fell about giggling.

The man with the moustache slammed the door shut, shooting Nathan a stern look, and they continued up a last flight of steps, emerging on the bleached timbers of the main deck. It was buzzing with activity. An army of sailors manned the sails, while at the centre, under pale awnings, the imperial court was gathered: navigators, scientists, botanists and artists; some at tables, calibrating instruments and marking down numbers, others making sketches and diagrams or poring over books.

The History Keepers were ushered through the throng towards the prow, where a flight of steps led up to a screened platform. Topaz realized that this was where she had seen the figure in gold and blue watching with his telescope. Here, a line of men stood guard, each with a sabre gripped in his hand.

An older man barged his way through the guards and approached them. He was obviously of a high rank, as the man with the moustache bowed very low before him. The new arrival wore a silver robe that matched his sleek hair, and his finely plaited beard was knotted with jewels. His gaze was haughty and he addressed them in stern tones.

Yoyo translated for Nathan's benefit: 'He says that he is the imperial adviser and that the grand prince – that's the emperor's son – has asked to see us.'

'Great.' Nathan beamed. 'Let's go.'

As he set foot on the steps, the adviser barked out an angry order, at which the guards put up their swords.

'He wants to know more about us first,' Yoyo explained, adding under her breath, 'I don't think it was his idea to invite us aboard.'

'Then explain to him that he's about to die,' Nathan suggested through gritted teeth.

Yoyo launched into her speech again, warning of the imminent danger. The man listened blankly, unmoved. She held out the Lazuli Serpent and told him what it was. Unafraid, he took the stone, inspected it briefly, and shrugged. Seeing that she was getting nowhere and fearing that time was running out, Yoyo tried again, even getting to her knees to make her point. Everyone within earshot craned to hear, but the imperial adviser clearly didn't believe a word of it.

He was starting to reply in condescending tones

when a high, bell-like voice called out from the dais, silencing him. He bristled with anger, but the imperial guards stood aside. Nathan and Topaz looked round at Yoyo.

'It seems that the prince will see us now,' she said.

24 THE EMPIRE CRACKS

They filed up onto the platform. It was quiet here, separated by screens from the rest of the deck. Under a single awning stood a throne, facing the vastness of the ocean. It was upholstered in royal yellow like the sails, but otherwise, unlike Xi Xiang's, it was modest – if ancient. There was a figure seated on it, surveying the sea, but they could see only a padded crown of sapphire silk, studded with pearls and topped with a little orb of gold.

The silver-haired adviser bowed and spoke, and the figure in the throne stood up, turning to look at the History Keepers. He had a handsome, striking face that took both girls by surprise (in fact, even Nathan did a double take). He was roughly their age, but affected a stern expression – his chin high and his brow knotted – as if he had studied how to appear regal. It didn't ring true: his eyes were those of any fifteen-year-old . . . uncertain.

The boy was dressed in a golden robe emblazoned with turquoise dragons. His belt was made of jet and his boots were studded with jewels. Tethered at his side was a live peacock, as regal as its master, peering out at the horizon.

'Now that's what I call dressing for the occasion,' Nathan sighed as his companions found themselves smoothing down their hair and adjusting their torn and dirty clothes. The prince stepped towards them, making his adviser scuttle forward, annoyed by the breach of protocol. The boy snapped at him and he reluctantly withdrew.

Topaz sensed that a battle of wills was being fought between the two of them, and she offered a smile of encouragement to the prince. He merely pursed his lips, then spoke in Chinese. Yoyo replied, and he looked at Nathan and Topaz and waved at them, the jewels on his fingers flashing in the sun. 'You are English?' he asked with a strong accent.

Nathan and Topaz were about to explain that one of them was French and the other American, but for the sake of speed they both nodded. 'English, yes.'

'The best clocks from English,' the boy replied, before adding grandly, 'I am Zhu Chanxun, second son of emperor.'

The History Keepers each responded with a bow, and the peacock gave a piercing cry and opened its tail into a fan of turquoise and emerald.

Zhu spoke again: 'I hear you talking. You say I am in danger. What danger is this?'

Yoyo explained for a third time, suggesting that immediate action should be taken.

Zhu waited for her to finish. 'You want me to turn round? The fleet? Go back to land?'

'That's right,' Topaz told him, 'and prepare the cannon—'

The imperial adviser interrupted again, shaking his head, but the boy waved him away; then suddenly noticed the Lazuli Serpent in Yoyo's hand. She passed it over and he examined it, running his fingers along the engraving.

'Why do you bring me this stone? The stone is . . .' He searched for the word, clearly frightened, and mimed an explosion. 'The stone is destruction.'

Anxious that the attack might be coming at any moment, Topaz piped up in broken Chinese, begging him to return to port. Nathan eagerly seconded the motion, though his Chinese was far worse than his sister's.

The adviser finally lost patience, insisting that these upstarts should be clapped in chains.

Zhu listened, but kept his eyes fixed on the three friends. For a moment they all exchanged a look that had nothing to do with the world of grown-ups and courtiers – a look of comradeship. Then Zhu turned and called to his captain, issuing orders.

Yoyo translated, her eyes sparkling with relief. 'He has told them to change course, to head for the nearest port, and to prepare the gun deck.'

The courtier's jaw had dropped open. His cheeks reddened and his face twisted with fury, but the angry young prince demanded the respect that he was due.

At Zhu's command, a series of trumpet blasts echoed around the deck, and replies swiftly came from the other craft. There was a creak as a hundred ropes tightened at once, and the seven gargantuan sails angled round as one. Suddenly a shaft of sunlight lit up the four teenagers in a pool of gold. The flagship started to turn north towards the mainland. The other vessels, strung out in a crescent, followed suit.

Following the movement of the fleet, Nathan suddenly spotted a small craft at the back – one of the water tankers – list to one side, her mast tipping until it pointed at forty-five degrees. It carried on, seeming to right itself.

Then he heard a boom as it exploded.

The cargo of water sprayed up into the air like a fountain. Nathan cried out in shock, and the others turned to see the boat being pulled down into the sea by what looked like two giant pincers.

The prince gasped, eyes wide with horror, then looked down at the Lazuli Serpent before turning to the History Keepers. 'Help me, please. What do I do?' His face was pale.

Yoyo and Topaz explained that he must use the cannons to try and hit the submarine as it approached. He nodded, then swept through the guards down onto the main deck, the others following behind. The peacock tried to hop after its master, but its golden leash held it back.

When the rest of the courtiers caught sight of their prince, they fell to their knees, heads bowed to the ground. Zhu had no time for that; he ordered them to get on with their business and sent a lieutenant to check that the cannons were ready. Nathan volunteered to go with him.

Just then, a cry went up from another part of the fleet. The prince and his courtiers swooped over to the rail to see what was happening. Now another supply boat was in trouble: the prow lurched into the air while the stern dropped sharply. Seemingly suspended in this unnatural position, it suddenly snapped in two, catapulting its crew in all directions and disgorging its load of timber.

The ship behind it, this one full of soldiers, smacked right into the wreckage, and the deck tilted crazily, tipping half the troops into the sea. Now a shout of alarm went up from every ship in the huge fleet; on the deck of the flagship, it was chaos.

Nathan charged down to the gun deck with Zhu's lieutenant. It was humming with activity: three men were stationed at each gun, loading charge and ball, and preparing the fuses. At the lieutenant's command, the guns were rolled forward, barrels pointing down through the port-holes towards the water.

Nathan went over to the lookout window on the starboard side and scanned the sea for any signs of Fang's metal squid. The water was still choppy where the fleet had started to turn northwards.

Then he caught a glimpse of a dark spidery blur moving towards them. He shouted out, pointing, and signalled for the guns to take aim. The lieutenant immediately seconded his command.

Torches were touched to the fuses; there was a crackle, and everyone put their hands to their ears as half the starboard cannons fired, delivering an ear-shattering noise and a backdraught of sulphurous heat. As the missiles hit the sea, a curtain of water spewed up into the air, sending a great wave out towards the rest of the fleet. The lieutenant immediately ordered the second round of cannon-fire.

There was a scurry of activity as the guns were reloaded, and Nathan waited with bated breath to see if they had hit the submarine.

But then it came: a solitary thump from below. Then a second; and a third, making him feel sick to his stomach – *rap, rap, rap* . . . He knew it was a giant metal tentacle trying to breach the hull. There was a splintering sound, and Nathan was sure that it had pierced the timber. From below, he heard water rushing in and sailors shouting. Then the deep rapping started once more, from another quarter of the ship.

On the main deck, the Chinese courtiers were rushing around in panic. Zhu, the boy prince, stood rooted to the spot, unable to formulate the words of command he needed. The troupe of ladies decanted from the empress's quarters below into the clouds of smoke left by the guns, their dresses bright in the midst of the chaos.

Suddenly there was a thundering crack, and the ship jolted. The yellow throne shunted through the screens and down the steps. Screams went up as it smashed onto the main deck. Topaz and Yoyo cleared a path through the courtiers, navigators, surgeons and mapmakers, many still with instruments and charts in their hands. Over the side of the ship they saw, below the surface, the end of a metal tentacle tightening its grip on the timbers.

Topaz found a length of rope, tied one end to the rail and cast the rest over the side so that it unrolled towards the tentacle. She repeated the process with a second rope, then slung a further coil over her shoulder and tossed one to Yoyo. Meanwhile Yoyo had seized a pair of hammers – chunky iron mallets – from the deck and passed one over to Topaz. They both abseiled down the ropes towards the tentacle, while Zhu, amazed by their bravery, looked on, his courtiers crowding round on either side.

Once Yoyo was close enough, she let go of the rope, catching hold of the metal arm. The joint contracted as it took a tighter grip on the ship, nearly crushing her fingers, but she slid down, taking a deep breath as she disappeared underwater, feeling her way along the limb.

Topaz followed close behind, plunging into the water and grabbing hold as Fang's machine clung to the hull of the flagship like a monstrous barnacle.

The girls worked their way along, until they were within reach of the cockpit. Fang – a fearsome shape at the helm – saw them and pulled a lever that made the tentacle suddenly shoot out, nearly throwing them off. Topaz looped her rope around it to give them something to hold onto, but Fang shunted the control back and forth, making it flick to and fro like a whip. Topaz lost her grip and dropped the hammer, but just managed to cling onto the end of the rope and pulled herself to the surface, where she took great gulps of air.

Meanwhile, underwater, Yoyo managed to reach the top of the glass cockpit; here she knotted the end of her rope to the base of a tentacle and wrapped it around her foot. She raised the hammer and pounded on the glass over and over again, until faint cracks appeared on the surface. Ignoring her, Fang sent another arm out to spear the ship's hull.

Yoyo continued to strike the glass with all her might, finally rupturing it. Even as water seeped into the cockpit through the crack, Fang continued to work the controls. Yoyo hammered away at the glass, and now a chunk gave way and water flooded in, the momentum threatening to carry the control pod away from the flagship – though three tentacles were still clinging on. Desperate to breathe, Yoyo spiralled up the rope, kicking towards the surface.

As she did so, Topaz pulled herself back down her own rope to the squid's cockpit. Just inside the opening that Yoyo had made she spotted a latch that held the glass roof in place. She reached in, but Fang drew her dagger and slashed at her forearm. Ignoring the pain, Topaz unhooked the latch, and the roof of the cockpit immediately flipped off and disappeared into the vortex behind. The cockpit was filling with water, and as the current took the metal squid, all but one of its tentacles were forced to let go of the hull.

Now Yoyo reappeared; she took Topaz's hand and pulled her away, pointing towards the surface. Topaz knew she needed air before she passed out, and had no choice but to head upwards. She shot through the roof of light and gasped for breath.

Down below, Madame Fang still held on doggedly, trying to control the squid and thrusting her dagger towards Yoyo as she clambered into the cockpit. Yoyo struck back with her hammer, then yanked on a lever: the last tentacle relinquished its hold on the ship, and the machine shot backwards. Fang and Yoyo were thrown together, dropping their weapons. They grabbed each other by the neck, expelling any air still left in their lungs.

Weak with lack of oxygen, Yoyo finally managed to smash Fang's head on the edge of the cockpit. As the old woman reeled, dazed, Yoyo took the controls, turned the squid round and opened the throttle. She aimed it at a steep cliff rearing up out of the sea bed and accelerated hard. Fang came to just in time to see the sheer wall shooting towards her, while Yoyo closed her eyes, anticipating the moment of impact.

On the surface, Topaz was still taking deep lungfuls of air. The fleet had turned round, but the little patrol boat was heading towards her. She ducked back down, trying to see what had happened. Was

Yoyo swimming for safety? Then, in the distance, she saw the pulse of light and heard the explosion.

'*Noooo!*' she spluttered as she surfaced again.

The patrol ship drew close, the crew reaching down to help her aboard. The bearded captain, previously so mistrustful, gazed at her in awe.

'We have to find her . . . find Yoyo!' Topaz wailed, treading water as she looked around frantically.

But there was nothing but empty sea.

25 COMMANDER GOETHE

Oblivious to what was happening out at sea, Galliana Goethe and Jake hurried down the stairwell; she was leading the way carrying a lantern in one hand and her arrow gun in the other, while Jake struggled behind under the weight of the bazooka. When they reached a rickety landing halfway down, Galliana checked their position on her map.

'This way,' she whispered to Jake. 'It will take us into the back of the ballroom.'

The landing was rotten, and they had to tread carefully. Dust trickled down into the stairwell below. Suddenly a great chunk gave way, Jake lost his footing and the heavy bazooka almost hauled him over the edge; but Galliana pulled him back from the void.

'All right?' she asked. He nodded, tightening the strap.

Heading along the corridor, they soon came to a rusty metal door in the wall. They checked their weapons before Galliana turned the handle and gently pushed it open. It gave a shrill squeak.

She was about to go through when Jake spoke. 'Commander?' She turned round and looked at him. 'I just wanted to wish you luck.'

Galliana smiled and ruffled his hair. 'And good luck to you too. Your family have always been the bravest of us.'

Jake coloured at the compliment. 'I also wanted to say . . .' he mumbled. 'What happened to your son must have – I can't even begin to imagine how you . . .' He trailed off, not knowing how to put it into words.

Galliana looked down and gave a sigh. 'It was a dark time,' she said quietly. 'The darkest of all.'

Jake knew that this was a strange conversation to be having at such a point, but if he was to enter this place again, he felt a sudden, urgent need to unravel at least some of her story. 'When you disappeared down those steps on your own just now, I realized I – I didn't know enough about you . . . even where you were born or – or how you came to be commander.'

Galliana seemed to understand. Her eyes were serious, windows into a world of extraordinary secrets. 'Would you believe I had great difficulties growing up?' she said softly. 'I was much more fragile and less clever than my four older brothers. And I was afraid of my own shadow, as my father put it. We lived on the Baltic, in the little German port of Flensburg . . . long winters and bright summers – a happy town. All my family were History Keepers, going back many generations. And we were boat builders too. Half of the fleet are still Goethe ships.'

'You were afraid?' Jake asked, finding it hard to believe: he thought of her as fearless.

'No one was expecting much of me, I can tell you.' Galliana's face darkened. 'You don't need to know the details, but my folks – parents, cousins, brothers – were all killed; burned in their beds after a family wedding. Under cover of darkness Sigvard Zeldt struck with his squad of executioners.'

Jake knew the name: though long-dead, Sigvard Zeldt was the father of Xander and Agata, both of whom he had come up against on previous missions.

379

'Only *I* escaped,' Galliana continued, 'hiding underwater with a length of clay pipe. I was the only Goethe left – I still am – so I couldn't be frightened of shadows any longer. I had to grasp life.'

The poignancy was not lost on Jake. Galliana's misfortunes were beyond anything he could possibly imagine – losing her family, not once but twice – but she had found the courage to continue, uncomplaining, always doing what was right and fair.

'There were many happy times too,' she said, gently pinching his cheek. 'I had a wonderful marriage and so much laughter; much of it with your family, whom I hold close to my heart.' She paused, her expression serious. 'Now, Jake, I am going to ask you one more time: will you wait for me here?'

He shook his head. 'Let's go,' he said, motioning for her to proceed.

Galliana passed through the opening, checking that the chamber was empty. It was light inside, so she put down the lantern and beckoned to Jake. The huge bazooka got stuck in the doorway, and clanged loudly against the metal as he pulled it through.

'That thing is more trouble than it's worth,'

Galliana said, taking it from him and setting it down next to the lantern.

Jake looked around. He had passed by this chamber before: here, the stone figures were frozen in a dance, while others looked on from the sides.

Watchful, they crept towards the open double doors at the far end. Jake glanced at the faces of the dancers, captured in the moment of action, eyes wide, mouths open with the thrill of the ball.

Galliana peered through the doorway and headed into the main corridor. Suddenly she heard footsteps approaching and quickly retreated. They waited behind the door, listening. The footsteps were heavy, thumping – it clearly wasn't Xi Xiang, but his mute executioner. The statues shook as he approached.

Galliana swung out, punching the sharp point of her elbow into the giant's chest, sending him reeling backwards. She raised her arrow gun, but he kicked out, knocking it from her hand. As she reached for it, he drew his machete from his belt and slashed at her. As she dodged once, twice, Jake tried to take aim with his own gun, but she was in his line of fire. Eyes burning with determination, she caught hold of the man's wrist, but she was losing the struggle and his blade came down towards her head. Suddenly she hooked her leg around his knee and pushed hard. He toppled backwards, gravity taking over; his head hit the wall and his neck twisted until his spine cracked like a nut. His mouth gaped open, showing the knotted stump of his tongue. Galliana dragged the body – her strength was astonishing – to the corner of the room out of sight. Jake stood watching her, dumbstruck.

'I'm sorry,' she said to him. 'I have taken you by surprise.' She retrieved her arrow gun and checked that the cartridge was still properly attached. 'You'd think that after four decades in the secret service I would be used to taking lives . . . Not so. It is something you never get used to.'

They set off along the passage, the commander facing forward, Jake guarding their rear. They twisted and turned, passing more stone attendants, until they approached the open door of the control room. Galliana held up her gun in both hands, but the place was deserted. The four arched windows looked out across the sea bed, now illuminated by a gleam of daylight from above. There was a movement in the huge tank, and Galliana swung her bow towards it – but it was only the octopus surfacing for a moment. Its eyes lazily inspected her, before it slipped back down, sending a stream of bubbles up to the surface. The room fell silent again. Jake had just noticed that the golden pistol was no longer on the control panel when the lights flickered; for a second the palace went dark, but then they blinked back on again.

Galliana looked at Jake, and he wondered if they should have brought the lantern. He reached for the flint lighter that Nathan had given him in Renaissance Venice, and found the reassuring chunk of metal in his pocket.

The commander referred to the plan: the main corridor, Jake saw, followed an octagonal path as it connected the principal chambers of the palace. She pointed to a room that was diametrically opposite the ballroom. 'The night suite,' she whispered.

They followed the corridor until they arrived at another door, this one slightly ajar. Galliana pushed it open with her foot as they took cover on either side.

For a full minute, neither of them moved. At last, Galliana swung round and saw a dark anteroom, where two rows of stone courtiers knelt facing each other. Their heads were slightly bowed, but their glass eyes looked back at the door, challenging anyone to enter. Beyond them, a round opening, a 'moon door', led into the main chamber. Galliana and Jake crept past the kneeling courtiers and went in.

In the centre, surrounded by more kneeling servants, was a giant four-poster bed with a blue roof like that of the palace itself. Silk nets hung down the sides around a sleeping figure.

Gun primed, Galliana motioned for Jake to stay back and soundlessly inched her way towards the bed. Jake checked the statues – after his previous experience he wasn't taking any chances – and they stared back at him accusingly.

Galliana drew back the net with the tip of her weapon and reached out towards the still shape under the covers. She yanked back the sheets, ready to fire, then let out a little gasp.

Jake stepped forward and saw that the sleeping figure was also a statue, this one of jade, its mouth gaping open – whether in pain or joy, it was hard to tell.

All at once they heard a giggle behind them – the unmistakable high-pitched laugh of Xi Xiang. They both swung round, aiming at the moon door. A shadowy figure flitted across the anteroom into the corridor. The door slammed shut and the lights flickered again.

'So he's playing games with us . . .' Galliana said softly.

They headed out towards the other side of the palace, but before long the lights blinked once more. This time they went out. It was pitch black; Jake had never known such total darkness. They heard a giggle, then footsteps scampering towards them.

Jake heard a twang as Galliana let loose an arrow; it whistled through the air before hitting a wall and clattering to the ground. Again she fired, then a third time, and Jake followed her lead, though they had nothing to aim at.

He reached into his pocket for his lighter. As he pulled it out, something touched his forearm, and he heard a soft snigger. He froze, terrified, as he felt warm breath on his face, and then the palest of shapes blinked out of the darkness – the white of a withered eye.

'Such a pity you never found your brother,' Xi Xiang whispered.

Jake sparked his lighter, only to see Xiang

pointing a pistol – his brother's golden pistol – straight at his heart.

'Jake!' Galliana screamed, throwing him out of the way just as Xi pulled the trigger. There was a flash, and a mushroom of smoke, and she took off into the air, struck a stone pillar and thumped to the ground.

Xi sniggered and scurried away, his feet tip-tapping along the passageway until there was silence again. Suddenly there was a distant clunk, and the lights came back on.

Jake looked around. The empty corridor curved away from him on either side.

Galliana lay on the floor, her body twisted, her breastplate punctured; blood seeped out into a thick puddle, clogging her mane of silver hair. Her face was pallid and her eyes filmy.

Jake stood there, shaking his head in horror. And then in fury. He tried to undo the buckles of her armour, but she gently pushed his hand away.

'Get out . . .' she whispered hoarsely. 'Please get out.'

Jake shook his head. 'Never.' He took her spare cartridge of arrows, swapped it with the one on his own gun, then unhooked her belt of daggers and slung them over his shoulder.

'I'll be back, do you hear? I'll come straight back,' he vowed.

As he set off, he heard the sound of music – strings – coming from a room along the corridor. He found himself back at the ballroom and blinked in amazement as he saw that the dancing statues were slowly revolving on the spot in time to the music.

Then there was another cloud of smoke as Xi fired at him from across the room. Jake ducked behind a group of statues, and the bullet struck one in the chest, shattering it into dozens of pieces. As the laughing Xi skipped from statue to statue, Jake's arrows hissed across the room, but none found their mark.

His cartridge was now empty, so he threw down his gun and started hurling Galliana's daggers. Something small and heavy landed at his feet – a firecracker shaped like a dragon, red smoke hissing from its mouth. Jake took cover as it exploded and red smoke filled the room. Xi cackled as he launched more firecrackers – purple, yellow, green . . . The stench was dreadful, and Jake could feel the smoke burning his lungs.

He caught a flash of movement as his foe

disappeared back into the corridor; then glanced round and saw the little metal door through which they had entered the room. *He could escape now, leave this place for ever* . . . But he gritted his teeth, and crunched across the floor in pursuit of Xi.

His nemesis was scampering towards the control room. As Xi turned and fired again, Jake ducked, and the bullet smashed into the ceiling, which started to fall in chunks, knocking over the stone figures guarding the doorway. Jake bent down and picked up a piece of broken statue – a fat hand and forearm – and, yelling a curse, hurled it at Xi. It struck him hard on the forehead, and he tumbled down the stairs, his pistol flying across the room. Dazed for a second, Xi looked around and saw the gun glinting under the throne. He pulled himself to his feet, but Jake had already leaped down the steps and caught him a blow on the jaw with his foot.

Xi reeled in confusion, and Jake picked him up and dragged him towards the tank.

'Where's Philip?' Jake yelled. 'You have twenty seconds to tell me . . .'

26 Mirror to the Past

He tightened his grip on the monster's collar and thrust his head into the water. As Xi fought back desperately, his octopus appeared, wrapping its tentacles around Jake's wrist, trying in vain to prise his hand off its master. It spidered up out of the tank and along Jake's arm, its suckers seeking out his face, curling into his mouth. As Jake grabbed hold of it, the creature pumped black ink into his face. Jake wiped his eyes and tossed the octopus across the room. Immediately it righted itself and slithered its way back along the floor.

Meanwhile Xi had managed to grab a lungful of air. He tried to speak, but Jake pushed his head down again, and his words spilled out as bubbles. Jake kept him submerged for a little longer, then pulled him up by the scruff of the neck.

'I'll tell you where he is! I'll tell you!' Xi cried, spluttering water. 'I'll tell you, I promise to tell, but I beg you to kill me some other way. Drowning is—' He broke off and vomited water and mucus over Jake's sleeve. 'Drowning is my greatest fear. Shoot me . . . Promise to shoot me—'

'Tell me where he is.'

Xi shook his head in fear; make-up ran in black streams down his cheeks, and his lip trembled. His two good eyes opened wide, while his bad one closed completely. 'He's dead. He died nearly a year ago.'

Jake said nothing; his face was expressionless.

Xi continued, 'I know you will never believe me, but I did not kill him. How could I? Even after everything that happened, I still loved him – like a father. He . . .' For a moment, he couldn't bring himself to say it. 'He killed himself.' Jake shook his head in disbelief. 'He had the freedom of the palace, you see. I told you I kept him locked up, but I didn't – no, no, not at all. I'm not a complete monster. I came down one morning and found him . . .' Tears streamed from Xi's puffy eyes, though still the mutant one remained impassive. 'I found him hanging by his neck.'

Jake's voice was cold. 'Where? Where did you find him?'

Xi pointed at the chandelier above his head. The memory was clearly too much for him and he started shaking. 'I cut him down. He still had a pulse. I gave him the kiss of life, pushing on his chest – breathing and pushing. He died in my arms.' He let out a strangled cry of pain.

Jake stood there, quite still. 'Thank you for telling me,' he said.

Xi tried to smile; but Jake simply pushed him back under the water. Xi wrenched his head round, spluttering: 'You *promised* you wouldn't drown me . . .' Then his words disappeared in a cloud of bubbles.

Jake used both hands to thrust Xi's head down to the bottom of the tank; he kicked and thrashed, but Jake showed no mercy. The octopus had made its way back across the room and started to creep up his leg, but he shook it off.

Soon Xi's face started to turn blue, his bad eye gazing up through the water, pleading. Suddenly Jake was appalled at himself; he remembered what Galliana had told him: *Taking a life is something you never get used to.* He pulled Xi out of the tank, and let his body fall to the floor. The octopus moved its master's head from side to side, but all three eyes merely gazed up lifelessly.

Jake felt the hairs on the back of his neck stand on end; bile inched up his throat. Had he killed Xi? He got down on his knees and shook him, forgetting what a monster he was. How could he kill someone in cold blood, pleading for their life like that? He was *fifteen years old*.

Through the windows, from far across the sea bed, came a distant flash of light. Jake went over and looked out, but couldn't see what it was. Then he noticed a reflection in the glass and his heart stopped . . .

The floor by the tank was empty: Xi wasn't there!

Jake cast his eye along the glass and found the image of his foe standing by his throne, dripping wet and taking aim with his golden pistol. He looked like a ghost, floating above the floor of the ocean.

'I lied . . . Pip's alive,' the spectre said, his voice hoarse where his throat had been squeezed. Jake suddenly remembered Galliana's warning about Xi: *Be wary. There are so many layers of deceit to that man.* 'Yes, your brother's alive . . .' Xi smiled. 'You were looking straight at him . . .'

392

Jake turned slowly and saw Xi's finger tighten on the trigger.

'Jake!' a voice shouted from the doorway.

They both turned as Galliana fired the golden bazooka. It struck Xi with such force that it blew off his right arm, sending it splashing into the pool. He screamed as his cloak caught fire.

Galliana limped down the steps with the huge weapon. 'And this one's for my son . . .' She fired again.

Xi fell to the floor, thrashing around, his mouth a shocking red hole in his charred body. 'Amateurs,' he croaked, lifting his gun and firing it twice at the window. Then his arm dropped. His withered eye swivelled to glare at Jake – and froze as he died.

Only now did Galliana falter, holding onto the edge of the tank. She clutched at her wound; she had removed the breastplate and managed to wind material around her chest, but blood seeped out from underneath it and her face was deathly pale.

Suddenly they heard a crack and looked round at the windows. The first of Xi's bullets had hit one of the four large panes, fracturing the glass; the second had made a hole in a smaller one, and a fast stream of water came pouring through the opening. Jake felt his ears pop.

'Come on!' Galliana panted. 'If that large window goes, we'll be dead in seconds.' She hobbled up the steps, but Jake was thinking about Philip. What had Xi meant when he said, *You were looking straight at him . . .* ? Where *was* he?

Water started swilling across the floor and down into the maze. 'Jake, we have to go. *Now!*' Galliana told him urgently. The crack in the window grew.

Jake nodded grimly. He wrenched the golden pistol out of Xi's blackened hand and followed her up the steps. He put his arm around her shoulders, and was struck by how light and frail she felt.

As they wound their way along the corridors, past the ballroom and the chambers of state, the stone courtiers looked on. *Is Philip trapped somewhere in this labyrinth?* Jake wondered.

They came to the courtroom, where the stone judge presided. Jake stopped, staring back down the passage.

Galliana sensed his torment, but spoke firmly: 'Jake, we *must* leave now.'

With a heavy heart, he turned and they limped on, starting up the grand staircase. They were almost at the top when suddenly it came to him: *You were looking straight at him . . .* Earlier Xi had dragged him over to the giant looking glass. *When you look into it, you can see your past,* he had said, giggling. *Can you see your brother?*

'The mirror . . .' Jake said to himself. 'He's behind the mirror!' He turned to Galliana. 'Just two minutes,' he told her. 'Wait for me, please. I'll be back.'

'Jake, *no* . . .' she commanded, struggling for breath; but it was too late anyway, for Jake was charging down the steps, two at a time. Galliana had to lean against the wall to prevent herself from fainting.

Jake splashed through the swirling waters, back along the octagonal corridor, past the royal chambers, weaving his way round the statues until he reached the war room.

The water here was waist-high. Xi's charred body floated on the surface, face down; his octopus clung to it mournfully. The throne bobbed close by. Jake glanced at the large window that Xi had hit. Fracture lines now radiated out in every direction. It could go at any time.

He waded across to the mirror and tried to peer through it where, over time, the backing had been scratched. There seemed to be a space behind. He turned and grabbed the throne, then hauled it back towards the mirror. Behind him, the window creaked, and one of the fracture lines extended a little further.

With every ounce of strength he had left, Jake launched the throne against the mirror. It shattered, and daggers of light rained down into the water, which poured into the empty cavity behind. Jake was carried along with it, over the jagged rim of glass. Then the water was still, and he managed to find his feet.

He was in a long, narrow chamber with dark walls; at the far end he saw a cage – and the silhouette of a man standing behind the bars, his gaze fixed on Jake.

As Jake waded towards him, he saw that the man's mouth was gagged, his hands chained behind his back. He was tall and broad-shouldered, but slim. His clothes were ragged, and he had a wispy beard.

'Philip . . .?' he whispered. The shadow didn't move as he approached the bars. Now Jake saw his face. It was black with dirt, but the whites of his eyes shone brightly. 'Philip—' he said again, but the word caught in his throat. 'Is it . . .?' He slid his hand through the bars and pulled the gag down.

The mouth immediately curled up into a tremulous smile. Jake let out a gasp, and hot tears sprang to his eyes.

'*Philip!*' he wailed, now stretching his arms right through the bars and throwing them around him – though it was hard to believe that this tall, bearded stranger was indeed his long-lost brother.

Philip opened his mouth to speak, but only strangled sounds emerged. He tried again, his voice so much deeper than Jake remembered: 'I wondered . . . when you were going . . . to get here,' he stammered.

Jake remembered the shattered window. 'We have to leave now. Where are the keys?'

'Xi . . . has them . . . on his belt.' Philip nodded his head. 'There.'

Jake turned. The corpse had been washed towards the secret room and was now lodged on the broken edge of the mirror. Jake rushed back and reached underneath it for the belt, pulling the keys free. As he turned back towards the cage, he heard another crack behind him. Like a jagged bolt of lightning, the fracture line was creeping towards the corner, and it seemed like the pane of glass was bulging inwards under the pressure of the water.

The first key Jake tried was too large, the next too small; then he dropped the whole bunch and had to fumble in the water for it. His hand shaking, on his third attempt, Jake unlocked the gate and then uncuffed his brother's hands with a smaller key. 'Can you swim?' he asked.

Philip smiled and ruffled his hair. 'Let's go, little brother.'

They splashed their way through the water, across the war room and up the steps into the corridor. Behind them, they heard the giant window rupture, letting in a tsunami of water. Philip turned and slammed the door shut. 'Run!' he croaked.

They took off along the corridor, Philip slightly wobbly on his feet. As they passed the ballroom, they heard the war-room door crashing open. The wave surged through, flowing into the corridor and overturning the army of statues as it went.

Jake and Philip raced through the palace, just ahead of it, then charged up the main staircase. As they neared the top, Jake looked around for the commander, but she was nowhere to be seen. They emerged onto the landing and continued up the final flight to the harbour.

'Here!' a voice crackled. It was Galliana, standing in the hatch of Xi's submarine.

Jake and Philip ran across the pier and clambered onto it. 'Commander Goethe . . .' Philip nodded, leaping over as the flood of water spewed up through the throat of the stairwell.

'Hurry, Jake!' Galliana yelled.

He cast off and dropped down after Philip; she pulled the hatch shut behind her just as the wave thundered down on top of the submarine, shaking it around like a toy.

Inside, Galliana fell down the ladder, but Philip caught her and laid her on a sofa. There was an almighty bang as the submarine was swept against the huge stone doors, cracking them open. It was carried through into the open sea.

Jake rushed over to Galliana. Philip was already examining her wound; her lung was exposed, blood pulsing out. 'Commander . . .' Jake glanced around desperately. 'We need to get help!'

Galliana clutched his hand, stopping him. 'Too late for that, I think,' she said weakly, scarlet blood bubbling out of her mouth, and gently touched his cheek. 'Jake was right all along. Welcome home.' Then she gave a little gasp and her eyes filled with tears. The two brothers glanced at one another in dismay, but Galliana was smiling through her tears. She held her hands out to them and said: 'Two brothers together, *two princes of Egypt . . .*'

Suddenly, bizarrely, Jake remembered his father's book – the one with a picture of pyramids on the front. What was the secret he'd been keeping from Jake?

The commander's expression became stern. 'Rose . . .' she whispered. 'Rose Djones: *she* must command now.'

And then she died.

27 CHINESE FIREWORKS

Miraculously, the flagship stayed afloat; her prow stood up out of the water, and her decks sloped, but the holes in the stern had been patched up, and she had survived, along with her imperial passengers. She dropped anchor halfway to shore, while the rest of the fleet gathered around, looking like a floating city.

The patrol boat ferried Topaz back to where Nathan was waiting, and they hugged each other, Topaz clinging onto him and sobbing. As they limped up onto the main deck, the imperial court of China bowed down to them as one. Zhu came to greet them with open arms, beaming from ear to ear.

'You save us,' he told them with a pointed look at his overbearing guardian. 'You save me – and you save China.' His courtiers gathered around like old friends and cheered.

Topaz was gratified, but it did not lessen her heartache at the loss of Yoyo or her worry about Jake. She and Nathan wasted no time in asking Prince Zhu to lend them a boat to return to Xi Xiang's island for their comrades.

Zhu replied: 'I will not lend you a boat – I will *give* you my fleet.' And with that he ordered the navy to follow Topaz's directions.

Just then, a cry went up from sailors who had spotted a figure drifting towards them, clinging to a piece of wreckage. Topaz's heart gave a flutter as she rushed over to the rail and watched half a dozen crewmen haul a limp figure out of the sea.

Yoyo . . .! Though Topaz couldn't tell whether she was dead or alive. Finally she received the news that her friend was still breathing, and she and Nathan punched the air in celebration. Now they needed to know that Jake and Galliana were safe.

A short while later, as the ships started on their journey to Xi's island, Yoyo was laid out on the main deck, with imperial doctors rushing over to attend to her. She had been cut badly across her shoulder and chest and was scratched and bruised all over. Topaz and Nathan took her hands. She looked up at them, blinking in the bright sunlight. 'That's the last we'll hear from her,' she murmured. 'The indestructible Madame Fang died as she lived: with a bang.'

Despite the assurance, Topaz found herself glancing back at the sea, checking that the old woman wasn't still lurking out there somewhere.

'Any news on Jake and Galliana?' Yoyo continued.

'We're on our way there now,' Topaz told her.

They had only travelled a few miles when Nathan spotted the submarine heading in their direction. At first, it threw everyone into a panic and the sailors started preparing the gun decks again, but Topaz noticed two people sprawled on top of it. One of them suddenly stood up and started waving.

'*C'est Jake!*' she exclaimed, leaping with joy. '*Il est vivant!*' She took a moment to inspect the other figure, and added uncertainly, 'Is that Galliana with him?'

Nathan took out his telescope and peered over. He was surprised to find instead a shabby, bearded young man. His mouth curled up into a smile. 'Well, I'll be—'

The Djones brothers came aboard the flagship to another emotional reunion, and Jake gave the others the devastating news of Galliana's death.

'She gave her life for mine,' he sobbed. Topaz fell to her knees in shock and Nathan's face streamed with tears – something Jake had never witnessed before. It should have been a moment of triumph: the missing Philip Djones discovered after four years, Xi Xiang vanquished, his schemes destroyed; but how could they celebrate when their leader was no more?

When the young prince understood what had happened, he immediately sent a team onto the submarine, instructing them to prepare the body as if Galliana were a member of his own family.

Philip stood with his arm around his inconsolable brother, as Topaz looked from one to the other, half smiling, half crying, and said, '*C'est un miracle* – to see you both together. Although, of course, Philip is the good-looking one.'

Jake surprised her by suddenly kissing her on the cheek. She blushed and locked eyes with him.

Philip looked at them, eyebrows raised. 'How long exactly have I been gone . . . ?'

Yoyo watched them, half smiling. Yesterday, outside the doctor's in Zhanjiang, she had guessed that Jake's feelings for her were not strong. Probably, in her heart, she had always known that he and Topaz were inseparable. She went over to join Nathan at the rail; he was staring at the submarine as an empty coffin of interlocking jade plates was lowered down into it in readiness for Galliana's body.

'I'll never forget her,' he murmured. 'She was the one person who never laughed at me. And she gave me my first compliment: when I was four, she said my cavalier boots with silver spurs were very daring.' Suddenly a terrible thought struck him. 'Or was that *jarring*?'

The submarine was tethered to the flagship, and they set off again, this time towards Zhanjiang. Its harbour was deep and repairs could be carried out there.

Jake and Philip, standing shoulder to shoulder in the afternoon sun, looked back at the archipelago. Xi's mountain, the furthest island, was easily identified – a sharp pyramid with a crooked peak. Neither brother would ever forget it – a place of almost unendurable pain, but also a place where they had found each other at last.

'Any idea what she meant?' Philip asked Jake. '*Two princes of Egypt?*'

'No,' he replied. 'I was hoping that you might know.'

As the fleet started to file into the port, word spread around the town, and the harbour was soon full of people gawping at the great flagship that wallowed into the bay. They hadn't received a royal visit in over a hundred years.

Suddenly a firework shot up from an unseen backyard, high into the dark sky. It exploded in myriad blue and pink stars. A minute later, another joined it, gold and orange this time. Soon they were rocketing up from all corners of the town.

Zhu clambered onto the listing platform at the prow, smiling regally. When the townspeople saw who it was, they cheered and clapped, finally breaking into song. The young prince waved back, even doing a little dance for their benefit.

Nathan turned to Jake and raised his eyebrows. 'Flamboyance? Are we responsible for that?' he whispered. 'Next thing we know, he'll be throwing a fancy-dress ball with a rococo theme.'

Hong Wu, the thin man in black who had first accompanied the History Keepers onto the ship, came to ask what should be done with the commander's coffin. Yoyo quickly took charge, supervising the sad task as it was transported to the *Thunder*, which was still moored at the pier. When the History Keepers went to say their goodbyes to Zhu, the smile left his face, and he looked them up and down.

'I will not allow you to go back to England now,' he said sternly, making Jake glance at Topaz in alarm. But then his face relaxed into a smile. 'You will have dinner with me first.'

Chinese lanterns were lit all around the deck and the large map table in the centre was laid out for a feast (one end had to be adjusted to compensate for the slope). More lanterns lit up the rigging, red globes with golden tassels luminous against the dusky sky.

Hong Wu came scurrying up to Yoyo and whispered something in her ear. She looked over her shoulder and Jake did the same. They could just make out, laid on the deck of the *Thunder*, a glint of green – Galliana's jade coffin, with a platoon of soldiers standing guard. Then Jake saw something else that made his heart quicken: a solitary figure standing at the end of the pier. He had a spindly moustache and a long white beard, and Jake realized that it was the fortune-teller they had met earlier.

One of you will die, he had said.

He had been right.

The History Keepers set off at first light. They had decided to take Xiang's submarine back to Point Zero with them; it could be added to the fleet. No one really wanted to crew it – Philip volunteered first, followed by Jake; but Yoyo said that they had been through enough – *she* would take it. Nathan insisted on accompanying her. To his surprise, she agreed.

Topaz and the Djones brothers watched them go off together, chatting amiably.

'They seem to be getting on better,' Jake noted.

'Maybe they have more in common than they realize,' Topaz replied.

They climbed aboard the *Thunder*, pausing for a moment in silence beside Galliana's coffin, then prepared to set sail. Ship and submarine went in tandem, skirting around the flotilla, across the bay and out to sea, heading towards Vietnam.

When it came to taking the atomium, Jake asked what they should do with Galliana. Topaz reminded him that inanimate objects were carried through the time flux by *living* things: they simply had to stay close to her.

'Yes – yes, of course,' Jake stammered, suddenly finding it difficult to breathe. Just yesterday Galliana had been commander of the service; now she was no longer a *living* thing. Philip put his arm around him as Topaz went off to write a Meslith to Point Zero. She needed to pass on the good news about Philip – and the bad . . .

As they approached the horizon point, just after lunch, Nathan came up through the hatch of the submarine and called across the choppy waters, 'Good luck, you three. See you on the other side.'

They all waved back, and within moments they were taking off out of their bodies, soaring high over the earth, into the silence of the upper atmosphere. Jake could see the islands of Indonesia, the expanse of the Indian Ocean, and across to the eastern coast of Africa. Then everything spun out of focus, like a wheel suddenly accelerating. The next thing

Jake knew, he was flying, his brother and Topaz close by. It felt as if they were moving at the speed of light, but still the Earth took a long time to come back into focus. At last they fell towards the pale seas of the eastern Atlantic – and Jake caught sight of the *Thunder*, north of the Spanish coast. Closer still, he spotted himself on deck, next to Philip and Topaz, standing guard over the green jade box.

He returned to his body with such a jolt that he stumbled back and would have fallen if the others hadn't caught him. He noticed a change in the weather: the breeze was fresh here. A few moments later, a little way off, the sea started foaming; there was a hiss of air, a sharp flash of light and the submarine surfaced.

They were on their way home.

28 THE LAND OF THE PHARAOHS

By tea time, the two vessels were approaching the Mont St Michel. Jake noticed a great mass of colour: the History Keepers were gathered for their commander's final homecoming.

'That's the biggest welcoming party I've ever seen,' Topaz said as she, Jake and Philip watched from the rail. Over her shoulder she carried a satchel containing the Lazuli Serpent and Caravaggio's portrait of Philip and Xi. They had all agreed that these priceless items needed to be kept safe in the castle vaults.

Jake surveyed the gathering. Over a hundred agents, each dressed in the finest clothes of their own time and place, stood to attention.

'The commander hated black,' Topaz commented. 'That's why everyone is dressed like that.' Even

Jupitus Cole wore white instead of his trademark dark morning suit. Charlie stood nearby, in an outfit every bit as bright as the parrot on his shoulder. Next to him, Oceane Noire, who looked much healthier, wore a dusky pink. Just behind them stood Fredrik Isaksen, his face stern but his eyes glistening.

As Philip Djones scanned the faces, he clutched the rail tightly and took a deep breath.

'They're not as scary as they look . . .' His younger brother smiled, aware that Philip hadn't set eyes on them for years.

Suddenly Jake had a terrible thought – *Olive, the commander's beloved pet. What would become of her?* At this very moment he saw Signor Gondolfino clutching the dog tightly in his arms, stroking her and whispering in her ear. Jake was certain, by the stoic look on the hound's face, that somehow she already knew . . .

The *Thunder* docked, and the submarine pulled up behind. No one moved or spoke as two gangplanks were put in place.

Philip alighted first, followed by Jake, and their feet had barely touched solid ground before a piercing shriek cut through the silence. Miriam, tears rolling down her face, had pushed her way to the front, Rose and Alan just behind her. The boys disappeared into such a flurry of kisses and embraces that you could barely tell one Djones from the other. Felson, barking with delight, jumped up and gave his share of kisses too.

Commander Galliana Gisella Ariadne Goethe was buried early the next morning, in the shadow of the willow tree next to the giant marble hourglass. Two paintings – one of her son, the other of her husband, both by Rembrandt and never seen by anyone except the History Keepers – were carefully laid beside her. Many people stood forward to speak, with funny reminiscences or tales of astonishing bravery. Rose Djones went last and spoke with great wit.

'None of you know this,' she said in conclusion, holding out her carpetbag, 'but Galliana gave this to me on my very first mission, when I was just fifteen years old. It belonged to her mother, who—' She broke off, then went on instead: 'It has protected me all these years. I would now like to give it back to her, so that it may protect her on whatever journey she is now taking.'

As she laid it carefully in the grave, a peculiar thing happened: the stern Jupitus Cole let out a sudden choking sob. Rose turned to him as he clamped his hands over his face, his shoulders heaving.

'Feelings . . .?' Rose whispered mischievously. 'Not made of granite after all?' He collapsed into her arms and wept.

The second extraordinary thing happened an hour later: as the pair of them walked along the shore, getting some fresh air, Rose saw a jewel glinting amongst the rocks. She knelt down and picked it up, staring in amazement.

'Jupitus Cole, something is clearly written in our stars . . .' She held up the engagement ring that she had tossed out to sea after the disastrous wedding. They looked at each other and burst out laughing.

They were married a week later, on the lawn at the base of the Mount, on a summer's afternoon every bit as beautiful as the previous wedding day. When it came to the moment for the rings to be exchanged, the whole party held their breath, but the ceremony passed without a hitch.

As Jupitus and Rose were declared man and wife,

a cheer went up, many of the guests jumping to their feet and clapping. Even Oceane Noire cried, '*Bravo!*' in operatic tones. (She had broken every History Keeper rule by bringing a companion – a handsome oyster farmer who had nothing to do with the secret service – but everyone decided to turn a blind eye.)

'*C'est merveilleux,*' she sang, giving Charlie a smacker on the cheek that made Mr Drake fluff his feathers up in annoyance.

Charlie rolled his eyes at the parrot and whispered, 'I may have created a monster . . .'

Afterwards there was a noisy feast and then, as the sun started to go down, lanterns were lit all around the island, the band struck up and the dancing began. The succession of quadrilles and waltzes grew rowdier as the heavens came alive with thousands of stars.

Jake and his friends took part in a Scottish reel: Topaz, Charlie – who was still hobbling, but determined to join in – Nathan, Yoyo, with Lydia Wunderbar to make up the six. (Despite being *as large as a tent* – as she put it – she was famous for being very light on her feet.) Fredrik Isaksen lounged nearby, regaling a group of adoring ladies with tales of his adventures. Signor Gondolfino, still clutching Olive, looked on benevolently as the dancers whirled around, cheering with delight. Next to them stood Felson the mastiff, and Dora the elephant with Mr Drake perched on her forehead – friends together, watching the antics of these strange humans.

When the dance finished, Jake realized that he hadn't seen Philip for ages. Unable to find him amongst the party, he glanced up at the Mount, searching the rectangles of light where windows had been thrown open. They were all empty – but at last he picked out a solitary figure on the battlements.

Philip waved back at him, so Jake went in and climbed the main staircase, past the portrait of Sejanus Poppoloe – restored after its accident – towards the ramparts. Philip turned, smiling, as Jake came to stand beside him. For a while they stared in silence at a far-off point where the stars met the ocean, listening to the revels below.

'Everything all right?' Jake said at last.

'Never been happier,' his brother replied. Jake knew that there must be more that he wasn't saying: you couldn't go through a ordeal like that and feel normal straight away. 'So . . . Aunt Rose elected head of the History Keepers' Secret Service! A land-slide victory! There'll be no going back to London now.'

'Would you *like* to go back?' Jake asked.

Philip frowned. 'It never felt like home to me.' He swept his hands around the twinkling Mount. '*This* is home.'

Jake was about to agree with him when a voice came from behind: 'There you are! We've been look-ing everywhere.' It was Miriam, carrying her shoes and limping, Alan at her side. Jake noticed that he had the book with the picture of the Egyptian pyramids on the front. 'It's getting out of hand down there,' Miriam giggled. 'In preparation for their honeymoon in Ottoman Turkey, Jupitus has put on hooped earrings and is doing a belly dance on the table.'

'It's the first time I've ever seen my sister blush,' Alan chipped in.

'What *is* that book?' Jake asked, unable to contain his curiosity any longer.

'What – *this* book?' Alan stammered as if surprised to find it in his hand. Husband and wife exchanged a glance.

'Well, the fact of the matter is' – Miriam used the

tone she normally reserved for tricky customers in the bathroom shop – 'we do have something to tell you, both of you, and now seems as good a time as any.' She took a deep breath and clapped her hands together. 'It's about where you came from.' She laughed nervously and turned to Alan for moral support.

'What she's trying to say is,' he jumped in, 'that you two thought you were born in Lewisham hospital. Well, you weren't. You were born in the past . . . quite a long time ago.'

'It doesn't *change* anything . . .' Miriam tried to make it sound like an everyday admission. 'You're still exactly the same boys. It's no different from the twins over the road who came from Toronto.'

'What do you mean, we were *born* in the past?' Jake demanded. Philip was smiling, as if he had just solved a puzzle he had been working on for years.

'We were living in Egypt at the time,' Miriam went on. 'In the time of Rameses the Second. We could travel anywhere in history back then: our *valours* were the best in the business. It really was the golden age of Egypt, wasn't it, Alan?'

'Oh yes, very lavish and upscale,' he concurred.

'Rameses the S-Second?' Jake stammered.

'We were stationed there, you see, running the Egyptian bureau, near the Valley of the Kings. I was pregnant with you, Philip, when we arrived . . .'

'Forty degrees, it was – not the best conditions,' Alan chipped in. 'Anyway, to cut a long story short, we foiled an assassination attempt on the pharaoh himself, and his government were so grateful they made us royalty.'

'We weren't *royalty*,' Miriam protested, though she beamed at the memory. 'That makes it sound much swisher than it was.'

'They made us governors of an entire province!' Alan pointed out. 'You had a throne of gold and turquoise and a thousand skivvies at your beck and call!'

'Yes, that was quite nice,' she conceded. 'What a relief it was not to have to worry about cooking.'

Jake's head was spinning. 'What. Are. You. Talking. About?' he asked, not knowing whether to laugh or cry.

Alan spoke softly. 'Boys, you were both born in a great big palace. And you lived as princes. And you enjoyed every minute of it. Here . . .' He opened the book and passed it to them. '*That* was home.'

There were illustrations of majestic buildings, of

grand halls and palm-filled terraces looking out across the Nile. 'And Egypt's where our name comes from – Djoneses, roughly translated. We simplified it, and it just stuck somehow. No one wanted my surname, Chapman.'

'We moved back after Philip's fourth birthday. From our sumptuous Egyptian palace' – the humour was not lost on her – 'and opened a bathroom shop in south London.'

As Jake ran his fingers across the pictures, suddenly all his confusion evaporated. This was epic: he wasn't an ordinary schoolboy after all. He and his brother were – they had *always* been – very different.

'Can I go and show Topaz and the others?' he asked, excitedly prising the book out of his father's hands. 'They'll never believe it, that I'm not from boring old Lewisham – but from history too!' He didn't even wait for his parents to reply, but charged back across the battlements. He stopped suddenly in the doorway. 'Wait . . . when *was* Rameses the Second?'

'Around 1250 BC, more or less,' Alan told him.

Jake counted it on his fingers, gave a big smile and clenched his fist in victory. 'That's nearly three

thousand years ago. I can't wait to see their faces.'
And he disappeared down the steps to the
stateroom.

'*Boring old Lewisham?*' Miriam sighed, turning to
her other son. 'I suppose that's how you felt about
it too?'

Philip wondered how to put it. 'I liked growing
up there,' he conceded, 'but it was hardly *the golden
age of Egypt*.'

Alan giggled, slapped his elder son on the back,
and soon they were all hooting with laughter.

Jake charged down the main staircase, two steps at a
time. When he passed Sejanus Poppoloe's portrait,
he stopped and blew him a big kiss. 'You're a genius,
old boy!' he announced, and flew through the
double doors at the bottom. For a moment he
stopped, panting for breath, looking at the people
on the lawns below. Everyone was standing in a big
circle, clapping in time as Rose and Jupitus – the
latter still sporting giant earrings – danced a polka.

Jake thought his heart would burst with
happiness. He loved the History Keepers. Every one
of them was fascinating and original. They weren't
spiteful like the bullies at his school or petty like

some of the customers in his parents' shop. They were kind and brave and adventurous. He thought back to the stormy night when he had first met them; when he had been kidnapped by Jupitus Cole and taken to the London bureau beneath the Monument. He had been wary of them then, even frightened. Now he was only frightened that one day he might be separated from them.

'Jake . . .' a girl's voice called out of the darkness beside him. It was foreign-sounding and familiar, but he couldn't place it. At first he thought it must be Topaz or Yoyo putting on an accent, but he could see both of them at the edge of the big circle.

'Jake?' the voice came again, and this time a caped figure stepped out of the shadows, beckoning with her gloved hand.

'Who is it?' he asked, still smiling, but a little spooked. The figure motioned again, so he stepped towards her.

There was a rustling sound from behind, and then he felt a sharp tap on the back of his skull. His vision went blurred, his legs collapsed under him, and the book dropped onto the ground. As he fell, someone caught him under the arms and he was dragged through the rose bushes, away from the party . . .

He was half aware of the figure in the cape looking down at him, her face masked. Then she pulled back her gloved hand and struck him again. He saw a flash of white light, and then no more . . .

He came to as he was thrown down onto a wooden floor. He heard people calling in urgent whispers – and suddenly he knew that he was on a ship. He heard the rasp as the anchor was raised and then dropped on deck, the purr of an engine. There was a jolt as the vessel started moving, quickly picking up speed, making his head bump about. Then the caped figure stood over him, pointing a steel rapier at his neck, and ripped off her mask.

Jake's neck mottled with goose bumps. Of *course* he knew that voice. He knew her face too: her black eyes, pale skin and crimson lips. It was Mina Schlitz. He had not seen her since the night he had killed her snake aboard the *Lindwurm*.

'Is he here?' a deeper voice enquired. The speaker limped heavily towards Jake, feeling his way with a stick. He looked like a giant raven dressed in a long trench coat of black feathers. His face, all the more shocking against the black, was stretched and disfigured. His left eye had been eaten away completely, revealing pale bone beneath. Prince Xander Zeldt – for that's who it was, unquestionably – observed him without expression.

'Take him below,' Zeldt ordered. 'Lock him up. Set course for my sister's and tell her we are on our way.'

As Jake was carried down into the bowels of the ship, he caught sight of the Mont St Michel; the dark pyramid of buildings that was the centre of his world. Across the water he heard the strains of music, and the hoorahs of delight, but they were growing ever more faint.

At Point Zero, Topaz went to look for Jake. Just outside the main doors of the castle, she found a book lying open on the ground. She picked it up and saw a colour picture of an Egyptian palace on the banks of the Nile. The caption above it read: *The Land of the Pharaohs.*

She looked round and saw Felson, and wondered why on earth he was barking at the sea.

ACKNOWLEDGEMENTS

As always, hats off to the sirens: Becky Stradwick, Clare Conville, Lauren Hyett, Sue Cook, Sophie Nelson and Kirsten Armstrong.

To Justin Somper for his fantastic work. To Ali, for being the man never discombobulated and to Martin and Rosie for their Cancale kindness and famous all-days. A special mention to Ting, for her inspiration, and to Sophie L, to welcome her back!

Finally I'd like to thank Sue Kerry, a guardian angel, to me – and many of us.

Author photo © Rufo Guerrero

Damian Dibben has worked extensively as a screenwriter on projects as diverse as *The Phantom of the Opera* and *Puss in Boots*. He is a keen explorer, inspired by everything from archaeology to cosmology, and loves nothing more than a great adventure story.

Nightship to China is the third in his *History Keepers* series after *The Storm Begins* and *Circus Maximus*. The books have been translated into twenty-six languages, with a major movie in development with Working Title.

Damian lives on London's South Bank with his dog Dudley.